Forever and For Keeps

The continuing adventures of

Lee and Bucky

Forever and For Keeps

By Jane Lebak

Philangelus Press
Boston, MA USA

Other titles by Jane Lebak:

Honest And For True
Seven Archangels: An Arrow In Flight
Seven Archangels: Sacred Cups
Seven Archangels: Annihilation
The Wrong Enemy
The Seven Angels Short Story Bundle
Bulletproof Vestments
The Boys Upstairs

Print version ISBN: 978-1-942133-11-7
Kindle ASIN: B00ZIMFD3O
Library of Congress Control Number: 2015939599

Cover: C.K. Volnek

Dedication

To Stephen.

Chapter One:

A Wheel-Shrieking Launch

When you haven't bought a swimsuit since leaving the college swim team, you forget little niceties like cutting off the tags.

I love the suit. In my aunt and uncle's bedroom mirror I admire the red halter top and the boyish red and black shorts, a style that came into fashion while I nursed along my dark blue Finals racer-back suit out of a fear of having to try on things in stores.

I love how this suit doesn't emphasize the fact that I'm too short and there are no curves along this stretch of the highway. I love how because my black hair is ultra-short, you can see where the suit ties in back of my neck.

But mostly, I'd love to wear it out of this room so I could rejoin the annual family pool party, except that after all my rejoicing, I never cut off the tag.

Only rude people go poking through their host's drawers and medicine cabinets, but I don't see much choice.

Although maybe I do have a choice. "Bucky?"

I can't say "he appears" because that doesn't describe the sensation. What happens is that one moment I'm alone and the next I'm aware of someone sitting on my aunt's side of the bed as if he'd been there all along, except that he wasn't. Or rather, he was, but I couldn't see him. But that makes sense because he's my guardian angel.

He flexes his brown wings so I get a glimpse of the yellow bars on the outermost feathers, the pattern of a pine siskin. "I like that swimsuit."

"You'd like it a lot better if I could remove the tags."

He rubs his chin, his hazel eyes losing their sparkle. "Wow. An insurmountable problem."

I fold my arms and regard him. He looks back at me. Then I laugh, and a smile transforms his face so he looks a lot more like I generally think of him: a dimple on one cheek, his brown hair neat but with a wispiness at the edges, his golden eyes flecked with light like opals.

To break the standoff, I lower my voice a notch. "O Glorious Angel, would you be so kind as to locate scissors? I don't want to go searching through Aunt Mary and Uncle Mickey's drawers."

Bucky looks shocked. "And it's superior if I snoop?"

I let off a long sigh. "You're an angel!"

"That doesn't mean I should be a rude guest."

I open my hands. "You're by definition a rude guest. You weren't invited."

He pouts a little. "I'm a social unit with you. And if I wasn't invited to look at food I'm not going to eat, then I certainly wasn't invited to root through the medicine cabinet."

I'm about to say "Then what good are you?" when the plastic loops part from themselves, and the tags fall to the floor.

I flash him a smile, but he pretends he didn't just do anything. I toss the trash into the can and then grab my bag.

In the kitchen I find my boyfriend expounding on the virtues of butter, real butter, lots of butter, and I pause in the doorway to drink in how intent he sounds and how well he presents himself. Hal is wearing khaki shorts and what they call a "sport shirt," although I think every shirt he owns has at least three buttons, so I should just say "a shirt."

He's instructing Aunt Mary on how to bake a batch of brownies dense enough to form their own gravity well. Standing this close to the dessert counter, I sense the mini-cheesecakes resisting a pull into orbit around the brownies like a culinary system of moons. Moons made of cream cheese.

Hal looks me up and down, and he grins. A good thing, too, since he was the reason I finally ditched the stretched-out old suit.

I take his hand. "Did you know some people write down their recipes?"

He looks horrified. "Did you know some techniques are complicated enough that writing them down would never work?"

Aunt Mary knows me through and through: she's already poured me a cup of coffee, and since adding milk into coffee requires no technique, I take the opportunity to top off my caffeine receptors.

Although the dessert counter sags beneath a load of six million calories, Aunt Mary believes starvation is imminent: before we demolish the desserts, we will have to level the snack mountains, and then work our way through the meat slabs (or tubes) Uncle Mickey deals up from the grill. You know that urban legend about the cramps you'll get if you swim an hour after eating? Uncle Mickey hosts an annual attempt to kill us all.

More power to him! I down the coffee and snitch one of Aunt Mary's hors d'ouvres, a half-dollar-sized spinach quiche.

My niece Avery bounds into the kitchen. "Whee! Cheesecakes!" Before anyone can remind her she'll be fed enough to drop a rhinoceros, Avery has a cheesecake square in one hand and a brownie in the other. Then she says, "Aunt Lee!" because she has her priorities straight. Food first. Relatives second.

I give a mock-frown. "Hey, honor that brownie! It's his."

She inspects it at arm's length. "Should I kiss it first?"

Hal murmurs, "I feel unappreciated. You never kissed my brownies."

I move closer. "I kissed the chef."

Before he can assert that he feels insufficiently kissed, my mother enters the kitchen. Avery shoves the brownie into her mouth and gives an enthusiastic, "Hff Gmmmmuh!" before trotting off to join her brother and sister in the back yard.

My mother pecks me on the cheek and casts a critical eyeball at my swimsuit. "Where on earth did you find that thing?" Before I can respond, she turns to Hal, and with a gentility reserved for queens, she takes his hand. "I'm so glad you could meet the whole family today."

Hal gives a solid handshake. "It's my pleasure, Mrs. Singer."

I say, "Did you have a good drive here?"

Without looking away from Hal, my mother dumps her jacket and purse into my arms. "How have you been?"

Right, this game. I carry her jacket into the bedroom where Aunt Mary has left everyone's things. *Bucky?*

She's not on one knee proposing on your behalf just yet. A pause. *But maybe you ought to hurry, just in case.*

I chuckle.

As my extended family arrives, there are many, many introductions: *this is Hal, we've been dating six months, yes he's cute* (that's to Avery, who dragged me into the hallway to bestow this information on me). Yes, he's got good-natured features you can't quite call handsome but which always get a second look, and no, I'm not going to object to the scenery when he removes his t-shirt to swim. But what causes everyone to double-take are his eyes, so blue and in stark contrast to his black hair. Or maybe it's the black hair that's the contrast. The traditional term for it is "black Irish," but when Uncle Mickey asked about his background, Hal said it's a mixture of Slavic, Germanic, old-stock American, and a half dozen generations back is some Spanish. If I had that kind of family history, on forms that asked my ethnicity, I'd totally write, "Yes!"

Uncle Mickey has sixty people for his annual party. If I were Hal and gotten this invitation, I'd have developed a pressing need to organize my sock drawer. *"Of course it will take all day. Should I roll them or fold them? Then I need to determine whether to alphabetize by color or brand name."*

Hal and I are helping Uncle Mickey set up tables when my brother Randy approaches. "Hey, if you don't mind, Aunt Alice needs some help."

"Sure." Hal and I follow Randy to the front lawn where Aunt Alice is saying to my mother, "Those careless construction workers!"

Ah yes, August: that splendid season when the highways bloom orange; when cones, saw horses, and reflective signs fill the heart with wonder:

WELCOME TO NEW JERSEY
CONSTRUCTION NEXT EIGHTY-FIVE MILES
FOUR LANES CLOSED, MOVE RIGHT

It's the time of year when healthy six-lane interstates become two-lane cowpaths. Hal and I arrived early to avoid overheating my car, which fails to comprehend the beauty of August. Or rather, gives its driver plenty of opportunity to enjoy the beauty of August while waiting for the radiator to stop boiling over.

Randy says, "Aunt Alice? Lee can help."

I bend to kiss her soft cheek. She's actually our great-aunt, eighty-five and white-haired. "What do you need?"

And her answer is why, five minutes later, I'm loosening lug nuts while wearing a swim suit. Because the reason to have Triple-A coverage is so you can guilt your great-niece into changing your tire rather than bother the nice man with the tow truck.

As I fit her standard-issue cross-wrench onto the first lug nut, I pat the black quarter panel. It's a three-year-old six-cylinder beauty, a Mazda 6 with 272 horsepower that she's never driven over 45mph. It's so shiny I may have left a handprint. And is that my imagination, or did I just hear the car whimper, *Save me! Please!*

I pat it again. "It'll be okay, baby."

The cross-wrench Mazda provided with the donut is even less useful than Aunt Alice's fourth and fifth gears: it wouldn't loosen a tie, let alone a tire. "Hey, Avery! Go grab my keys. I need better tools."

My mom says, "Let's call roadside assistance."

In response to Aunt Alice's cry of dismay, I protest, "I can do it."

Mom sniffs. "You'll get grease on your hands." She turns to one of my other brothers, standing beside Randy with a can of Coke. "Morgan, you help her."

Morgan puffs up. "You want a real man to do it?"

I gasp. "You have *A Real Man* on speed-dial?"

Behind me, Hal laughs. Morgan grumps, "Dude, she just insulted you too."

Hal shakes his head. "I know I'm no Real Man. I'm merely a CPA. Call me when you're comparison-shopping for a new car."

Hal works out—he could change a tire if he wanted. I'm just not sure anyone could manage with this stupid equipment.

My oldest brother Randy chuckles. "And I'm just an Old Man." He pushes Morgan's shoulder. "Go on—show us you're stronger than the accountant."

And thus, in front of our relatives, Morgan horrifies my mother by being unable to budge the lug nuts any more than I could. He grunts as he pushes. "It's the wrench."

I take it from him. "Of course it's the wrench, you idiot. I already said that."

Aunt Alice says, "I really don't want to call Triple-A."

Avery returns with my keys.

"You won't have to call anyone." I could use my own lug nut wrench, but considering who's watching, I'd rather go for impressive. In the trunk of my restored 1965 Mustang I keep an entire auto supply shop's worth of spare parts, among which is a two-and-a-half-foot section of PVC piping. This I slip over one of the cross-wrench's arms.

Avery cocks her head. "What's that supposed to do?"

I gesture to my niece. "It's supposed to enable *you* to change a tire."

Doubtful, she puts her hand on the end of the pipe. Fortunately she trusts me enough to give it a push.

The wrench moves, and the nut loosens.

Once you have the right tools, anything's easy. So while my mother battles horror, I talk Avery through her first tire change. I show her how to position the jack so it supports the car without raising it. Next we remove the lug nuts, plinking them into the hubcap. We jack the car higher to slide the wheel off, then lay that beneath the car so if the jack gives out, the car will fall onto that rather than someone's hand. She slides on the donut, then replaces the nuts on the axle. I tighten those myself because Great Aunt Alice shouldn't suddenly find herself driving a tricycle, then heave the flat tire into the trunk.

Avery high-fives me. My mother shakes her head. "Go wash your hands. You're full of grease."

Have I introduced my mother? I could single-handedly tune up every car in the Presidential Motorcade while it rolled down Fifth Avenue, and she'd wonder aloud why I did it wearing jeans.

Great Aunt Alice pats me on the head. "Thank you so much, dear. Here, take this."

She hands me a Dunkin Donuts gift card, the modern equivalent of when your Nana used to carry a roll of Life Savers in her purse for just-in-case. I thank her even though Hal would use it as a burnt offering to appease the vengeance of the Gourmet Coffee Deities.

It's while I'm jacking down the car that Morgan says, "So when are you two going to get hitched?"

Even as I glare at my brother, Hal replies, "Isn't six months a little soon to be talking marriage?"

"You know how one year is seven dog years?" Morgan glances at my brother Randy with a grin. "Six months dating Lee is the equivalent of three years dating a normal woman."

Hal says, "Is that in man-years, or Real Man years?"

He's playing it light because I've gotten to my feet. And you thought the tire blew up? "You mean a normal woman who can't change a tire?"

Morgan grins. "I mean a normal woman who hasn't dated three hundred guys."

Uncle Mickey drops his arm over my shoulder before I find out whether Great Aunt Alice's cross-wrench can remove the lug nuts bolting Morgan's minuscule brain into his skull. "Good work, Lee. Hey, how about everybody come out back and swim? Seeing as this is a pool party and not an auto rally."

Avery yanks my hand. "Hey, remember you challenged me to a cannon-ball contest?"

Randy's eyebrows shoot up. I grab Avery around the shoulders in a hug while making it look as if I'm strangling her. "I would *never* have suggested such a thing, *would I?*"

"Of course you— Oh." Avery freezes. "I was just thinking, Aunt Lee, if you wouldn't mind, maybe you could come with me to the diving board for additional swimming lessons?"

Uncle Mickey sighs. "Please try not to soak your uncle this year."

I turn to follow Avery. "Like it was my fault you were so close to the pool."

"I was grilling burgers twenty feet away."

Oh, sure. No one else ever makes a little mistake like that. How was I supposed to know where the water would go? Am I a sea goddess who controls it with my mind?

Hal follows me to the pool.

"You're going to swim, right?"

Looking serious, he rubs his chin. "Well, I don't know. Swimming with you for five minutes would be the equivalent of swimming three hours with a normal woman, and—"

I laugh out loud, and Hal takes my hand. I can't help it: I kiss him.

At about four o'clock, while two of my great uncles discuss* the Kennedy assassination, Uncle Mickey taps me

---

* That really should say, "Thundering their half-baked opinions at 195 words a minute with occasional gusts of up to 250," but I would never malign my elders.

on the shoulder and asks to see my car. He does it this way: "I'm going to go look at my car."

I'm wearing a t-shirt now over my swimsuit, but I haven't bothered putting on sandals or combing my hair. I'll probably swim again. It's quiet underwater. Everything moves together. Who wouldn't like that?

I trail Uncle Mickey to the street, Hal at my side. "Surely you forget who paid you money, towed that wreck out of your garage, and invested eleven million hours restoring it?"

He laughs.

I add, "And has paid for insurance on it ever since."

Hal says, "Plus a garage as expensive as some apartments."

I pause. "Where can you rent an apartment for four hundred bucks a month?"

He lays an arm over my shoulder. "Someday, Lee, we will explore the world beyond New York City."

We've reached the Mustang, its paint glimmering in the sunshine. "We're in New Jersey. How much further could we go before we run into sea monsters?"

Uncle Mickey slides into the front seat and lets off a long breath. "This brings back memories. I love it when you bring her out here."

"It needs the highway driving. Helps open things out in the engine." I lean against the hood while Uncle Mickey runs his hands over the restored leather seats, the steering wheel, and the high gloss of the dashboard. Last night, I gave this car the detailing of its life. No dust mote has dared settle on the metallic blue exterior, even after a ninety-minute highway drive.

Maybe it had a little help? I think pointedly, and momentarily I sense a friendly rejoinder: maybe just a little, and thanks for noticing.

I smile to myself.

Uncle Mickey asks about the car's known trouble spots. He rubs at a worn area on the upholstery and massages his fingertips over the stick shift.

He doesn't need to ask. I present him the keys.

He snaps them into his palm. "I'd love to."

Hal steps back onto the sidewalk. "I'll pass, if you don't mind. Lee already broke the sound barrier on the way here."

I hop into the passenger seat. "Only once."

He kisses me through the window. "Don't be gone long. If you're driving for five minutes, that's like three days' driving with—"

"You're getting a lot of mileage out of that."

Hal nods. "Approximately fifteen times the mileage of—"

Uncle Mickey starts the engine with a roar, and Hal laughs.

"I think that's his way of saying the joke's about fifteen times too old," I call to Hal, and he only says, "I'm outgunned."

Uncle Mickey puts the car in gear, and we venture into uncharted waters, except that they're streets, and they're not uncharted. Instead they have names like "Pleasant Oak Drive" and "Whispering Pine Path."

I say to Uncle Mickey, "If the pines are whispering, I don't think I want to be here."

"Who's going to hear a few whispering pines when we've got a whinnying Mustang?" He chuckles. "I should have got the upgrade kit. This is so tame."

Only 95 horsies and three speeds for me. Even with a bum tire, Great Aunt Alice's Mazda would view me as nothing but a shrinking speck in the rear-view mirror, assuming she ever did more than idle up Sleepy Grove Avenue. But that's okay. How often are you going to have a real wheel-shrieking launch from zero to sixty, the accelerator pressed flat to the carpet?

Well, except for that time at the Verrazano bridge toll plaza at three o'clock in the morning. But *other* than that, I mean? It's one of the real losses of modern life, the way the SRS systems and traction control keep the tires doing what they're supposed to. And the final indignity: the EZ Pass. Sure you can get through the tolls in three minutes, but you lose that Kentucky Derby feel when the barrier goes up and your pony shoots from the stall like it's the Run for the Roses. Or the Run From New York's Finest, who are not notable for their senses of humor. (Although that one guy did apologize for ticketing me after we'd dated a couple of times.)

Uncle Mickey sold me his dying Mustang when I got out of college. I needed a hobby. Actually, I needed to have my head examined, but I imagined everyone gawking at the bombshell driving the vintage sports car. Uncle Mickey and I invested in tarps and too many tools to count (but not enough) and spent the next two years making the car start.

Now, though, it launches into the subdivision while Uncle Mickey glories in what I've done to his baby. This was his first car, and since I rescued it, I must be some kind of hero. I submit for your consideration Superman's kid sister, only with a tool box and a maglight rather than a cape.

He doesn't do what I'd want to and "see what this baby can do." He probably saw it all when he was fresh out of the army and the proud owner of a 1965 Mustang, racing other guys on the south Jersey back roads, or maybe heading into the city for drag racing out by the cemetery at McDonald Avenue. First guy to the elevated train tracks gets a ticket.

He also obeys the traffic laws nowadays. While waiting at a light, he says, "I like Hal a lot."

I grin. "You just like his brownies."

"You know what I mean." Uncle Mickey gives me a wink. "I know marriage is a topic off-limits, but you two look cute together."

I chuckle. "You can talk to me about marriage, but I'm safe. Mom says women over thirty are unmarriageable."

"I'll chip in three goats and a pig for the dowry." He's got a perfect deadpan. "Living way out here in the country and all."

Rahway, if you're curious, is a bedroom community to New York, Newark, and Philadelphia. The only thing the farm lands yield out here are townhomes and subdivisions with curvy roads.

I act shocked. "No bales of hay?"

"I gotta feed my family something." The light changes, and we move again. "He seems like a nice guy, and if that's not the kiss of death, he also sounds very responsible."

"I already got that from Mom. He's *good for me,* the way bean sprouts, dental cleanings, and running on a treadmill are good for you."

Uncle Mickey can't help it. He snorts. "She means well."

Why does everyone feel the need to say that about her? No one ever says Randy means well, and yet he does.

"He's not totally safe, though. I saw the way he was looking at you."

"I doubt that." Pretty swimsuit or not, there's nothing to see here. It's not only my hair that's short and straight.

Not that Uncle Mickey would care, but we've never Done The Deed. I made a deal with Bucky a long time ago not to have sex unless I got married. Both Hal and I agree I'd never remember to take a pill every day, and the last thing I want is to "honey-trap" Hal. Or, for that matter, honey-trap myself. Fortunately we're both smart, so for the past six months we've found ourselves entertainment of the clothed variety. Hal doesn't object. He doesn't want to pressure me.

"Have you talked about marriage?" asks my uncle.

I roll my eyes. "Why would we? It's been since February."

Morgan is probably wrong that I've dated three hundred guys, but he's right that I pick up guys quickly, serially, and juggle multiple partners whenever I feel like it. Sometimes I date no one at all. There's nothing wrong with that, and I don't understand why my mother thinks my life won't be fulfilled until I'm married. I've lived on my own for almost a decade. I've got a stable job, a 1965 Mustang, and an apartment in Park Slope with my best friend. With two of them, in fact. Why mess with success by trying to shoehorn in a husband?

Uncle Mickey says, "Does Hal know how you feel about marriage?"

I shrug. "I'm sure he's figured it out."

"He deserves to know if you're not in it for the long haul. Let him cut his losses."

I laugh. "Uncle Mickey! He's having a good time. That isn't any kind of loss."

"He's an accountant. He thinks of it as an investment when he endures your family gatherings and rides in a noisy sports car that smells like burnt oil if you idle it too long."

"I fixed that!" I nod. "It doesn't overheat any longer, either. You wouldn't believe—"

"Don't change the subject on me, little lady." I can't believe how smoothly he shifts gears as we turn back onto Placid Sparrow Circle. I always fight the stick shift, even when I'm in practice. "If he thinks he's paying into a long-term mutual fund, you need to let him know if you're going to short-sell him."

I frown as Uncle Mickey kills the engine in front of his house. "You just majorly mixed your metaphors."

"My point got across." My uncle unbuckles and exits the car. "Your mother and Morgan aside, you need to be clear what your expectations are. And his."

Chapter Two:

It Rocks

Changed but smelling of chlorine, Hal and I enjoy the crackling of the Mustang's AM radio while I terrorize the Garden State Parkway.

"Your family is something else." Hal's voice has its regular cadence, smooth. He puts his hand on my leg as I drive. "I'm glad you warned me about your brothers. You didn't tell me your Aunt Mary would try to force-feed me enough cheesecake to stun a goat."

The highway lights wane and brighten as we pass. I wrap my fingers around his and give a squeeze. It's dark enough in the car that I can barely see him, but in a way, that makes it more comfortable.

We'll reach home at ten o'clock. Unless I can convince him ten is too early to call it a night, I'll drop him off at the Ansonia Clockworks on Seventh Avenue (a factory transformed into condo units so expensive that Bill Gates would have to phone his accountant) and then bring my car to its garage on Garfield Place. Once it's safely stored, I'll head back to 246 Sixth Avenue, the brownstone where I have an apartment on the top floor.

We exchange typical party post-mortem comments.

From Hal: admiration for the mountains of food and rivers of drink.

From me: "I'm really sorry Morgan hassled you about the accountant stuff."

Hal laughs out loud. "Oh, trust me, my father's friend deals out worse every time I meet him. If you return the favor and come to my family's Labor Day barbecue, you'll need to wear armor."

I would love to rent armor. I might even visit the junk yard and build my own! "And will I get to change a tire?"

"God, I hope so. I love watching you work on that stuff."

Hal puts his hand on my shoulder. It stings, and I flinch. I say, "Well, at least that's over. You met everyone."

"Not everyone." He sounds confused. "I didn't meet Bucky."

I stiffen. "Did you think you would?"

"Beth showed up for a while, and since you've known Bucky longer than Beth, they said he had a standing invitation."

Whoops. This wasn't exactly something I'd considered. That, you know, while he was with my family, they'd talk. *I thought you said you weren't invited,* I think out into the ether.

Hal chuckles. "At least one relative had placed bets you were going to marry Bucky."

I burst out laughing. "Which one?"

"Some cousin. As if I can remember them all."

"You met sixty people today. Be glad we only do this once a year."

I look in the side-view mirror before changing lanes. We pass another car, but I stay cruising in the middle, enjoying the roar of my Mustang's engine and the rattling of a dashboard dating from the days when "interior noise" was a badge of honor and real men didn't care about tinnitus.

Hal says, "Will I be invited to next year's party as well?"

He's tentative. My breath catches.

"It wasn't just Morgan who asked when we'd be getting married." Hal's looking away, rotating the grooved plastic ring on the window handle. "It also struck me that they consider it a given because they're asking *when*, not *if*, but I have no answer."

I shrug his hand off my shoulder. "I don't care what my family thinks, and neither should you. If it was hard for you to hear this today, imagine what it's been like for the last twenty years."

"How many guys have you brought to these things?"

I flinch. "Only two."

"And was one of them Bucky?"

I sigh. "I never dated Bucky."

I've dated men with just about every other name, but none unfortunate enough to be saddled with *Bucky.*

"Then why do they think you'll marry him?"

"They always misunderstood everything about him. Just drop it."

I sound defensive, so Hal presses on. "But I have one more question, which is, are you so eager not to get married precisely because they'd marry you off to your childhood friends if they could?"

Whoa, we're at 75 mph. The highway is doing far too rapid a thump-thump beneath our tires as we pass the seams in the pavement, and the rattle is going to drop the rear-view mirror into my lap. I pull into the right lane and ease up on the accelerator.

He's been quiet for too long.

I reach for his hand. "Why are *you* harping on this? I never said never."

"Then when?"

Breathing hurts. Beneath my fingers, his hand is limp when I squeeze.

"I'm not proposing right now." He sounds tense. "I'm not ready for that either. But in theory, when would you be ready?"

I squeeze his hand again, and finally he has mercy and squeezes back.

"Look, about Bucky—" I bite my lip. "I've known him since I was three, and he's been clear for as long as I can remember that he's not my boyfriend. He's never kissed me."

"But you're in love with him." Hal's voice goes flat because he got burned that way once before. "And despite the wretched tale of heartbreak, you're holding out hope—"

"Will you let me tell my own story?" I look over my shoulder. "Bucky is my guardian angel."

It takes a really long time before Hal says, "What? He used to help you cross the street?"

"No, that's a crossing guard. Bucky's an angel. Like in the Bible. His assignment is to look out for me. It's a long story, but I can see him and talk to him."

I glance away from the road, and I can see the whites of Hal's eyes.

I swallow hard. "I know it sounds crazy. But I can't have you believe I'm pining after some other man when that's the furthest from the truth. He's like having another brother around all the time."

Hal sounds tentative. "And it's got the whole deal—wings, halo, robe, harp?"

"Wings, yes. The rest, no. Maybe it's Casual Century right now."

Hal maintains silence for the entire distance between two exits.

Finally he says, "And everyone in your family knows you see angels?"

"One. One angel."

"Because they think you're carrying a torch for him."

"Nobody but Randy knows he's an angel. Bucky's just so much a part of everything it's hard to leave him out of conversation, so I talk like he's a friend, the way I did with you." I grip the wheel harder. "Now you think I'm nuts. This is why I don't tell people."

"I'm not sure you aren't screwing with my head."

I sigh. "What would prove it to you?"

"Can it read my mind?"

"He can't even read mine." For which I assume he's grateful. "Randy 'tested' him for me when I first started seeing him, though. He made it recite things I don't know."

"Okay, then. Does it know Satan's first monologue in *Paradise Lost*?"

What a thing to pick. "What about *Hamlet*?"

"Everyone knows *Hamlet*. I want something I know that you probably don't."

I shake my head, then repeat the words I hear in my mind:

"If thou beest he; But O how fall'n! how chang'd
From him, who in the happy Realms of Light
Cloth'd with transcendent brightness didst out-shine
Myriads though bright: If he Whom mutual league,
United thoughts and counsels, equal hope
And hazard in the Glorious Enterprize,
Joynd with me once, now misery hath joynd

In equal ruin— And I think that's enough to prove a point, don't you?"

Whoops—I forgot to stop repeating.

Hal says, "Can it do Homer in ancient Greek?"

"He can do Gilgamesh in the original Sumerian. Do you want him to juggle plates and bend spoons, too?"

Inside, I feel the faintest affirmation: if he did, then Hal would want him to make the interior of the car glow. I grin.

Hal says, "What does it do other than recite poetry and make smart remarks?"

In my head, I hear, *It rocks.*

Hush, you. I shrug. "He warns me if I'm going to get hurt and helps me when I'm making decisions. Things like that."

He sounds tart. "That's not an angel. That's a spirit guide."

"Thanks for that vocabulary lesson. And in your vast experience with angels, what do they do?"

"In my vast experience, I've heard about angels killing entire armies single-handedly, causing plagues, slaying firstborn Egyptians, feeding people in the wilderness, and fighting Satan. Poetry never entered into that."

I frown. "Why did I loan you my angel books?"

"Because you supposedly love me and you wanted to make it easier to talk to me about your obsession. You failed to mention," he adds, "the reason behind it."

Sure, he read a book or two and that's supposed to trump an entire lifetime of experience? I could kick him out of the car and make him walk home. Come to think of it, that would also stop my mother from pestering him to marry me.

Hal sounds baffled. "This makes no sense. You said a long time ago that Bucky can destroy you at Carcassonne."

"Brutally."

"You can see an angel, and the only thing you can think to do with it is play board games? Has it entered your mind how crazy that is?"

I shudder. "Not as crazy as trying to play chess with an angel."

Hal sounds momentarily grim. "No, I imagine that would be no fun at all."

"He doesn't like Monopoly. There are too many impediments to playing Scrabble. And we've decided the only point of two-player Cosmic Encounter is to find a third player."

Hal snickers. "Granted. And its name is actually Bucky?"

I sigh. "He won't tell me his real name, so the first time I asked, he said to give him one. It's a lousy nickname, but I was three."

No commentary as I keep driving through a night whose silence is shattered by a Mustang engine and a confused-if-not-angry boyfriend.

Hal says, "Is there anything else you'd care to divulge? Perhaps on Saturday nights you summon the four winds before trading jokes with Thomas Jefferson via a Ouija board?"

My eyes narrow. "More like I've summoned Doubting Thomas via a diving board."

"I'm just having a hard time wrapping my mind around this. Didn't you say Bucky has this hopeless fascination with the *Rumours* album?"

"Always has."

"Not Mozart?"

I snicker. "He can *talk* to Mozart if he feels like it. Lindsey Buckingham isn't dead yet, so he can only listen to the album."

"I...wow, that never would have occurred to me." Hal doesn't sound exactly enlightened. "Does it ever tell you anything about the end of the world?"

"Most of the time we talk about important and practical stuff. Like my life."

"So let's talk about your life." Hal's voice sharpens. "Does Bucky think you should get married?"

Oh, God. Why this? Why now?

"Is that, *I've asked and he's told me not to marry,* or *I've asked and he's told me not to marry you*?"

I still don't respond.

"Or conversely," Hal says, "your silence could mean *I've asked and he says I should get married, only I don't want to think about it, and I hate you for bringing up the subject.*"

Unfortunately, that's nearer the truth. Bucky wouldn't tell me whether I *should* or *shouldn't* get married. He's warned me against dating certain individuals, whom I assume had chainsaws and large empty duffle bags in the trunks of their cars. Although come to think of it...

"If it helps, Bucky did encourage me to ask you out."

"That's something." His voice sounds flat. "Let me know if it ever encourages you to look at the long white dresses."

"Please don't do this to me!" I'd smack the dashboard, but I know this car too well — I might have it in my lap. "This is exactly what my brother wanted. He doesn't give a damn if I marry you, but he loves to stir the pot. Why are we fighting over something neither of us is ready for?"

"We're not fighting," Hal says.

"Then what are we doing?"

His voice sounds tight. "Long-range planning."

"Don't ruin today by thinking about tomorrow." I've breezed through three decades this way, and I can make it through another three no problem. "Don't let a few stupid questions wreck the fun."

When we pull up in front of the Ansonia Clockworks, I idle in a bus stop with the hazards flashing.

Hal turns to me. "Thank you for inviting me. I'm sorry I got so upset with you before."

And then he kisses me, lingering. We're both chlorinated, but he's got his fingers in my hair, and he pulls back just a bit. "When will I see you again?"

Our old nemesis, commonly known as "the work week," may separate us for a few days. I'm pretty sure that's why they invented email and the phone, though. "Maybe dinner sometime?" I trace a finger over his sharp ten o'clock shadow and down to the dimple in his chin. "Out or in?"

He smiles. "Out is fine, but maybe I'll cook."

I wink. "I'm flexible." My accountant may think sporty means the Camry XLE rather than the LE, but he's the Indiana Jones of food. He'll order the strangest thing on the menu just to experience it, whether it's Thai, Indian, Singaporean, Afrikaans, or in one very memorable instance a traditional meal from Samurai Japan that had my eyes bugging out.

A beep startles us, and I find headlights filling the rear view mirror. Oh, right, we're in a bus stop, and incomprehensibly, a bus wants to stop in it. Hal gets out, slams the door with a solid thunk you don't get in imports (which sound more like *shhhhfd,*) and I pull onto the street before Mr. Bus tries to climb over my bumper.

Twenty feet later I'm waiting for the light when I hear, "That went well."

I face Mr. Sarcasm with a look of mock-toleration.

Bucky shrugs. "You didn't end up in an all-out fight, nor did you call things off." His hazel eyes glow against the nighttime and the street lights pick up the white in his wings. He rubs his jaw with one hand as he leans against the passenger side door. He's buckled in. Of course he is. "I found it intriguing how you distracted Hal from the marriage question by telling him about me, which would have been brilliant had it succeeded."

The light changes, and I advance along Seventh Avenue. I'll head over to Garfield Place and turn there.

Bucky says, "You haven't told anyone about me since you were five and you first figured out people didn't believe you. This makes me uncertain whether your revelation was a declaration of trust or an act of desperation. Would you mind clarifying?"

I make a face. "Did you actually memorize *Paradise Lost*, or did you have a copy in your pocket?"

Bucky laughs. "Here's the greatest parlor trick ever: memorize the first five hundred lines of any epic poem. Then tell everyone you've memorized the whole thing and start reciting. Even other angels will stop you long before you reach that threshold. I was going to try it on you in the next year or so, but I didn't mind doing it today."

I sit at the stop light on Seventh and Garfield, my left turn signal on.

"You're sunburnt," Bucky says. "You'll want to put lotion on your shoulders before you go to bed tonight."

I resist exclaiming with wonder, *That explains the stinging and the stiffness.* "I suppose it would have killed you to remind me to reapply the sunscreen before I got roasted?"

"Exactly as much as it would have killed you to read the bottle and notice when it would wear off."

I say, "And malignant melanoma—that won't kill me either?"

Bucky nods. "It could kill you, which is precisely why it would have been a good idea to read the bottle of sunblock."

A tap at my door startles me. I look up to find a black-haired and dark-eyed man, his face angular and his ripped t-shirt loose over his muscular upper body.

"You and your Mustang look sharp." The light turns green as he hands me a slip of paper. "Why don't you give me the ride of my life?"

Whoa—that is so incredibly not the smoothest pickup line I've ever heard.

"Thanks." I pluck the paper from his fingertips as I rev the engine. "I'll give your offer all the consideration it deserves."

I'm in luck—no oncoming traffic to prevent a dramatic pull-away onto Garfield Place.

I'm a quarter of the way down the block when I slow the car. "Bucky, did he want to kill me?"

Bucky shrugs. "Don't hold me to this, but I think he wanted a joyride."

I pull into a space.

Bucky sits bolt upright. "What are you doing?"

"Use your superior angelic intellect and figure it out." I grope for my cell phone in my backpack, and I hold the paper up to the light to make out the numbers and his name. Bet me it's his cell.

He answers immediately.

"Francisco? Maybe I'll take you for the ride of your life after all."

Chapter Three:

One Expensive Joyride

Four hours of sleep is more than enough because on a short-term basis, coffee replaces sleep. Of course, this is difficult to believe when you're struggling to brew your first cup of coffee without having already consumed a cup, henceforth known as The Coffee Bootstrap Problem.

I'm exhausted, and I look it. I'm sunburnt and feeling it. It's only six-thirty and I've already turned three times trying to catch whomever is staring at me, only to realize that oh yeah, it's Bucky scolding my soul. Shooting it dirty looks. Whatever it is angels do when they're disgusted.

Drinking my coffee—at least, struggling to drink the coffee instead of sleeping on my feet—I go back over last night to figure out what exactly made Bucky so angry. Francisco and I cruised in my Mustang, but I wouldn't let him drive it. We ended up at a dance club where the music didn't deafen us only because, as it turns out, two hundred people on a dance floor the size of a Ford Excursion absorb a hundred decibels. *("IT'S A BIT LOUD!" "WHAT?")*

When it got too smoky to breathe, we pushed toward open air through the throng to an outdoor snack-bar.* It's

---

* I drank a Coke and paid $2.50 for the honor. It wasn't three times as good as the two-liter bottle from the grocery store, nor was it served in crystal by a white-gloved butler who spoke French.

not like I fooled around with the guy. Well, maybe I kissed him once right before I kicked him out of my car right around midnight. Well, about two hours after midnight.

At seven-thirty, as I force my body to bike up Sixth Avenue, I catalog the pains shooting through assorted body-parts. Why did I think it would be a good idea to stay out until two in the morning after a full day of driving, swimming, and changing a great-aunt's tire? More importantly, will I be able to raise my arms above shoulder-height to do my job?

Oh yeah, my job. I'm a mechanic at Mack's Auto Repair on Fifth Avenue and Ninth Street.

There, I said it. It didn't used to be that easy, and to be honest, sometimes people do ask if I'm sure. But usually they think it's cool. Everyone except my mother.

When my boss Max comes to me, I'm still trying to determine whether what's in the coffee pot was brewed today at a thickness of crude oil, or whether it's basked on the burner since last Saturday. Max says, "Guess who phoned in her resignation again this morning?"

Oh, let's play along. "I did?"

Max rubs his stubbled chin with a finger that's only 3/4 there, a constant reminder to his mechanics that medical coverage is good, but paying attention is better. "Apparently you're going to work in the mail room at Random House. I refused to accept your resignation, but before you call me a heartless jerk, it's because I saw you clocking in."

I would dump the coffee sludge, but Max is so tight he needs a shoe-horn to draw a deep breath. I don't need a lecture about literally pouring his money down the drain.

He leans against the wall. "It also didn't work because this is the fiftieth time your mother resigned for you."

I beam. "That's like an anniversary! We should order pizza!"

He grunts. "Everyone needs a hobby. Mine is preventing you from dumping perfectly good coffee so you can make a second pot."

I fold my arms. "Who made the first pot? George Washington?"

Uncoffeed, I meet the first customer of the day. She's shifting her weight, and a toddler clings to the leg of her worn jeans. "What can I do for you?"

She swallows hard. "I need...um...an estimate. My tailpipe fell off, and I think I need a new muffler, but I need to know what it costs first."

The child at her leg squirms, and she picks him up. He's wearing what look like hiking boots even though it's eighty-five degrees, and his t-shirt is too small.

I say, "Sure, let's go take a look."

I suspect what I'm going to find, and our customer doesn't disappoint. The car's at least fifteen years old with rust all over the quarter panels plus a huge dent in the front fender. In her arms, the customer's little boy whines about being hungry, and she asks him to hush. She's skinny as a rail herself. I crouch until I can see the tail pipe. It's rusted through just below the trunk.

She's showing me the ragged half-foot of tailpipe she retrieved from the side of the road, along with the chrome tip, babbling as she asks if it's cheaper just to weld the two edges together.

Well, thank goodness I'm me and not Max.

"This is an easy fix." I reach into my wallet for Great Aunt Alice's Dunkin Donuts gift card. "Go get him a donut, and when you get back, I'll be done."

She frowns at me. "But how much will it cost? I might have to wait until my next paycheck, and—"

I wave her down. "This will cost less than is on the gift card. There's two ways to do this: my boss would replace the whole muffler and tailpipe assembly for three hundred bucks, or I can use a hack saw and cut off the ragged end of the tail pipe and bolt the chrome tip back onto it for free. Guess which option I recommend you take?" When she just stares at me, I say, "Plus, there's a free Dunkin's gift card for our first brand-new customer this morning. I'll be done in ten minutes."

She whispers, "You're not supposed to be doing this."

I smile. "I recommend the chocolate glazed. Grab yourself a large coffee and drink it in my honor. I haven't had any yet."

The car goes on the lift as if I'm about to do an actual estimate, and it's the work of about two minutes to fit the chrome tip to the tail pipe so it doesn't look like an invitation to the NYPD to give the rest of the car a once-over. I also kneel in the car seat to tighten it all the way down. The car goes right back out into the sunlight, and by the time she's back in the waiting room with a large coffee and a toddler sucking chocolate frosting from his fingers, I've got an estimate in front of me with "No repair necessary" scrawled across the middle.

I hand back her keys. "You're all set. The tail pipe is fine."

Beaming, she sets the cup of coffee on the counter. "I hope you like hazelnut."

Oh, wow. That was nice of her. She didn't have to do that. While I was fixing the tail pipe, one of the other mechanics had stealthily dumped the old sludge and made new.* But this stuff's better.

As she's leaving, I get my first swig of coffee, and then I call up the other waiting customer. I know Mr. Hartman, one of our regulars. "Hey, there. What brings you?"

"I had my car towed here last night." In his early fifties, Mr. Hartman has thinning straw-colored hair and a lean

---

* *It's still sludge. Just new.*

build accentuated by his faded Yankees t-shirt. He's also got a sweet Maxima that aches to meet my Great-Aunt's underused car so they can form a support group. "My son drove through a construction zone Saturday night and got two flat tires."

"Ah, the August disease." I bring up his account on the computer. "If you'd like to wait, I'll take care of it right now."

He glances to the side, where I find a younger version of my customer. The unlucky driver, perhaps? "I hope you brought your phone to fiddle with."

The son shrugs.

Tire changes aren't a challenge, as I've already proven for my great aunt, but this Maxima's tires are shredded. Apparently due to budget cuts, the city's DPW is doing construction with cheese graters. Regardless, a tire change is a tire change, so I'll do it outside. I'm in my element, and more to the point, the air is cool and the sky clear. I jack the car and pull off the driver's side front wheel.

As I do this, it feels strange. I can't define why. I could call it gut instinct, but it's in my hands rather than my stomach. I slide the tire back on, then pull it off again.

No, something's definitely wrong. It's in the scraping sound, the play in the wheel. I move to the front of the car and do my best impression of roadkill while squinting beneath the car. It's too dark. Clear day or not, I'm putting this girl on the lift.

Raising it gives me confirmation with my eyes of what my hands told me first.

Yeah, good morning. That will wake you in a hurry.

I take another long drink of my coffee, then push my safety goggles onto the top of my head. "Max, I need your input."

Max doesn't have to take more than one glance before barking with laughter. That, ladies and gentlemen, is the sound of two hundred dollars turning into two thousand.

Carlos, Ari, and Tim all leave their repairs, and to a man, they stare at what's obviously a broken axle.

Carlos has a part-time job at a race track. "Holy crap. How fast was the old man going?"

"The story," and I arch my eyebrows, "is that the customer's son drove through a construction zone."

Max and Ari guffaw. "Maybe if he drove it off a building under construction!"

"Don't laugh so hard." I lower the cup. "If we can see this much damage, the hidden damage may total the vehicle."

Max's lips purse. "Oh, God, I hope not."

Carlos shakes his head. "It's a sure thing both wheels need to be replaced. The whole front end should be checked."

I fold my arms. "I figured as much. What do you think happened?"

"I think exactly what it looks like. He hit a pothole at ninety miles per hour." Carlos runs a hand through his hair. "I've seen this kind of damage at the track."

I lower my voice. "Could it have been a hit-and-run?"

Ari shakes his head. "Hit anything big enough to harm the car that badly and the engine would be in the front seat. He might have run over a cinderblock, but with both tires flattened—"

Tim grunts. We turn to him, and he says, "Speed-bump."

Later tonight, I'll record this in a notebook I stashed in the back of my sock drawer. I started it three years ago. On the front cover it reads, "Things Tim Has Said," and tonight, the number of words on the inside will exceed the number of words on the outside.

Ari says, "How drunk was he?"

Carlos shakes his head. "If he'd've been drunk, he'd have kept driving on it and destroyed the whole car."

I look down. "I feel bad for the kid."

"I don't. Stupid people deserve to buy new axles." Max harrumphs. "I'll handle this, Singer. It's going to require a certain finesse to make sure they get it repaired rather than donating it to some charity."

Heaven forbid *some charity* get the car. "I'll come with you. I need to learn about finesse."

Mind you, I'll still need to learn about finesse after Max finishes, but I'm going anyhow.

Out behind the counter, Max looks the customer's son dead in the eye. "Were you the one driving the car?"

The young man shrugs. "Yeah?"

Max laughs out loud. "Son, you are screwed!"

Looks like we're out-of-stock on the finesse.

Mr. Hartman stands. "What?"

Max jabs his gnawed-off finger at Hartman's son, a man in his early twenties. "Whatever he did with your car, he did it fast enough that he snapped the axle. We can't just replace the tires. It'll be the tires, the wheels, the axle, and quite probably a few other things."

I add, "Sometimes there's hidden damage when a car takes an impact at that speed."

Mr. Hartman turns to his son, who exclaims, "I wasn't going that fast!"

Max chuckles. "Carlos estimates you were doing a hundred and ten when you slammed into a pothole."

Before my boss enjoys himself too much, and before our esteemed elder customer makes me eligible for subpoena in a murder trial, I say, "Mr. Hartman, is there an accident report? You may want to file a claim with your insurance."

No, there is no accident report because until thirty seconds ago, there was no accident. Mr. Hartman keeps insisting his son wasn't doing anything wrong as Max verbally juggles numbers, time frames, options, and so on. I jot down all the numbers and make a list, grabbing them from the air as they pass Max's lips at random.

Here's why I came up front. By "finesse" Max means, "Not telling the customer everything he needs to know in the order he needs to know it," on the grounds that sometimes the customer will agree to a repair confused about what it costs. Even Hal would have a hard time keeping track of these numbers.

Max hates me getting it all on paper (the form prints even as he pressures the customer for a decision) but fortunately I'm too stupid to learn that he never wants estimates written. Customers, on the other hand, love estimates, even when they're not legally binding because you don't have all the part numbers. Max can't yell at me for giving them what they want. At least, not in front of them.

I hand over the hand-written paper, dodging Max's evil eye. "Eighteen hundred dollars?" Mr. Hartman mutters. And that's only the lower end of the range.

"Yeah." I look to Hartman's son, for some reason lacking his cavalier smile. "That was one expensive joyride."

I'm biking home now, thinking about that snapped axle. "The kid's lucky he didn't slam into something."

Bucky drifts at my side, not using his wings for the moment. "After-hours decisions made by thrill-seekers are rarely known for their wisdom."

Oh, right, he's not done scolding me. Do we think that's a hint? A giant hint? A "blot-out-the-sun-with-its-hugeness" hint?

Not huge enough for Bucky. "Speaking of expensive joyrides, let's talk about Francisco."

"What are you going to say? That I should never see him again? I'm not going to." I'd tell Bucky to save his breath, but he doesn't breathe. "It's the perfect one-night-stand. A bombshell drops out of the sky in a hot car, they run around town, and she vanishes into the stratosphere. No strings, good memories."

Bucky sounds unconvinced. "Why did you do it in the first place?"

"I told you, it was fun." I would shrug, but shrugging while biking causes falling while biking. "It's not a big deal."

"I think it is."

I stop my bike in front of my apartment. "Well, I disagree."

The steps outside the brownstone are made of (take a wild guess—you know you want to) brown stone, scuffy beneath my feet. Steep, too, but I carry my bike to the landing, then haul open the heavy outer door in order to unlock the even heavier inner door, and then I wait while my eyes adjust. My landlady, bless her heart, knows we don't live in the hallway and therefore feels no compunction to light it. Fifteen watts and sunshine is what we get for two grand a month.

After I can see again, I chain my bike to the stair railing, then haul my sunburnt self up steps that serenade me with an alternating groan and squeak. At the top floor I fit my key into a lock three times as old as I am. It thunks open, and after I get inside, the Master Lock clunks shut with a resounding solidity.

I expect to be alone, so I'm startled into a scream when I'm facing an unknown angel.

Chapter Four

She's smarter than both of us combined

The new angel sits on my table holding one of Beth's origami cranes in manicured fingertips. "Juliet Singer, otherwise known as Lee the Mechanic from Mack's Foreign Auto on Fifth Avenue, owner of a 1965 Mustang and breaker of hearts—greetings."

By the time she's finished, my back is pressed against the hardwood door. I can't breathe.

She stands, her hands extended. "Don't be afraid, Lee. I'm here to bring you a message of hope."

I can't look away. She wears a floor-length prairie skirt and an unadorned shirt, both silk. Loose like the skirt, her hair ripples to her waist. She raises her golden feathers as she steps closer. "Listen, Lee. Listen and learn."

Bucky? I think frantically, but there's no answer. She's close enough to touch me, still holding the paper crane.

"Who are you?" I rasp.

She replies, "Why do you ask my name?"

That's what Bucky says when I ask his real name. I try to relax.

She spreads her wings, and the crane in her hands spreads its own. "Lee, love, you must listen to me. I have a message for your heart about your future."

The air carries the scent of roses, so faint that I keep trying to catch a whiff of it, and then when I think it's gone, it teases my mind away again. So beautiful. Her midnight eyes, her graceful movements, the smell, her voice as golden as her feathers. The silk rustles with softness, and I think about something that smooth against my own skin.

Bucky? Where's Bucky?

Even as I start to say "Where—" she says, "Read deep into your heart and your inner peace."

She's amazing.

The paper crane on her palm pirouettes with its neck arched. Bucky never does things like that. I'm so tired. Where is Bucky? But her eyes, her amazing eyes—

She extends her hand toward me. "Let me into your heart. Open your thoughts to me and allow me to slip inside."

Wow—so easy. Just open my heart to her, just invite her inside and give her control and let her figure it all out for me. Bucky won't do that. He always makes me puzzle things out for myself.

My mouth is watering. "I—Where's Bucky?"

"This is my assignment, not his." Again roses tease at the peripheries of my senses. "More to the point, he *must* not be here now. Bucky is keeping you too tightly attached to himself. You have to reach beyond his parlor tricks and not rely on him for everything. Relax and let me show you your true potential."

I shudder

She says, "You have to send Bucky away for your own good. And for his."

My heart plummets into my gut. I love Bucky. He's my friend—he's always been here.

"He's standing in your way." The angel looks sad. "He's been warned, but he ignores it. He's going to send you to Hell if you don't cut yourself loose. And if he causes your downfall, he's going to burn too."

Bucky, in Hell? Getting hurt because of me?

I'm about to reach for her hand, but then my heart hurts again, and I pull back. I don't want to let him go either. It's selfish, but maybe we can figure this out. Maybe we can make it work so he can stay and no one gets hurt.

The roses are still bewitching, but I close my eyes and make her brilliant eyes and golden glow leave my mind. How can I put this off? I need a delaying tactic.

Randy tested Bucky all those years ago. How did he do it? What was it I'd told Hal?

Oh, right. "Pray with me. I'll talk with you if you pray with me first."

She smiles. "Pray, love. That's what your Father wants. Pray to the God who loves you."

Wait, what? "*You* pray with me." I'd sound a lot more confident if I weren't still backed against the door with my arms in front of my chest.

Her eyes, already black, darken perceptibly. Or maybe it's the apartment itself that's darkened.

Wait a minute. What if she's not really an angel? What if that test...what if she just failed it? What are you supposed to do if you're facing a demon?

I saw this in a movie once. "In the name of God, get out of here."

It's like I'm the Exorcist or something, minus the green slime. Abruptly I'm speaking to no one. I drop back against the door, breath heaving.

In the next moment, my head jerks up. "Bucky? Bucky, where are you? Are you okay?"

Nothing.

"Bucky! Show yourself!"

Where is he? I can't do anything for him if he's hurt or trapped. How do you help an angel? Or did I drive him away too? What if she wasn't a demon after all and she took Bucky with her?

I put my face in my hands and try to stop panicking. In the next moment, I feel hands on my shoulders.

I whip away, only to find it's Bucky afte rall. "Oh!" I lunge toward him as if to hug him and have to catch myself when he's not physically present because I'm just that brilliant. "What happened to you?"

"I got overwhelmed." He sounds breathless. "We need to talk."

You can't sit an angel down on the couch and give him a mug of hot chocolate with extra whipped cream, but I would. I'd even put sprinkles on it, and I'd bring him a blanket too.

Instead it's just me and him sitting up against the hardwood door on a hardwood floor, unable even to hug because he's immaterial.

I don't think angels can get hurt, not the way we can. They're spirits. And that's all nice in theory, but this is reality where I'm sitting with my breath heaving, staring at Bucky who looks whiter than the porcelain on our bathroom sink. His eyes are reddened. His wings are limp.

I put my hand up to his, and he raises his to meet it, as if we're on opposite sides of a mirror.

"Can I do anything?" I whisper.

Bucky regards me for a moment. Angels have the most amazing eyes, and they tend to look right at you when they talk.

I'm still seeing his eyes, but now I'm also seeing hers, the shadow angel sitting on my tabletop. I get a sense of her, sinuous and rippling, and the impact of her will crashing against his. I feel him in her restraint, terribly worried for me because she had gotten between us and he couldn't protect me.

The Bucky I can see with my eyes rather than my heart looks more than a little worried.

I swallow. "Did she hurt you?"

"No." I get the impression that he can take being restrained, but he didn't want me separated from him.

"Was that a demon?"

He nods.

My hands tremble. "Is she going to come back?"

He steels himself. "If she does, we fight her off."

"But I didn't do anything."

"You did the right things." He shakes his head. "You can't outsmart her, and you can't strong-arm her. Don't talk to her. Let me fight her while you run from her."

My brow furrows. "How do I do that?"

He swallows. "Just— Just don't listen to what she has to say."

"What did she want?"

He leans forward and drops his voice to the merest breath. "Don't quote me on this, but I think she wants you in Hell."

I sit back far enough to give him a dirty look, and he offers a smile that's disarmingly cute. I fold my arms.

"I mean, what did she want from me right now?"

"She was quite clear about that. She wanted you to let her into your heart so she could take up residence, then separate you from me. Ultimately she would own you, own your thoughts, and own your will." He clenches his fists. "She had you enthralled like a snake-charmer, and as soon as you allowed her access into your heart she was going to start coloring your perceptions, introducing doubts where you had none before, and making you cynical."

I raise my eyebrows.

"More cynical than you usually are," Bucky amends. His color has picked up, and his eyes sparkle again.

"I didn't mean that. I mean the doubt thing. Doubt isn't necessarily bad." I rub my chin. "I doubted her, right? For that matter, I also doubted Patrick Edgars when he told me he'd definitely marry me if only I took off all my clothes for him."

"Doubt is a good thing in the correct doses at the correct time. But," Bucky adds, sitting up on his knees and raising his wings, "what if you doubted me every single time you saw me? Yes, you can and should challenge me, and if I ever say anything that sounds as if I shouldn't have said it, *please* challenge me. But on an ordinary basis, what if you woke up every morning doubting God's existence and demanding that God prove Himself to you again today? And then again the next day? And the day afterward?"

I sit back, palms on the floor. "But then wouldn't I also doubt that God *didn't* exist?"

"That's a good point." He looks intrigued. "A true atheist questions God's existence *and* God's non-existence." Bucky has his smile back. "So yes, healthy skepticism is a terrific thing and can give a huge boost to your spiritual life. That's not what she would have had in mind."

I shift backward a little so we have more distance between us. "Okay, so speaking of healthy questions—was what she said true?"

Bucky looks pained. "It really depends on what she said. Was it categorically untrue? Sadly, no. One of their favorite tactics is to say something that's true but you're not ready to know it yet. Another favorite tactic is to tell you something so close to truth that you might already believe it—except it's twisted enough to cause harm."

Both those options stink. "Don't they ever just lie? Tell me if what she said was true."

Bucky flinches. "And—I have no idea what she told you."

Oh. I figured he'd be able to hear what she was saying, being my guardian angel and all. "What good are you?"

"I'm wondering that myself. You could remedy this gap in my knowledge if you wanted."

I make a face. "She said—" My throat closes up, and my eyes burn. I blink, then stare at my lap. "She said...you..."

"Hold on. If it made you that upset, I revise what I told you before and say it's categorically untrue."

"But—" I swallow. "She—"

"She's a demon." He tucks up his knees. "If you're this upset, it's because she wanted you to be."

"Wouldn't something terrible but true also have me this upset?"

He bites his lip. "I can't for the life of me think of anything that terrible in your life."

I shiver. "What if I'm endangering you?"

His eyes widen, and he smacks his hand into the floor. "You know, I understand God lets them roam the Earth to test people, but there are times I really wish they were chained down in Hell." He shakes his head. "You're not endangering me. I told you how I got assigned."

The tears spill over. "But listen. She said I love you too much and we're getting in each other's way. And that if I end up in Hell, then God's going to take it out on you and send you to Hell too. And I don't want that!"

He blinks, then leans closer. "You're more worried that *I'd* be thrown into Hell than that *you'd* be thrown into Hell?"

I cover my face with my hands.

"Lee, that's really sweet. Really. Look up." He has his face right near mine. "I'm perfectly safe. I run my conduct by God at just about every opportunity. He'd warn me."

I put my face back in my hands.

"It's easier to feel love for someone you can see and talk to than for an abstraction you're praying to. God understands that. You're doing fine."

I swallow. "She said you'd say that."

"She's smarter than both of us combined, Lee. Of course she knew what I would say." Bucky shakes his head. "But she can't change the collateral evidence."

I think for a moment.

Bucky forces a small smile. "You're going to ask me what collateral evidence is, aren't you?"

"See, you're smarter than me too, so..."

His look softens. "Are my actions more consistent with her story or with mine?" He tilts his head. "Has the net effect of our relationship been to make you generous or to make you selfish?"

My brow furrows. "I— I think you've been good for me."

He reaches up to touch my hair, and there's the mildest tingle as his fingers cross my forehead. "If it made you feel better, I'd back off. I would recommend against it. But I don't want you to doubt me, and if distance will reassure you, that much I can give. I can pray with you too. Let me know what you want, and it's yours."

I look at him again. "Thank you."

He tilts his head, and his eyes glimmer. "You don't know what you want, do you?"

I want her not to have appeared in the first place. I want her not to come back. I don't think Bucky can give me either of those.

He hugs me then, an angelic contact that always leaves me reeling. There's the feeling of being stared-at, but at the same time it's a gentle tingling across my shoulders and a tightness in my throat.

When the pressure eases, my cheeks are wet, and I hunt for a tissue. Bucky has vanished, but I know I'm not alone.

Chapter Five

The Kingdom of God is like a hex nut.

Of course, I'm not really sure I'm not "not-alone" with two angels rather than one, so I take the hammer out of the kitchen drawer and patrol the apartment.

Stupid invisible enemies. I hate this. I feel like there's a hidden mike around me, catching everything I say to analyze for potential chinks in my armor.

Actually, come to think of it, they're probably looking for potential armor around the chinks. Bucky's right: she's bound to be faster, smarter, stronger, wittier, and better able to manipulate me than anyone I've ever dealt with, and that includes that guy who stinks of cigars but always tries to weasel his way to a free oil change.

But for now, I'm going to go looking for something I can't see, armed with something that can't hurt her. This is a superb plan.

I should mention how our apartment is laid out. You can see from one end to the other if all the doors are open because all the main rooms are laid out in a line. The walls don't even go the whole ten feet up to the tin ceiling (I guess because the pretty design would have been messed up, and privacy is for other people?)

You enter at the rear of the apartment, facing the back yard (half concrete, half ivy) where there's a dining room joined to a minuscule bathroom and an even smaller kitchen; following that forward you encounter the first bedroom, the living room, and if you continued moving forward you'd fall four stories to your death, so you stop at the French windows. There's a second tiny bedroom off the side of the living room. The building itself is billed as an "extra-wide" brownstone, at a stunning nineteen *and a half* feet. We pay a premium for those six inches.

Ladies and Gentlemen, welcome to New York. This is why we gasped in awe when Uncle Mickey moved to New Jersey and had grass not only in back of his house, but also in front. And his house was fully-detached.* With a pool. And a driveway. And no alternate side of the street parking. That's what it must be like in Heaven, only you don't have to live in New Jersey.

Oh, right, I'm supposed to be hunting a demon. I check out the windows looking downhill toward Fifth Avenue, Fourth Avenue, etc, all the way to the East River. Today is clear enough to see Manhattan, but the skyline is remarkably demon-free.

It's stupid to hold a hammer while hunting for a demon, but I want to hold onto something. Don't Catholics use Holy Water and a crucifix for this?

Then I remember, I kind of do have something I can hold. I head to the china cabinet and get out my ceramic Bucky.

---

* *Housing primer for non-city-dwellers: row houses like our brownstone are all together in a row with only a firewall between them, at least if you believe city code. Windows are only at the front and back. Semi-detached houses are a premium because, coming as they do at the end of the row of row houses, they have windows on the other side and a marginally wider lot. A fully-detached house would have space all around it. It must be disorienting to have windows on all sides.*

It's not really Bucky, but I bought it in late January in an overpriced gift shop, the only real-looking angel among the knickknacks.

I lift my delighted little figurine and hold him against my palm. *You're coming with me,* I think to it. *You're going to remind me what's real and what's not.*

There's a prompt inside: am I aware that this is a ceramic representation of an angel rather than the real thing?

I say to the empty apartment, "And are you aware I can't hold your hand?"

Inside: *Touché.*

I stop. *This isn't a graven image, is it? I mean, it was only ten bucks.*

Don't pour honey over it and you'll be fine.

"Oh, sarcasm, my love?" I head through the French doors into the living room, flip on the light, and look in the corners. No demon.

You know, I hear in my head, *I'd tell you if she was still around.*

"You didn't tell me the first time."

That's not fair. I was kind of tied up.

"And how do I know you're not tied up now?"

Fine, keep looking.

I head off the side into the second bedroom, and that's also clear. No demon. No roommate either. I've got the place to ourselves.

I take a long breath and lean against the doorframe. Half the time this bedroom belongs to me, but because it's summer, it's my roommate's so she can sleep in late. The one in the middle with no privacy is currently my bedroom.

With one insurmountable problem surmounted, I look at my phone and discover I've got another. Namely, two voicemails. Caller ID tells me they're both from Francisco.

Well, that sucks. In that sleep-deprived haze after the club kicked everyone out, I forgot about cell phones having caller ID. Dating was easier ten years ago.

His message is cheerful. He wants to see me again, which is quite a bit sooner than when I wanted to, since I'd have opted for "never."

I could call him back and break it off. *I'm sorry, but Sunday night I took leave of my senses. I have a long-term boyfriend, and that night he and I were discussing marriage, if you can believe it. Yeah, me. Very funny, right?*

The next option is the Miss Manners option, whereby I fail to return any calls forever. Yet another option is to keep seeing him and tell Hal I want more space.

None of these are good options.

In retrospect, my best option would have been to a) feel flattered and then b) throw away his phone number and c) get a good night's sleep. This would have resulted in a clear conscience, or at least a non-nagging guardian angel, and no need to dump a guy who's fun but has bad timing.

I delete the messages and go with option 2. Francisco will figure out my lack of interest from lack of response. I'll screen my calls for the next month, and that should do it.

The next morning, I'm up to my elbows in transmission fluid and grease and little parts I'm pretty sure will all go back where I think they belong when I realize—the Shadow doesn't have to be visible to be around. She could be right here, staring at me. Boo!

This is like a game of chess, and I already know not to play chess with an angel.

My cell phone rings in my back pocket when I can't possibly answer it, so I let it roll to voicemail. An hour later, drinking coffee and celebrating to myself the fact that five million transmission parts are once again on speaking terms with one another, I find the call came from Hal. *Lee, if you don't mind, please call me back. I need to hear a sane, rational voice right about now.*

Hah—so he called me? Or maybe he was about to add "But I called you instead." He sounds bushwhacked.

I dial his work number, get his voicemail, fake a Australian accent and demand that he bring me to his leader or I'll be forced to read him Shakespeare in the original Sumerian, and then get back to work. Next up: squeaky brakes from which I've been asked to remove the squeak.

This job is the best. There's something new every day, like a car still on a lift with a shattered axle and two shredded tires, even though you do get a lot of the same-old-same-old. Oil changes and state inspections are a staple, but tune-ups are more challenging, and then every so often you get the prize: the mystery car suffering from "won't go" and "it makes a funny noise sometimes."

Plus, just take a look at this place! Four repair bays, four mechanics, the owner in a room so full of papers that you'd swear an office supply store sneezed all over it, and the owner's wife who comes in every so often to ensure we'll actually make payroll the way the law kind of demands.

And tools! So many tools you wouldn't believe it—and good tools, too. Torque wrenches, ball hex wrenches (both fractional and metric), ratchet wrenches, impact wrenches—we got them. Awls, nut-threaders, extractors, twenty-six types of screwdriver, drills with one thousand drill bits, air compressors, grinders, ratchets.

Jesus is a carpenter, and when I get to Heaven, I want to see his workshop because maybe it has even cooler tools than this place. But not by much. If Jesus were born today, he wouldn't have taken up carpentry. He would have been an auto mechanic.

"To what shall I compare the Kingdom of God?" he would have posted to Facebook. "The Kingdom of God is like a hex nut. Alone it is the smallest and plainest of the parts of the car, and yet without it, the car would fall to pieces in the road and go nowhere. Or the Kingdom of God is like a good oil change. Some of the oil burns away or leaks out, and without its slipperiness to lubricate all the moving parts, lo, the engine seizes and even the finest vehicle will go nowhere. You who have ears to hear, remove those iPod earbuds so you can actually hear me for once."

I can't use earbuds in the garage, so I pop the *Rumours* album into the tape deck (yes, in the twenty-first century even!) and let Bucky listen while I keep working.

As I'm raising our good friend the Axle-Shattered Maxima on the lift, the phone rings in my back pocket. I pick up with, "Hey, guy. Your boss is driving you nuts again?"

"Not as nuts as you are," says a voice that isn't Hal's.

It takes a moment, plus a frantic look at caller ID, to realize I should not have picked up this call.

Crap, crap, crap. "Hello, Francisco."

"I was beginning to think you were avoiding me."

Well, I was. "Now isn't a good time."

"Where are you?" He's barely audible over the sound of one of the other mechanics banging on a wheel frame. "On a construction site?"

"Car's in the shop," I'm hot between my shoulder blades from Bucky's stare. "I'll call you back later."

"I want to see you tonight. I won't take no for an answer." He laughs. "Let me give you a lift home."

"Already arranged. Sorry. I've got to go."

Francisco says, "Do you shoot pool?"

Behind me, the *Rumours* album shuts off. No one is near the radio. Subtle, Bucky. Subtle.

"I'll meet you tonight. On Fifth Avenue and Tenth Street there's a bar and grill with a pool table in the back."

Just my luck: I can see it from here. "I—"

A beep. Hal's on call waiting.

"Come on, Babe. I'll go easy on you."

"I have plans."

"I'll be there. Show up."

I drop his call and stand there, breath heaving. Then I pick up Hal on call waiting. "Hi, guy. What's up?"

"Is it a crime to kill your boss if she honestly deserves it?"

"You'd have to ask your attorney." I bite my lip. "Is it jeopardizing your job to say something like that while you're in the office?"

"Probably. Right now, I don't care."

For five minutes, Hal gives me the lowdown on his accounting woes, which I hear in between blasts from a pneumatic riveter. His boss has mood swings that would leave Vincent Van Gogh shaking his head. She tends to conduct conversations either in a mousy whisper, leaving out little details like a project's deadline because she doesn't want to stress her employees, or at top volume because they missed the deadline she never told them about. Hal can handle her, but it's a strain when she asks him to complete a task by noon, then comes to his desk screaming questions about why he isn't working on a different top priority project that she never mentioned.

It's kind of like working with distressed automobile owners, except I get to deal with at most fifteen a day and he has only her with her fifteen rotating faces of doom.

"Which one's open on your computer?" I say as I loosen the lug nuts. "A spreadsheet or your resume?"

"Neither—I'm walking to Starbucks to get a cup of coffee I don't particularly want." He sighs. "I'm leaving tonight at five even if she's standing in the doorway with a machete. Do you want to come over for dinner?"

The last of the lugs is off the wheel, only without a hand free I can't get the tire off. "You shouldn't have to cook if you're this wiped out."

He sounds irritated. "If I cook a meal, at least I can do something right."

In all fairness, Hal claims cooking relaxes him. I have no clue why because it's not as if he sticks a hot dog in the microwave and then, if he wants an extra special treat, toasts the bun. He'll cobble together a wild, experimental dinner from whatever he has in his fridge—the worse the day, the more exotic the meal. We may end up eating crayfish that's still alive but lightly dusted with sage on a bed of apricot halves.*

"You're doing everything right. She's a few lug nuts short of a tire change." I sigh. "I've gotta run now, but let me know what time you're getting home and I'll meet you there."

"I will. I love you." He sighs. "I'm sorry for dropping this all over you."

"I love you too. Hang in there."

With my cell phone in my back pocket, I return to removing axle parts from the DeMaximized Maxima.

At five o'clock, I'm shooting pool with Francisco.

---

* *And which would taste amazing, for the record.*

At six o'clock, I'm waiting at Seventh Avenue and Ninth Street for Hal to exit the subway station.

People stride past with their heads tucked and their eyes on the pavement, purses safely under the arms of the women and hands in the jacket pockets for the men. It's the New York City shuffle, not meeting anyone's gaze but at the same time staying out of everyone else's way. It's how you have space when there are eight million of you in fifty square miles.

Bucky won't tell me where Hal's train is, probably irritated at me for meeting Francisco again, but all we did was play a couple of games of pool. He didn't even touch me other than a couple of those "Here, let me show you how to make this shot" moves where guys think they're so sneaky. He beat me both times, and he wanted to take me to dinner, but I ditched him and walked here instead. He didn't follow. I've been in one place long enough that I'd have seen him if he had.

The stairwell from the subway gushes its once-every-three-minutes hemorrhage of commuters, so I turn my attention to the crowd scanning for Hal.

In the next moment, *she* is standing in front of me, her eyes absorbing, her breath the scent of roses. I can't hear the traffic only ten feet from me. It's the Shadow and it's me, and we're on a street corner except that we're not. We're on the brink of eternity. I don't look away from her eyes, but if I did, I know the world would be grey and formless.

"Lee Singer," she says, "don't you care that you're jeopardizing Bucky?"

My arms and chest weigh a thousand pounds each. Bucky said— If she returned, Bucky said—

"He loves you too much to let you go, but you need to release him. He's breaking the rules by continuing to appear to you." Her voice drops so low I can hear it only if

I strain, like a flute played two apartments away. The depths of her eyes sparkle like stars at night when you're out in New Jersey. I swallow, and my mouth is sweet as if I'm recalling a peppermint tasted hours ago.

She raises a hand right before my chest. If I raise my own hand, I'll brush her fingertips. "You're harming him by keeping him tied to you. You need to release him for his own good."

Tears come to my eyes, and I blink so I can keep seeing her clearly.

"Lee, I know how much this must hurt you, but he's stalled out. Angels need to fly, otherwise they're swept backward in the stream of time. He's fixated on you to the point where he no longer grows in his spirit." Her eyes dim, and their sudden emptiness leaves me hungry for lost light. "Angels need constant motion. Give him motion. Let him go free."

I want to run. I want to stay. A chill winds its way up my spine even though all day I've walked around drenched in my own sweat. My vision blackens, and I can't feel my own arms and legs. *Oh, God.* What did I do last time?

"Pray with me," I whisper.

"Sweetheart," she whispers in return, "pray for yourself. You must, *must*, pray for yourself."

And then she's vanished.

"Lee?"

My vision clears, and I see Hal. He's wearing a look of horror. "What's the matter?"

My cheeks are wet with tears. I hadn't realized.

I can't even talk. I just collapse on him and bury my face in his shoulder.

Chapter Six

The thrill of watching me create havoc out of nothing

It took ten minutes rather than five to reach Hal's apartment because he let me cry against his shoulder for five of them. I couldn't even talk, but once he realized, he did nothing other than hold me.

When I finally pulled away, he handed me his little packet of Kleenex, and I mopped up as best as I could. Without looking up, I let him guide me to his apartment, one arm around my shoulder and the other holding my backpack. And then, once we were here, I told him to get started cooking. He didn't want to leave me, but I told him he had to.

That's how I ended up here, on his couch while he rummages in the kitchen.

Bucky? Where are you?

He hasn't answered since the Shadow appeared. I don't know if she restrained him again, if he's chasing her off, if he's injured or even dead—but I don't think angels can die.

But even worse, what if she's not a demon and he's really defying God by appearing to me? What if she's bringing official charges against him or whatever angels do, like a lawyer testifying to a grand jury that he's being harmful to me? And do I have any right to protest if she is? They say God does what's best for us, although no, it's really Bucky who says that, and then Bucky usually laughs that sometimes we're not sure how difficult *the best* will actually be.

Maybe I don't want the best. Maybe I just want Bucky.

Bucky?

Do angels get lawyers? Would he get a phone call?

Hal returns from the kitchen to upgrade me to a full-size box of Kleenex.

"I can make dinner now, but—" He sits beside me. "Can you talk?"

"I can't reach Bucky." I swallow. "I saw another angel. I think a fallen one, at least he said she was the first time she appeared." Hal looks as if I've just said — actually, he looks as if I've just said I saw a fallen angel. "But she said Bucky's angering God by appearing to me, and now I can't reach Bucky."

There's a long pause, and then Hal offers, "Oh."

I put my face in my hands. "I just want him to reappear and explain to me what's going on."

Hal says, "What do you do to...summon him? Do you need anything?"

"Yeah, I need a purple chalk circle and four parrot feathers for the cardinal points."

"Look, what do I know about this stuff?" He sounds a little defensive, or maybe it's me. "Should I just make dinner, then, while you're getting him?"

Right then I shiver because if I can't reach Bucky, I might have no guardian. Hal's guardian is looking out for the two of us, or maybe he's fled for help and the two of us are exposed. Maybe the angels from the surrounding co-op units are taking up the slack. I don't know how this works—but once Hal goes into the kitchen, I'll be totally alone.

Well, suck it up. I put my arms around Hal's neck and nod against his shoulder. "I'll join you when I can."

Is Hal mildly relieved that he doesn't have to take care of this? I'd be.

I take a deep breath. *Bucky, please come back. Please. I need you.*

It's as if heat shimmers over the matching single seat cater-corner to the couch. In between one moment and the next, the shimmering gathers form until it resembles Bucky, but again with his wings drooping and his eyes the color of apple juice.

I gasp. "Did she hurt you?"

"No," he whispers. "You did."

There are times I wish my life was a TiVo unit, where I could record conversations and run them back afterward to make sure I caught everything the first time. You know, like when the doctor tells you something and you don't remember afterward what she said about how she's going to follow up on it, or when you wander downstairs as a little kid and you can only remember that you were told your father is dead only you never, no matter how hard you try, can remember who told you, and when you talk about it later with someone else, the people you remember being there simply were not there at the time.

I'm blinking. "How did I hurt you?"

"You keep summoning her." Bucky's gaze is like an arrow into my head. "You're putting yourself in bondage to her, and that's crimping my ability to protect you."

I sit backward. *I'm not summoning a demon!*

"Aren't you?" he says. "Did you ask her name?"

"She said what you always do, that I'm not allowed to know."

"You can demand her name because it's her *function,* not her *identity.* She's just not telling you." He leans forward. "And every time you summon her, you're empowering her to push me aside."

What am I doing? I sit forward. *I'll stop—but how can I be summoning something evil without knowing about it?*

Bucky's eyes are fire. "Are you totally unaware that you're cheating on Hal with Francisco?"

My eyes bug. "I'm not—" *I'm not cheating on him!*

"Then tell him about it." Bucky sweeps his arm toward the kitchen. "Tell him you were bored by accountancy agonies and so you wandered over to a pool hall with a guy who thought you and your Mustang looked hot. Tell him you went into the Ladies' room so you could talk to him on your cell without Francisco overhearing." His mouth is a line. "For that matter, tell Francisco you have a steady boyfriend whom your family is pressuring you to marry."

I sit, elbows on my knees, cheeks in my palms, eyes closed. Bucky in my heart rages like a downpour.

"Do you want to know her name?" He stands. "It's Betrayal. And you're right to call her the Shadow, because she's going to cling to your heels for as long as you follow this path."

I bite my lip.

"Even if you don't care about hurting Hal, which I don't understand at all, and you don't care about hurting your immortal soul, why not think about it as you're hurting *me* when you do this kind of thing?"

"I don't understand." I grope for another tissue, which hisses out of the box with a subtle *ffft* even as another one pops up behind. *I've dated multiple guys before. She never showed up then.*

"Didn't Hal know about Bill? Everyone always knew about everyone else. You can't be unfaithful to someone to until you've promised faithfulness." Bucky folds his arms. The yellow has returned to his wings, but the white and brown are still mottled. "Why am I telling you this? I'm sure you know it."

I remain with my head cradled in my fingertips.

"You're restraining me worse than she is." Bucky flares his wings. "I've always managed to keep her in check because you weren't listening to her. Now you're courting her even as she's courting you. Every time you listen to her, it's going to get harder for me to push her back, easier for her to shove me aside, and harder for me to reappear to you afterward. Think well on it."

Bucky vanishes.

Wow. This just got ugly in a hurry.

Not wanting to be alone, I mop up my face and make my way to Hal's bathroom, a tiny nook just as neatly apportioned as the rest of the apartment. For the record, I hate how faces look like they've been crying after you're done. Humans should be able to get it over with and walk away from the icked-up tissues with no residuals.

Out in the kitchen, Hal looks up from the cutting board. "Everything okay?"

"He's cheesed-off, but I guess he's fine." I slip onto the stool alongside the kitchen's center island. "I don't think it's possible to hurt an angel, other than hurting his feelings."

Hal continues chopping.

"I'm sorry." I touch his guiding arm as he chops. "You had me come here because you'd had a rotten day yourself, not because you wanted me to fall apart."

"I can't think of a day I *would* invite you over to have you fall apart." He looks up, utterly serious but his eyes sparkling. "I'm just glad you're feeling better. It's not like I can do anything about this." He reaches into an open jar for a red slimy thing that looks like it should come pinned with "*spleen.*" "And trust me, despite what you may think, your problems are actually sane in comparison to my boss."

"Why do you stay in that job?" I walk my fingers up his arm while he continues chopping the roasted pepper. "You work in Manhattan, not West Cupcake, Montana. You'd be able to find another job in a heartbeat."

Hal says, "I've thought about it."

I watch in silence as he proceeds to do something that I, in a thousand years, never would have done. He concocts an entire meal out of Portobello mushroom caps, some kind of cheese, roasted red peppers, spinach, and breadcrumbs. I can see there's half a loaf of Italian bread heating in the oven, and a can of mandarin oranges sits empty on the countertop; I presume the evicted residents are chilling in the fridge. Tiny shrimp are thawing in a bowl of water. While I maintain an awed hush like a pilgrim entering the Temple area in Jerusalem, Hal chops fresh parsley and mixes that with the other ingredients then proceeds to stuff the mushroom caps.

I wonder if Bucky felt this way watching God create the universe out of nothing. I'd ask, but he'd probably mutter something about the thrill of watching me create havoc out of nothing, and who needs that?

After arranging the mushrooms on a baking sheet for a vacation in the oven, Hal turns to me. "So."

"So?" I open my hands. "Rewrite your resume. You need to get out of there."

He chuckles. "What makes you think it would be better elsewhere?"

"You wouldn't have to deal with Julie of the Jungle."

"Instead I'd have to deal with Insane Ingmar or Sadist Sam." He puts his hands in his pockets. "They're not all bad days."

"But they could be all good days." I rest my elbows on the tile top of the island. "You could be a chef."

He laughs out loud.

I slip off the stool and get plates out of the cabinet. They match. "You're good enough that you could get a job cooking anywhere."

"It's my hobby," he sing-songs.

"And no one ever got hired to do her hobby for a living?"

"It would kill the enjoyment."

"It hasn't for me," I say, and he flinches.

"I'm sorry. I forgot for a minute."

"And you're in a better position than I was when I started. You've already been taking classes." I put my hand on his sleeve. "I'll help you find a position as a chef."

"Let me give you fifty reasons. No," he said, "let me give you only five. One—starting from the bottom, working entire days chopping carrots. Two—very stiff competition. Three—not catering to the whims of the public."

"As opposed to catering to the whims of Julie of the Jungle."

"She's not as fickle. Four—an unbelievable pay cut. Five—the loss of all my accounting skills."

My eyes brighten. "Open your own restaurant!"

"Ah." Hal points at me. "I see Julie is not the only one who lost her mind."

"You could open a restaurant, be your own boss, do your own books, and have a blast!" While I set silverware at our places, Hal washes his cutting board and knife. He's the only one I know who cleans up while in the act of cooking. "I could ask Max how to make a business plan."

"I'm glad you mentioned the business plan, because until you said that, I wondered where this castle in the air was grounded in reality, if at all." Hal looks up from the sink. "I can't cough up six figures to open my own restaurant. I have no restaurant experience. I don't know the first thing about it."

"You could read books and get backers."

Hal addresses the wall. "Pardon me, but do you have a hundred grand I can borrow? I'll name my restaurant after you." He turns back to me. "Actually, the one thing I do know about the restaurant industry is that you can't pick up what you need to know from a couple of books and a love of cooking."

"What would it take?"

"It would take someone else. I'm content cooking for you and the occasional dinner party." He sets the knife in the dish rack. Have I mentioned it's as long as my forearm? "It's one thing to repair cars all day. It would be another to open your own garage. I'd rather not trawl the markets at four AM looking for bargain fish, or research how the patrons want their pan-seared beef seasoned this year, or figure out how to take reservations without shutting the place to walk-ins. New restaurants have a sixty percent failure rate. Accounting has closer to zero."

I sit, frowning.

He sets the cutting board in the rack, then turns to me. "I appreciate what you're saying. But I honestly enjoy what I do most of the time. It was different for you."

I hated my previous jobs. Actually, I shouldn't say *hated*. I should say, "wished I wouldn't wake up alive in the morning if it meant I didn't have to go to work."

He puts his arms around my shoulders, and I raise mine so we're standing in a frozen slow-dance. When he kisses me, I savor the feel of him, the scent, the way he's all right there. He pulls away, but I linger for what I know comes next, and then there it is, a light brush of his lips against mine before he releases me.

He always does that. It's as if he doesn't want to let me go, so he does this half-kiss to make it easier.

This time, I don't let him go. Pulling him closer, I kiss him with a ferocity that surprises even myself, and in the next moment he has his arms wrapped around me, and I'm backed against the island. He smells of Old Spice and olive oil and Manhattan office supplies, and he's intoxicating. His hands are in my hair, and I clutch his shoulders while kissing him urgently.

Eventually he gets a breath. "We can talk about my job more often if it does this to you."

I kiss him again, but then I just pull him close for a long hug. I think he realized before I did, that it's not about him right now. It's about a very scared me needing something solid to keep away the shadows.

An hour later, I'm home again. This time it's not a fallen angel at the table, but a crestfallen roommate.

"Stupid dragons." She glares up from a crumpled square of red paper. "Saint George had the right idea. Put a spear through the heart of all of them."

"Good evening to you too." I shut the door with a scratching thunk; because it doesn't quite fit in its frame when the humidity rises, you have to lean against it most of the summer. "Why do you make dragons if you hate them so much?"

"They sell like hotcakes." Beth crumples the red paper and grabs another sheet. "I can't walk away from a moneymaker, but I'd rather spend all day making frogs than half an hour making three dragons."

Beth clutters our apartment with both origami and preschool projects. The preschool projects are for the class she teaches during the year and the day camp kids she takes on during the summers. She also sells origami on Etsy, since Forbes has never found the need to feature multi-millionaire preschool teachers on its cover.

"Did you have dinner already?"

"Hal stuffed some Portobello caps with every single thing he could find in his refrigerator." I squint uneasily. "Somehow it tasted good, but I'm afraid to list the ingredients, so just use your imagination."

Beth has resumed folding the paper on our dining room table, a monstrosity suitable for folding a life-size origami alligator; we picked it up at a stoop sale three years ago when the previous table became a tetanus hazard, and it took both of us and three of my boyfriends to shoved it up the stairs.

She frowns at me. "You look like heck. Did he poison you?"

"I missed if he had cyanide in the fridge."

I go into the living room and raise the lid on the laptop, but then there's a push inside: we need to talk.

I grimace. *No, I need not to be talking to you right now.*

I push the button, but the computer fails to start.

My eyes narrow. "I'm going to kill you if you fried my computer."

Again that push inside: we need to talk.

"You're such a jerk sometimes." I stalk away from the computer desk to sit on the couch. "Are you going to fry the television as well?"

Bucky appears standing against the book shelf, home to our DVD collection, our board games, and our video games. "Would you care to define *jerk* in this context? Does it mean that I prefer not getting tied up, or does it mean you don't want to have a conscience?"

"It means you should have flipping well *told* me who she was and why she was able to appear the first time, and then we would have avoided our next little fling with 'Bucky gets his butt kicked while I get seduced by a demon who's five times smarter than I am.'"

Bucky's got his arms folded. "I wasn't aware it was my fault that you cheated on Hal."

"Don't play games with my head." My eyes narrow. "What kind of guardian would let me walk into that kind of situation without so much as a warning?"

"First of all—" and Bucky's eyes flame up even as he tilts down his chin. I gasp because it looks as if his hair will catch fire. "First of all, *I* am not responsible for your bad choices. *I* told you not to go out with Francisco, if you can recall back as far as yesterday morning. *I* urged you not to see him again. That's the first thing. Secondly, if I'd told you who she was and why she was able to subdue me, you would have felt awful. If I have any culpability in this mess, it's that I counted on your better judgment to prevent a repeat performance."

I draw a breath, but he raises his hand and stops me cold. "Thirdly—" His voice has dropped half an octave. "You seem to have forgotten which of us needs to get into Heaven. Regardless of what the Shadow told you, I'm in no jeopardy whatsoever. God won't hold it against me if you screw up your life. Is that perfectly clear?"

I bite my lip.

The flames subside and his wings relax. "You want to know what kind of guardian would let you walk into that kind of situation? A good one. One who expects you to learn from your mistakes. Don't let me down again."

He vanishes.

The computer boots up. I sit on the couch with my arms folded for a long time.

Chapter Seven:

An act of watching a tournament

There's no perfect way to tell a guy you aren't interested, and half the time if you tell a guy you've already got a boyfriend, he's going to pursue you even more. When a woman cools off toward a guy, he senses it and turns up the romance. This is why playing hard-to-get works so well for some women and why women who come across as desperate remain desperate. The negative side is that if you really are trying to cool things off, he turns up the heat regardless.

Thus the only way to tell him "no" is to say "no," and then nothing else. Just to put a bullet in the heart of the affair and allow it to die.

And for Exhibit 1 of this problem, let's look at Bill.

Bill and I have dated on and off forever (and yes, Shadow, he and Hal have met). Because he works at the gym where I'm a member, he and I still see one another three times a week, but he's kept it friendly. There's no rancor because there were never any expectations. Kind of the way I like things.

I'm just finished with the treadmill when Bill stops by and hands me my towel.* "You looked pretty grim there at the end."

---

* It's very easy to demystify a relationship by working out at the same gym. There's "hot" and there's "sweaty."

I shake my head rather than speak.

"Everything okay?"

I'm still winded. "For the most part."

"Politicians getting you down?"

Yeah, um, I told Bill I was a secretary for a political action committee, and I kind of never told him what's actually greasing my palms. When I hesitate, he must attribute it to being out of breath, because he adds, "Don't stress yourself to death."

My voice is thin. "At least it's not as hot as it was last week."

"I wouldn't know. Half the time it's freezing in here." Bill leans against the handle of the treadmill. "Listen, if you don't have anything to do tonight, there's a Brazilian Jujitsu tournament over at one of the high schools. I have tickets."

"Really?" I had no idea they did jujitsu in Brazil! Was there some mass migration of Samurai warriors to Brazil a thousand years ago during the great Samurai-Brazil War? I never paid attention in history class. Or is it one of those false cognate things, where "Brazil" is actually a corruption of Brahzeeru which is a street in south Tokyo. "What time—" I stop cold. "Oh, wait, I don't think I can go."

He shrugs. "It's not a big deal if you can't come, but I have to go because my sister's in it, and I thought you might like it."

I would. I'm just not sure how I'd like the after-effects. "Let me think about it."

Bill nods before walking away. "The tournament begins at seven."

I find an open weight machine and start working my arms. *Bucky? Do I have to say no?*

Inside, I feel a question mark.

Would it be an invitation to the Shadow?

Bucky appears on a nearby ab machine. He's wearing a grey sweat shirt and a pair of shorts. "Hal and Bill know about one another, and as far as you know, Bill's intention is not to seduce or date you as much as it is to have someone to sit with at the tournament."

I nod.

"Can you not see the difference?" Bucky frowns. "Would you tell Hal about going with Bill to watch a martial arts display?"

I shrug. *I don't think he'd care. Oh!* I could call Hal and ask if he minds—except I don't actually need Hal's permission to watch people get pummeled senseless with one of my friends, even if it's someone I used to date.

"Don't wrap yourself in knots figuring this out," Bucky says. "They have machines here to do that for you."

I know—he's rescued me from some of them. *So this wouldn't be an act of infidelity?*

"It would be an act of watching a tournament." Bucky rubs his chin. "Are you actually this confused, or are you jerking my chain? I can't tell."

My arms hurt now, so I do one last rep and then sit forward on the bench. *I'm actually this confused.*

"Then go. Have a good time. Enjoy the tournament. It's not a big deal." Bucky shrugs. "And maybe you need to think a bit more so you understand the difference between having friends and having an affair."

Bill drives to the gymnasium in his black Monte Carlo SS, a car he's unnecessarily proud of. I wish I could tell him about my Mustang, but he's so delighted with his "NASCAR Wannabe," and it's kind of a nice ride with a comfortable grey interior.

As it turns out, one of the other personal trainers is also along, so we're totally safe because a date is two people and we are three; even I can handle this much math.

How did I even get into this trap? I never promised to be faithful to Hal. It's just that once I realized I loved him, I didn't want to be with anyone else. He made it clear he wanted to be the only one, and I know he wants me to be faithful to him.

But when you say "faithful," I think "cocker spaniel," and that's the trouble. Hal's "faithful," as if I can call Hal and his tail wags and he fetches me a pizza.

Oh, right, pizza: so we'd been dating a month when I suggested we go out for pizza, and he said with all seriousness, "That's for Fridays." No. If I want pizza at seven o'clock in the morning on a Wednesday, I'll have it. I'm not faithful to my pizza. And that night, I got Hal to be unfaithful to Fridays.

So would that be it with Hal? Every Friday is pizza night, and every curve in the road is visible long before you take it at the speed-limit in your sensible sedan with plenty of trunk space?

Or some nights, would it be okay if Hal came home with tickets and said, "Follow me," and I just went along and discovered some exhibit at a gallery I never even knew existed? Because otherwise, I think I'd die.

At the tournament, Bill and I sit on wooden bleachers with no backs. Bill opens a bag of Doritos, and we turn our fingers orange while highly-trained athletes politely and ritualistically beat the snot out of each other. At the end of every match there's polite applause, except for when Bill's sister wins hers and there's one lunatic in the stands cheering like crazy. She waves at me, and I beam because her waving is better than her killing me barehanded.

Although seeing what she can do, I'd be honored to have her break my neck.

Afterward, Bill drops off the other trainer, then brings me home.

"You've been quiet. Tired?"

I shrug. "Sorry. I had a good time."

He nods. "I wasn't sure if you were mad about something."

"Everything is so complicated." I bite my lip. "If I like things the way they are, why do they have to change?"

"They don't." Bill looks at me as we idle at a red light. "What's eating you?"

"My family wants me to marry Hal. I don't want to get married."

"Oh. Who cares?" He chuckles. "Did he propose?"

"No." I wonder when his calendar schedules him to do that. "But he wants to get married eventually."

Bill says, "So cut him loose. Let him find someone else."

I flinch.

"Oh, you're in trouble!" He laughs out loud. "You can't keep him around and tell him he can't have what he wants. Either you give it to him or you let him go somewhere he can get it."

"It's my stupid family's fault." I fold my arms as we head up Carroll Street toward Sixth Avenue. "They instigated this."

"Do you really think he had no idea what marriage was until they henpecked him?'"

I run a hand through my hair. "From the way my mother talks, you'd think so."

"He'd have laughed it off and never mentioned it again."

I glare at him. "You're no help."

He puts his hand on my knee. "I'm just saying. I've been where he is, Kid, and I laughed it off."

I bet. Bill and I might have dated for ten years before it even occurred to us that people expected us to settle down.

But still—Bill was handsome. Is handsome. He's got a great sense of humor, lacks a little in the planning department but would do anything for a friend. I can see him ogling my Mustang or being impressed that I change tires by myself, and it would confuse him to no end that I can see my guardian angel. "Kid," he'd say, "are you sure you're all right in the head?" I'm not sure if that makes someone long-term material. But then again, I'm not long-term material either.

I wrap my fingers around his hand. "What should I do?"

He pulls into the fire hydrant space on Sixth Avenue, down the block from my house. "How should I know? He's a great guy."

I still have his hand in mine, and I bring the other hand over them. "Thanks. I—"

He leans closer. "It's okay."

Bill was a great kisser. My heart is pounding. The streetlights frame his face in gentle shadows, and the engine idles with a regular hum. I tighten my hands on his.

He lets go of me. "Don't worry about. It's not like you have to make a decision before the return period is up on the ring."

"You're right. Thanks for bringing me tonight." A moment later I'm walking toward home while he's pulled away down Garfield Place.

Maybe I made the wrong choice in February when I let him go and settled on Hal. I'm thinking about how good he smelled, his manly shoulders and confident stride.

The inner glass doors weigh a thousand pounds apiece, so it's slow going to open them. They close heavily at my back.

I turn to go upstairs, but the Shadow sits on the steps, a rose in her fingertips. "Lee, my love."

Chapter Eight

No slot in the daytimer for "spiritual warfare tactical development."

I haven't called yet for Bucky.

It's almost midnight, and I don't know what to do, so from my bed I'm watching street lights move across the ceiling.

It's the tin kind, with squares and ridges as if it's a tile floor. Since the walls don't reach all the way to the top, the movement of headlights on Sixth Avenue creates patterns as things shift. I can hear the swish as a car passes four stories below—all our windows are open—and then the lights all swing on the ceiling. A moment later, another one. A radio blares, then distorts as if dragged away, the bass lingering long after I can no longer hear the treble.

Bucky.

Shadow.

Infidelity.

With my hands knit behind my neck, I watch the semi-darkness. What happened to my world? Why don't I know where I am anymore?

Exhibit A: Bucky, lifelong friend and guardian, always right and yet now inexplicably wrong because he said she wouldn't come back if I went out with Bill, but there she was.

Exhibit B: Shadow, so persistent and attractive, so earnest and urgent that my holding tight to Bucky is harming both of us.

Bucky said a little doubt was okay, so I'm doubting him right now even as I'm doubting her. I've prayed a bit, too, but I don't know what to ask.

I'm afraid she hurt him. Or I did. He said it was me hurting him, and I don't want to see him beaten down again.

I wonder what it's like for other people who don't even know they have guardian angels. Maybe they don't care that an angel gets pummeled in the line of duty because it's just a soldier on the line and not their best friend.

It's not fair.

You shouldn't be jealous, but sometimes I'm eaten alive with envy for the people who can ask God a question and get an answer. Wouldn't it be cool to go to God.com and send Him an email, then get back a response in your inbox?

To: God@heaven.el
From: the.amazing.lee.singer@gmail.com
Subject: What's going on?
—

Dear God:
What the heck is happening here? Is Bucky okay? Why does this keep happening?
Love,
Lee

To: the.amazing.lee.singer@gmail.com
From: God@heaven.el
Subject: re: What's going on?
—

Dear Lee:

This keeps happening because you're making stupid choices. Bucky is fine, but I've gotten an earful from him in the last five hours, and I'm getting tired of it. Would you mind straightening up and flying right?

Love,

God

PS: The milk is about to reach the point where you'll get sick, so you should use up the rest of it making pudding tomorrow.

The Shadow makes so much sense. When she's here, she feels so good, so pretty.

Bucky told me not to listen to her, but Bucky would say that either way. Either she's evil, and Bucky wants her to leave. Or else she's good, and Bucky wants to protect his territory.

I want to call Hal and ask him what he thinks, but there's no slot in the daytimer for "spiritual warfare tactical development." Maybe I should call Randy because Randy knows how to talk me through stuff like this. This is what would happen:

Randy: "So after thirty years of hanging out with Bucky, you see this other angel who's prettier and does parlor tricks, and Bucky says she's a demon even though she says Bucky is offending God. And you had the nerve to call me at midnight asking me which one I think is telling the truth?"

It's just that he didn't see her eyes or hear the way she explained.

And if Bucky was right, why did she come back tonight?

Another car passes on Sixth Avenue, and I awaken with a start. I must have dozed off, and Bucky still isn't visible.

I whisper, "Bucky?"

Inside, a response.

"Are you okay?"

A rueful feeling: he's been better.

"I'm scared."

An overwhelming yearning inside, an urgency, a wistfulness.

"Pray with me." My hands are knotted around one another behind my neck. "Please."

Agreement inside, and I close my eyes, but for a few minutes I can't come up with any words. Only, *Help*. And, *Please*. I don't deserve it, but please.

I extend a hand to Bucky, and he raises his fingers enough that we brush by one another. I'd guessed by the relative time lapse between passing cars that it was three, and a squint at the clock confirms it.

I think to Bucky, *You lied to me.*

Inside, a series of question marks.

You heard me.

Multiple confusing urges inside, along with a marked irritation.

When I open my eyes, Bucky looks grim. "Don't hit me with that. Just ask whatever you want."

You said if I went to the tournament with Bill, that wouldn't give her a foothold.

"She *has* a foothold. She just needs to keep her hand on the doorknob and tug until it gives a little." He sighs. "That's how bondage works. Otherwise we'd call it *camaraderie,* and for really tough cases, you'd only need call blocking rather than an exorcism."

That would have made for a sucky movie: "The Call Blockist." The whole movie might have been shorter than its trailer.

My mouth twitches. *That's it, then? She's going to keep reappearing forever?*

"It's not a once and for all thing. But souls do get acclimated to demons just the way they do to angels. It gets easier to listen the more you've been listening, harder to turn it off when you want to. Going with Bill wasn't a problem. But she was whispering to you the whole time, and my guess is, you were listening just enough that she could begin speaking louder."

I pull my pillow tighter.

"You're frightening me." Bucky's voice sounds thin, as if the entire apartment has emptied out leaving the faintest of echoes around his voice. "You're spiraling downward in ways I can't comprehend. It makes no sense to me. What's doing this to you?"

I swallow hard.

A tingle over my forehead, along the line of my eyebrows, then over my cheekbone and down my jaw. "Talk to me. What's going on?"

"Who are you really?"

The tingle vanishes. "You're worried you can't tell the difference between me and her?"

"It's more than that." I hope Beth isn't awake, but Bucky would warn me if she were. "What if you're in danger because of me?"

Bucky adds, "And what if *you're* in danger because of *me*?—both valid concerns. I've offered already that if you want me not to manifest to you, you can say the word and I'll back off. I have no interest in keeping you confused."

"What if God told you to back off?"

"I would immediately proceed to back off."

"And if God told you to leave?"

"If God were to replace me," Bucky says slowly, "I would obey, but I would pray for you from a distance until you got into Heaven."

"You wouldn't fight for me?"

Bucky's shoulder sag. "It's a tightrope, you know? There are times God is looking for us to resist Him, where He wants us to ask, and ask again, and keep on asking. It's a given among the angels that if you're ordered to kill someone, you kill him, or else you plead for mercy. You don't give the intended target a serious wound and hope he recovers."

My head jerks up. "You would kill someone?"

"I would never kill except on God's orders."

Oh my God. It never occurred to me, but of course angels kill people in the Bible.

"And I could never kill you because that's forbidden." Bucky looks as calm as if I asked whether he can peel an orange. "In the same way, the Shadow can't lay a hand on you unless God says she can. One of the conditions for that would be you permitting it. Which gets back to the question of what's opening you up to her."

I say, "What if she's right?"

He shakes his head. "I mean what was bothering you before she appeared. I'm guessing you're flirting with her because—"

I snap, "Flirting?"

"Of course you're flirting," he says with a hand wave. "I'm guessing it's a result of that discussion about marriage, but if that's the case, then—"

"Stop." I've clenched my teeth so hard they're hurting. "I am not flirting with her!"

Bucky glances toward Beth's room, and when he turns back, his eyes are amber rather than hazel. "You're playing with her, with what she represents. When she shows up, you're enthralled by what she has to offer. You're not flirting *then*. Then you're just her plaything until you break free. It's the times in between when you're calling her back, playing a bit without ever giving in or really saying what you want. What would you call that, if not flirting?"

I drop to lie flat on the bed, my chin on my wrists. How can he say I'm flirting with evil the same way you'd say "Looks like rain"? Or has my whole life been like watching a train derailment in progress? *Wow, how'd that caboose get all the way up there?*

"If it's that you don't want to commit to Hal," Bucky says, tracing a hand over my shoulder, "then the way to chase her off is to break up with him."

I clench my eyes shut.

"I know it hurts, but it's better to enter the Kingdom of God with a broken heart than lead a parade of broken hearts into Hell."

I give him a dirty look. Usually he'd look pleased over a play on words, but now he's just grim. "The very idea of marrying Hal is giving you the urge to run. But don't run to *her*." Bucky rests his hand on my forehead again. "I want you to get some sleep tonight so you don't fall apart tomorrow. But I also want you to think about what I'm saying."

"Not yet." He can put me out in a second if he lays his hand over my eyes. "If she's so much more successful when she doesn't appear than when she does, why does she do it?"

"Because there isn't a demon in existence that can resist showing itself. They crave an audience, even if it undermines their own goals."

"You said they weren't stupid," I murmur. He's got his hand halfway over my eyes.

"They aren't stupid." He brings down his hand, and the last thing I hear is, "But they're undisciplined and want to have a good time."

Friday night, Hal walks to my apartment because yes, we must have pizza. We'll also have to rent a movie.

Since Beth is here, they also have to have an argument over pizza toppings for ten minutes while I dial in, order the pizza, and get out the plates. By the time they finish their half-baked argument and agree on half-mushroom, half-Hawaiian, Pino's Pizza had a pizza of exactly that description also half-baked because I'm just this total genius woman.*

Hal and I wait for the delivery downstairs. By now the tie is gone (I'm not sure why you need a tie to work a calculator, but hey, my previous job thought I needed heels to work a telephone) and we sneak a kiss while we're waiting. Well, a couple of kisses. Actually, he's breathless by the time the pizza guy is coming up the steps, and there's only time for a quick check in the hallway mirror before I open the door, tip the driver, and hand off the pie to a flustered-but-delighted-looking Hal.

Upstairs, Hal disparages white button mushrooms and Beth folds the pizza menu into two turtledoves. All she says is, "You're nuts," and that starts a volleys of "facts" and opinions at various volumes and different stridencies. I have no idea why they do it, but since they do, I enjoy setting them off on each other. Beth and I never tangle about anything except which of us found something *more* repulsive, or which of us was more amused by our landlady's latest concern for our well-being.†

Beth says, "They're mushrooms, not violin concertos."

---

* When Hal makes his own pizza, you can never identify which breed of mushroom is on the pizza. Or breeds. He has jars of dried mushrooms the way a wizard has jars of dried eyes of newt.

† Last week our landlady, Mrs. Goretti, heard about the hanta virus and was afraid the pigeons nesting on the roof might kill her top-floor tenants. It's illegal to electrify the roof, so she paid a man to hang plastic owls off the side. Now I awaken to the dulcet sounds of pigeons recommending good sunbathing spots for owls.

To which Hal replies, "The plural of concerto is *concerti*."

Beth's eyes flare. "Whoa! It just got pretentious in here!"

Hal shrugs. "If you're going to bother saying plural-of-concerto, you might as well say it correctly."

Beth makes another crease in the menu. "If you're going to bother talking about *concertos* in the first place, you might as well say it in a way normal humans understand."

Hal gasps. "Italians aren't normal humans?"

Beth hesitates, so it's time for me to step in. "Crap, Mrs. Goretti is using the wrong name because there's only one of her. Shouldn't she be *Goretto*?"

But it's too late to save the argument, so Beth digs a DVD out of her bag. It's a shame.

Right about the time we've finished skipping thirty-two previews for movies we wouldn't see on a bet, Beth gets a phone call. Three minutes later she and her cell phone and her purse are out of the apartment, and Hal and I are watching the opening credits of a movie I know nothing about.

It's hot even at eight o'clock at night. I hated watching the branches go to bud this year and then the mercury climbing. Guys just don't snuggle the same when it's 90 degrees and 90 percent humidity. Instead we sprawl on the couch, my legs thrown over his lap, holding hands at long-distance.

"We should have gone to a theater," I say.

It's New York City's best feature that we can absorb people from every country and culture on Earth and help them find a means of making a living. For example: a man arrives in JFK from Siberia, Greenland, or the Bering Straits. He wonders aloud what he should do, and immediately the kind folks at customs tell him he needs to open a movie theater. This he does, delighting thousands of New Yorkers by bringing them entertainment where they might otherwise have been reduced to playing hopscotch. Sadly, these men miss their homes, so they set their thermostats to help ease the homesickness.

Thus: an entire theater crowd wearing sweaters and mittens during the hottest week of August.

Hal pulls me close with a kiss. "We can't really do that so much in a theater."

The opening is a whole lot of scenery, so there's more kissing. Then the opening scene with a horse galloping.

Hal says, "Really? Horses?"

"Horses are cool. Every girl goes through a phase where she's horse-crazy and wants nothing more than to live on a dude ranch riding horses every day."

Hal raises his eyes. "Thank you, God, for making me a boy."

I shift on the couch so I can kiss his neck. "Thank you too, God, for making him a boy."

We have to back up through one chapter of the movie so we can actually see the beginning, but we didn't have to bother. You've probably seen this movie too. There's footage of galloping horses, someone overcoming all odds to win at the end, the friendly rival who ends up helping the hero because it's honorable even though in real life the friendly rival would be laughing his way to the bank while the hero digs the knife out of his spine. There's the instrumental soundtrack, the song they intend to become a smash hit that sounds exactly like every other credit song. There's the obligatory bed scene, the obligatory self-realization, and the obligatory thrill when the main character wins at the end. It's a blast.

Very predictable, not very exciting, but still kind of good, and I'm still kind of confused.

Chapter Nine

No bicycle is going to defeat me.

"You *are* out of your mind, right?" Yes? No?" I look up at Mr. Hartman, he of the Maxima With No End Of Damage, and yet in his eyes I find no glimmer of humor. Bad sign. "You're not really considering doing this?"

Mr. Hartman's insurance company has had a brilliant idea. Their insurance adjustor, a lovely man who cries real tears recalling when milk was five cents a gallon, can't find enough damage to total the car. He tried, tried so hard, a veritable Fred Astaire of that dance where you want to either identify as much damage as possible so you don't need to pay to repair it or else find as little damage as possible for the same reason. But our dear friend the younger Hartman cruelly destroyed only half the book value of the car.

Mr. Insurance Adjustor probably went to his boss, forms in hand and trembling with terror, as she glanced over his estimate, and then she came up with an idea to save money.

"A Frankencar," I say. "That's what they want."

Mr. Hartman looks glum. "I said I wasn't sure this was a good idea."

I'm not sure this is a good idea will get you out of a second dessert with your Great Aunt Mildred, but saying that to an insurance company is kind of like declaring, "Sure, go right ahead."

Mr. Adjustor has left his phone number on the form. I should totally speaker-phone him into this discussion. "Let's look at what your insurance company wants us to do. They've got another Maxima, same year as yours, that recently got rear-ended, and the damage totaled that car. Your car's damage is clustered at the front end, so they in their wisdom want to cut the front half off the other car and replace your front half."

Dr. Frankenstein would be proud. Me, no. "That's not safe."

Mr. Hartman says, "They said it's safe."

"They're an insurance company. They should know better. You're going to have no end of problems with this arrangement, and the car will never run right ever again."

My client bites his lip. "They said my car's frame might be bent."

"And that's improved," I ask, "by welding a second, differently-bent frame onto the first?"

He shakes his head. "I don't want to give them trouble."

I smile. "I, on the other hand, adore giving people trouble. Please take a seat."

My insurance-agency counterpart, Mr. Tight Fist, is pleased to take my call after I climb three limbs up the corporate phone tree. Yes, it's Mack's Auto, just wanting to verify the work order you've written for your client's Maxima with front-end damage after a single-vehicle accident. Would I be correct in assuming you've opted for the cheapest possible fix on the grounds that your client may or may not know the difference between a working vehicle and a nonworking one? Are you aware that as the insurance agency authorizing this work, you are taking full responsibility for any loss of life resulting from this drunken debauchery of a repair order? Or is your hope that your esteemed client, whose safety you value so much, will unload the car on some unsuspecting second owner when the car is peppered with lots of little, seemingly unrelated problems that in actuality all stem from a half-body transplant?

No, it won't actually work out okay. Do you know why it won't? Because I say it won't.

"You're failing to understand." I sound so polite in print that you'd never know I had to raise my voice in order to interrupt the guy. "I'm going on record, here and now, saying your suggested repair is not safe. I'm willing to testify to this in court. I refuse to do unsafe work. You will issue a new authorization that permits a full repair of all the damage, or else you will become intimately involved with my ex-boyfriend over at the State Insurance Commission."

Applause behind me. I turn to find two more clients in the waiting room, laughing. In my peripheral vision Max nods with approval. You might think that's because he admires polite self-assertion, but in actuality he just doesn't mind doing things the right way if screwing over the customer gets us less revenue for once.

Hartman on the other hand looks like a lone mouse in the home of the Crazy Cat Lady.

The adjustor says something about having to talk to his supervisor. I put a little sugar in my voice. "Don't you have the authority to approve your own work orders?"

I think Max just took notes. Seriously, this is New York City. Don't cut corners on us. We invented cutting corners. We also invented dodging responsibility by saying you need to check with your supervisor.

And finally, we invented the stone wall. No, I will not do that work. No, I will not say it's safe. No, your client—my client—will not go somewhere else for the work.

I'd hate having to do this every day, but every so often it's refreshing to get on the phone and unleash your life's frustrations on the person who's so generously offered himself up as the point person for an obnoxious decision. Politely. Bucky would break a vinyl copy of the *Rumours* album over my head if I didn't keep it polite.

But for the guy on the other end, politeness only makes it worse. They can deal with cursing. They're a bit confounded by socially exacting iciness.

The adjustor does attempt a little blackmail of his own. "You and I both know that damage isn't innocent. We could deny the whole claim on the grounds that it got into an accident during some kind of illegal activity."

"Then you've got to prove the driver was doing something illegal," I say, which brings an angry red to Mr. Hartman's cheeks, "and that would require a police report you don't have."

When I get off the phone, I'm all smiles. "We're good to go, Mr. Hartman. We'll both have a copy of the new work order by the end of the afternoon."

Hartman only says, "My son wasn't engaged in anything illegal. He's a good boy," before he leaves.

And me? Sure, I've been scolded, but I get to start ordering parts to rebuild a Maxima.

Out in front of Avery's apartment, I find Corinne with a bicycle, a tool box, and a look of fury. "I've started an online petition to have the designer of this bicycle hanged, drawn and quartered."

I stop in my tracks. No, no, it's okay: no matter how I wrack my brains I cannot remember a stint as a bicycle designer, so I'm in the clear. "What's going on?"

"Training wheels!"

My brow furrows. "What are you training them to do?"

She smacks the bicycle with the flat of a crescent wrench. "This piece of garbage came with training wheels. When Suzanne outgrew the training wheels, I did something stupid, something you never, ever should do. I *took off the training wheels.* And now a friend of mine could use the bike, but the training wheels won't go back on."

It should be a matter of unscrewing a nut, sliding the training wheel frame onto the axle, and screwing the nut back on. "Want me to take a look?"

"Be my guest." She stalks back into the building, dropping her wrench on the sidewalk. (Ack! Don't mistreat a tool!)

Avery trots out. "So what are we doing today?"

I pick up the wrench. "First we're installing a pair of training wheels."

Here's the glitch: it turns out Mr. Tight-Fisted Insurance Adjustor has a younger brother who designs bicycles. The first thing our frugal designer did was figure out how to save $0.00005 per bicycle by shortening the rear wheel axel a mere .2 inches. When you put the training wheel up against the side of the bike, there's not enough bolt protruding for the nut to bite on the threads, so you can't drive it in.

And therefore I, fresh from rebuilding a transmission, cannot install training wheels. I've got a metal tool box supporting the bike and Avery standing on the bike frame to squeeze it together, and I can't make it work.

"Go tell your mother to add my name to that petition," I say, "and then get in my car. I figured out what we're doing this afternoon."

By the time Avery's back outside, I've thrown the bike in the back seat. In twenty minutes we're back at Mack's Auto, which only thought it was closed for the day. I let myself in, and now we've got tools.

Avery's mouth is open. "So this is where you work? What are we going to do?"

What I'd like to do is raise the lift, lay the bicycle carefully underneath, and then smash it into tin foil; then I could buy another bike and give that to Corinne with, "I fixed it. I painted it too. And changed the brand name." It would be pretty cool if I could lower the lift just enough to compress the bike frame and get the nut back on the end of the bolt, but that would take a degree of finesse no one had in mind for this machinery.

Instead I raise the lift to shoulder height, string bungee cords from both supports, and then hook them back through the bike frame so the bike hangs at a nice, workable height.

Avery says, "That's so cool."

"I'm lazy," I tell her. "I hate bending over."

And no bicycle is going to defeat me. Sorry, but if I can crane the engine out of a Pontiac Sunbird in order to replace the spark plugs, then I can get training wheels on a 16-inch bike.

"First we look all over the thing and figure out how it's supposed to work." I show Avery how the training wheel would hang off the axle and how a clamp would lock it into the frame to keep the posts perpendicular to the ground. "Without that clamp, the wheels would get dragged backward with the forward motion of the bike." Now to diagnose the problem: The wheel assembly is held together by a nut, and the frame doesn't get quite flush to the inner nut, and therefore the outer nut can't get a good bite on the bolt.

"See, without the training wheel, you can drive that nut in enough that it compresses the frame against the inner nut." I show Avery how it works with no training wheels attached. "But when you take off the outer nut to put on the training wheel, the frame expands just enough that you can't put the nut back on over the training wheel assembly."

Avery says, "So it won't work."

I say, "It won't work without some creativity."

Our options are many. I could remove the whole wheel assembly and try to find a longer bolt for the rear axle. I could find something to compress the frame enough to get the bolts back on. I could grind the training wheel clamp just enough to slip the nut back on. "We only need a tenth of an inch clearance," I say. "It's almost nothing, but as far as the nut and bolt are concerned, it's everything."

Avery laughs. "Like a tragic love story! They'll fit together perfectly, only something's keeping them apart!"

"Ooh," I say, "A mechanical Romeo and Juliet minus the mayhem and death. I could go for that." I point at the bike with a screwdriver. "Okay, you two. Time to get married."

First I need to remove the chain guard because it's entirely in the way. The screws holding the chain guard are inaccessible in the same way your spleen is. I imagine the assembly line producing this bike begins with "Step One: CHAIN GUARD." I use a small hand saw to cut off the end, leaving the front and top of the chain guard still in place. Next I try several clamps until I find one that will compress the frame enough to get on the first wheel.

The second still won't bite.

Avery giggles. "You ever tried to ride with one training wheel?"

"That sounds like a metaphor for my life." I frown. "Okay, next option."

I could get these pieces together in any number of ways, but the problem is keeping them together in a stable configuration. It's a safety issue. Yes, I could force the bike to do my bidding. But there's going to be a child riding this bike, and I don't want it to crash. Which may be a metaphor for Bucky's life, come to think of it.

Avery and I spend the next five minutes playing with the clamp. I fit the pieces together, take them apart, fit them together again, and then say, "Bingo."

A couple minutes later I'm outfitted with welding equipment, and it's the work of two minutes to install a tiny metal flange onto the side of the training wheel post. That's going to lock into the frame, which eliminates the need for the outer clamp, which gives us two-tenths of an inch clearance. On goes the nut; the nut marries the bolt; the training wheel is stable.

From behind her safety goggles, Avery whispers, "Can I have one of those for my birthday?"

That's what you really want: your fourteen-year-old niece welding things in her bedroom. I can predict my brother's paroxysms of delight. "Put it on your Amazon wish list. We'll see." Her birthday isn't for another six months. That's enough time for me to leave the country.

We put away all the equipment (no, I never clean my apartment, but it's just not professional to leave tools helter-skelter) and then I lock the garage and toss the bike back in my car.

Avery checks the time on her phone. "We're not going right back home, are we?"

"I thought you had a great time."

She makes a face, and I laugh. So instead I drive my niece to the place you know all the coolest teens go: the cemetery.

Avery stares at the Greenwood Cemetery gate as we pull in. "Why a graveyard?"

"Oh, come on," I say. "People are dying to get in here!"

She gasps and rolls her eyes. "Aunt Lee!"

I navigate the little roads until we pull up in front of a commemorative plaque on an unassuming boulder. (Are there assuming boulders? What do they assume?) Avery reads the plaque, then thanks me with a hearty, "You've got to be kidding me."

The plaque informs us this boulder is stamped with *the hoofprint of the devil himself.* No, really, it's written in stone: one fine day four hundred years ago the devil got into a fiddling contest with a man named Joost, and when the devil lost, he stamped his foot and left behind a hoofprint.

Avery says, "Isn't that supposed to be a fiddle made of gold?"

"A fiddle made of gold would weigh five hundred pounds and sound awful." I shrug. "I'd rather have the hoofprint."

Avery says, "You think the devil really has hooves?"

"The devil doesn't have a body. He can have training wheels if he wants them. But this is New York, and there's no reason to live here if you're not going to see all the ridiculous things it has to offer."

We examine the hoofprint, touch it, take selfies with it. Avery's already got five likes on Instagram before we've left the cemetery, and I've got a text from my brother reminding me I'm three clowns short of a circus.

Chapter Ten

I'm not a lonely hearts charity for single guys

Labor Day weekend—three days of fun, fun, fun. Did I mention the fun?

Saturday morning, I tinker with the Mustang. At lunchtime I clean up and drive my safe-to-park-on-the-street Acura across Brooklyn to spend the afternoon playing Ultimate Frisbee with Randy and the kids. Afterward, we gorge on chicken nuggets while playing a board game where you pretend to be superheroes beating up a super villain.

Sunday morning I meet Hal at the early Mass. At the coffee hour afterward he does this little thing where he holds my hand beneath the table. Probably this is obvious to everyone around us, but he makes it seem like a secret. With a little squeeze of my hand, in the middle of a conversation about the Yankees (who somehow managed to snatch defeat from the jaws of victory again this year) he sends a hidden signal saying he loves me. I squeeze back, tight in my throat.

Ah, but afterward...afterward the true fun begins. I'm meeting my mother for lunch.

It was only in futility that Randy invited her to his house yesterday; she had thirteen excuses why she couldn't possibly come: the weather, her hair appointment, a show she wanted to watch, the phase of the moon, her neighbor might need her, a three-hour-only coupon for Macy's. She must have Sunday lunch with me, and only me.

Earnest as she was, you'd think she's about to propose.

So after church, I drive Hal back to Eighth Avenue. While we're parked at the fire hydrant, he and I kiss for a while. "I may have to go back to church after that," he murmurs, and I kiss him again to make sure.

Eventually he breaks free long enough to remind me he'll pick me up tomorrow to go to his parents' barbecue, and then I'm on my own.

My mother warned me to dress nicely, so I'm a little more upscale than "midsummer slob," my normal look. I've discovered a boutique on Seventh Avenue where the sales gal knows me and makes sure to handle my mother's sporadic calls for gift certificates.

Today's outfit is a knee-length cotton skirt and a denim sleeveless blouse with a silver pendant that picks up the blue of the denim. Neat, presentable, and not frilly.

My mother, by contrast, is wearing a peach-colored dress, her hair perfectly curled, her makeup visible from across the street. She sets her handbag on her knees in the front seat, the scent of lilacs filling the car.

"Italian okay?" I ask.

"Let's go to Glenwood Manor."

There are eighty-seven million restaurants in New York City, and you can name yours anything. You can name it after the food ("The Speared Olive") or you can name it after yourself ("Carlo's Café And Pretzel Counter") or you can name it after...what the tables are made out of? Whatever. If I were home, I'd be surfing the web while eating Apple Jacks straight from the box ("Lee's Apartment Of Edible Garbage.")

Mom asks about Randy and the kids, about Hal, about Beth. She doesn't ask about my job at all. Instead we go right to hers: "There's a new chaplain doing visits with the residents." She flashes me a smile. "He's single, you know."

"How interesting. We both realize I'm not, right?" At this point it must be habit.* She sighs and hands me the chaplain's business card. I shove it into the change compartment with five others from our last five trips.

At Glenwood Manor (my bad—they didn't name it after the tables; they named it after the *street*) the hostess says something to my mother about seeing the manager. "You've been here before?" I say. "Got something comped?"

She straightens. "Juliet! Don't be rude."

"It must have been one heck of a complaint if you made it." Some mother-daughter lunch, huh? *I hated this place. The service took hours and I found a cockroach leg in my soup. So I brought you here to use my coupon. We probably won't be sick all night this time.*

They seat us quickly, and the menu is all standard stuff. Chicken cordon bleu. Steak in a mushroom sauce. We'll be having shrimp cocktails for appetizers, and I order a frozen slush-type drink because my mother never let me do that when I was a kid. "I want an umbrella in it," I say to the waitress. Mom glares. I'll offer to pay, but she'll refuse, and that will make it all the sweeter.

And now it's time to move through my carefully-rehearsed conversation topics.

- The weather
- Her job
- My more-respectable siblings
- The evening news

---

* *"Hi, Mom! How are you doing?"* *"Great, but quick, write down this number: 647-1522. He's waiting for your call. His name is either Paul or Phil, and he delivers the Poland Spring water to Manorside Residence."*

I've scanned Google News three times since last night in order to sound current, and I could (if pressed) hold conversations on "that situation in France," "that corrupt politician," and "the polar bear at the Bronx Zoo that's wearing a hand-knit sweater."

Buttering a roll, Mom says, "Are you taking Avery after school once a week this year again?"

I nod. The rolls give off steam like hot springs once broken open, and the butter melts on contact with the fluffy insides. At the very least, Hal would approve that it's real butter. "Randy and Corinne weren't sure what her schedule would be, but once we find a good day, I'll do it again."

Avery decided to remain in the private school where her ex-friends were bullying her last year. After Avery melted down last February, Corinne memorized their anti-bullying policy and recited enough phrases like "unsafe learning environment" that suddenly the school administration remembered who were the adults and who were the children. Strangely, it turns out the administration *can* do things about "girls being girls" whereas before they thought they couldn't. It's amazing what you accomplish by resembling a walking lawsuit.

Anyhow, they've worked out a game plan with Avery to avoid a repeat of last year, although that means she's ditching the volleyball team. She's made friends with a girl from drama (and I thought there was drama enough!) and ridden the girl's coat-tails onto the masthead of the school newspaper. Her ex-tormenters are now majorly worried about what gets into the paper, and my beloved niece has discovered geekdom.

Specifically, that geeks make good friends. Over the long term, they're far more accepting of your quirks and much less likely to stab you in the back. Plus, they'll always be able to suggest quick helps for your computer when it turns into a very expensive door-stop.

So I say, "I'm looking at Wednesday afternoons again."

My mother looks concerned. "Won't that interfere with Hal?"

"She's my niece. Hal has nothing to say about it."

She straightens her napkin on her lap. "But you're not available to him."

"If I had to be constantly available," I say, pointing at her with my butter knife, "I'd answer my phone with *9-1-1: what's your emergency?*"

"Maybe he could come with you?"

"Why are we having this discussion?" I lean across the table and drop the tone a notch. "The whole idea is to give Avery a female role-model. Are we forgetting that he's perfectly capable of taking care of himself?"

My mother raises her hands to stop the argument. "Don't be so over-sensitive."

"He's not a baby," I snap. "And she's a depressed fourteen year old. I know where I belong."

I'm still smoldering when our entrees arrive. I take three bites before I register that I'm tasting my food, and even then it's only because I can hear Hal in my head: *The presentation is lacking; while the meal is not disappointing in any respect, the cook took no chances, rendering it unmemorable.*

My mother fishes in her hand-bag. "I wanted to show you something." She withdraws a catalog, folded back to a center page and then folded again so it's quartered. She smoothes it on the table between us and shows me a floor-length lacy dress, such a light peach that in the dim overhead light* it looks almost cream-colored. It has a

---

* *I believe the term is "ambiance" rather than "saving on the electric bill."*

shawl to match and a sheer overtunic that drops to just below the waist.

"Nice."

Her whole face brightens. "Really? You like it?"

I blink at her. "It's okay. Kind of fancy."

"It has to be fancy." She holds the catalog at arm's length to admire the dress. "Do you think Hal's mother wanted to wear peach?"

I blink. "What?"

"You'll want Beth as your maid of honor, and given her skin tone, you certainly weren't going to choose peach as your wedding color, but I wasn't sure about Hal's mother."

I have to look into the science of making food perfectly unswallowable. That can't be my mother's superpower.

"I checked Miss Manners, and she says the mother of the bride should pick her dress first and then contact the mother of the groom, but I don't want to upset Mrs. Baxter."

No, it's Mom. I slam my hand on the table hard enough that the plates jump.

My mother tilts her head. "You don't like the dress?"

I've remembered how to swallow. "Did you purchase this dress?"

"Not yet."

"You are not," I say, "not, emphatically *not* to buy a dress for my wedding until I show up at your house wearing a diamond on my left hand." I'm shaking. "Moreover, I do not want you picking out my wedding colors, checking with my fantasy-fiancé's parents, or selecting my bridesmaids."

My mother gazes again at the catalog. "It's a lovely dress."

"It is. For some other mother of the bride, it's perfect. You don't know what season I'd be marrying in. I don't have a *groom.*" I stand. "Right now, you don't even have a bride. I'll be back in five minutes."

As I'm leaving, I hear my mother say, "You always get so worked up."

Of course. She's trying to change the entire course of my life to suit her fairy-tale mentality, but it's my fault for getting worked up.

In the ladies room, I yank a paper towel from the dispenser and rip it to shreds.

"It's really not healthy to imagine doing that to your mother." Abruptly Bucky's sitting alongside me at the row of sinks. The mirrors don't reflect him. "I'm glad you're releasing stress, but not—"

"She had the catalog in her purse. You let her blindside me." I keep shredding. "And don't tell me that you wouldn't snoop. If someone came into this restaurant with a sawed-off shotgun, I'd hear about it."

Bucky folds his arms. "As it turns out, her guardian did warn me. It would have ruined the entire meal to make you tense even before the appetizer. I worked hard to get her to hold off as long as she did."

I let out a long breath and half-close my eyes.

It's only one o'clock. I'm supposed to spend the rest of the day with her, at least part of it shopping at Kings Plaza because she wants to hit a sale at Macy's. They don't sell bridal gowns, do they?

Back at the table, I find my mother speaking with the manager. Great—he saw me storm off and must be asking if he should call the police.

He fusses over me, asks if everything is to my satisfaction, what I think of the meal and the service. So far so good—maybe he's just making sure I didn't leave to go puke? Maybe I was right before and my mother had a problem with this place.

My mother asks about reservation times, and he says there's one afternoon and one evening, with various options for menus and live entertainment or a DJ. The emcee comes with the facility, he says. My mother asks about menu choices, and he talks about a choice of three entrees, choice of five, or a buffet, which sounds odd because the menu was more like a choice of thirty. They have three styles of cake.

Oh no. No, no, no.

"Excuse me," I say softly, "but would you be talking about options for a *wedding reception?*"

Afterward, I feel sorry for the manager. He didn't deserve to witness the things I said to my mother, but perhaps I've enriched his vocabulary and enlightened him as to the psychology of mother-daughter relationships. I leave a really nice tip for our server, who also didn't deserve to deal with us afterward. And I don't speak to my mother during the entire ride to Kings Plaza, other than a muttered, "The thing you want to look at in Macy's had better not be a set of wedding rings."

I should have expected this: I return home to find Francisco on my steps writing a note.

Before I can bolt around the corner, he looks up. "Lee! I was going to leave this for you, but here you are!"

Go away. Just go away. Please, go away now.

He sticks his pen in his back pocket as he approaches me. I'm rooted to the concrete. "Are you trying to dump me?"

I nod dumbly.

"I'm not that easily put off." He puts his hand on my shoulder, sending tingles down my body and up my neck. I step backward, but he follows. "You need to give me an explanation."

"I don't *need* to give you anything. You haven't paid a dime." I fold my arms and step backward again. "I didn't want to dump you, so I figured I'd just let you move on."

He makes eyes that would inspire jealousy in an SPCA Poster Puppy. "What did I do wrong?"

See, that's why I hate this kind of conversation. At least he doesn't look hurt. "You didn't do anything wrong."

"What do you mean?"

I mean exactly what I said. "Can't we leave it alone? I don't want to go out with you."

Don't gasp. You're going to have to say it eventually, so you might as well blurt it out early in the Fateful Talk. "I don't want to go out with you" covers a multitude of situations, from "You're a creep and I'm afraid for my life" to "You smell like fish."

And I've learned that if you give a reason then inevitably the guy will come up with why that isn't a good enough reason. It might be a lame reason ("But Babe, just because I murdered my last three wives doesn't mean I don't love you!") but it keeps him talking when you want him gone.

Francisco waits because he has nothing to latch onto. Finally he says, "Why?"

I raise my eyebrows. Dude, I'm not a lonely hearts charity for single guys.

Francisco says, "Can you at least tell me?"

Someone passes us on the street, and I move so I'm standing closer to the buildings. He shifts right up alongside me. "Don't be like this." He puts a hand on my arm. "Let's go grab Chinese food and see what we can work out."

"I don't want to go out with you." Even I can hear it's not as firm as before. He traces his hand up to my shoulder. "Just let it go. It was fun, that's all."

"There's nothing wrong with fun." Francisco's voice is low, his face near my ear. "We'll talk, nothing more. Just a fun dinner. Aren't I at least worth a chance?"

There's heat all over me. My eyes half-close.

"Just dinner. If after dinner you don't want to see me again," and he snaps his fingers, "I'll be gone. For good. But if you don't come with me tonight, I'll keep pursuing you until I find out why. You'll find," he adds in a dusky voice, "I can be very persistent."

I should turn and run. I know I'm making a mistake, and I'm making it anyhow. "Fine. Just dinner, just tonight."

Francisco takes me to a Thai restaurant instead of Chinese, and then it's a sit-down meal rather than take-out. Afterward, it doesn't take much to convince me to go for ice cream, and all along I hear myself agreeing even though I keep telling myself I won't.

Bucky must be furious. Francisco won't be put off by tonight no matter what he promised because now he knows he can turn no into maybe. And I can tell you what Bucky would say: why would I want to spend time with someone who doesn't respect when I say no?

Even if I don't pay for this with a visit from the Shadow—or worse—I'm going to pay for this right here and now on Earth because I'm going to have to dump Francisco again. And again. And again until it sticks.

God, please don't let Bucky pay for this. But here's a worse thought: maybe Francisco overwhelmed my common sense because Bucky already went down for the count.

Or maybe Bucky has nothing to do with this, and I'm just having a little frolic with a nice guy, something I've done a thousand times.

Regardless, here we are, splitting a chocolate-almond shake and debating whether this season of Francisco's favorite show is better or if it's only riding the wave of energy brought by a new character.

Francisco reaches for my hand. "We have so much fun together." He squeezes my fingertips just enough to send a shiver up my arm. "Are you the kind of woman who plays hard to get? You want a man to get on his knees and beg for your attention?"

"No!" I lean forward. "It's just—"

"Shh." He lowers his voice. "No excuses. Just enjoy tonight."

He kisses me, and when he puts his hand in my hair, I'm lost.

Chapter Eleven

I never saw a judge laugh himself to death before

I awaken the next morning hating myself, unable to shut up my nagging conscience. The person I have to look at in the mirror is a liar with the self-discipline of a magpie and the honor of a coyote.

Bucky hasn't appeared. What's he going to tell me that I don't already know? Even if he doesn't lecture me, his eyes will swirl with a gaze as penetrating as a spear, and I'll know he's talking to God about what to do with a human who seems bent on ruining her life.

Based on Francisco's wolfish look when he dropped me off after a long, lingering dessert, I suspect he's going to camp on my front steps if I ignore him again. He'll start sending flowers by the armload, maybe stalk me to my job, schedule me to do a long repair on his car, and proposition me there. It's a mess. I'm a mess.

A hot shower does little to clear my thoughts; hot coffee does it better. This mistake wasn't fatal: I ate a meal and half a dessert on his dime. I kissed him. That's nothing irrevocable.

Oh, but Hal would hate that. The best thing would be to cut Francisco off at the legs. Don't give him a chance to interrupt the Pizza Topping Wars with a mariachi band beneath my window. The question is, how?

A restraining order would do nicely.

"Your honor, Francisco has left a few messages on my voicemail, and he asked me to go to dinner with him. But you see, I have no self-control, so I figured if you could issue a court order— No, I'm afraid I never saw a judge laugh himself to death before, you honor. No, I don't want to see it now either. Understood. You have a nice day too."

Plan Number Two involves pure cowardice. I can wait until a time I'm sure Francisco won't answer his phone and leave a voicemail telling him that I expect him to respect my wishes and not contact me again. It's brilliant. It's exactly what I tried to do last night, only this time it's going to work. He can't seduce me over the phone. I'm a genius. I'll do it after breakfast.

I'm such a genius that when Hal phones from downstairs, I realize I've totally forgotten we have Labor Day plans.

As I tear down the stairs, I keep repeating, "I'm sorry!" into the phone. "I should have been downstairs to let you in."

"I'm okay using one of my minutes to call you." He sounds amused. "Don't kill yourself."

He can hear the rapid rate of stair-creaks and then the too-brief silence as I pelt around the third floor landing and down the next set of steps.

When I see Hal through the double glass doors, he's holding a bouquet.

I drop the phone. Oh, crud. Francisco stepped up the romance and returned last night to tape flowers to the door.

Hal's eyebrows arch, and I pick up the phone with fumbling hands. "I'm sorry," I choke out.

"Apologize to the phone, not to me." I can see him talking but can't hear his voice for real. "I'm fine, really."

I'm dressed for sleep still, but luckily my sleepwear during the summers is a pair of comfortable shorts and an old Brooklyn College t-shirt. Hal slips inside and hands me the bouquet.

I brace myself. "And these...?"

"The lady at the Korean grocery store stopped me and said, 'You want to keep your woman? She needs roses.'" He laughs as I stare openly. "She's just a really good saleswoman. I bought them." He's also carrying a paper bag so maybe she's a better saleswoman than even he thought. "I figured Beth had a vase."

I wrap my arms around his neck, all but shaking with relief.

"She was right." Hal sounds surprised. "You did need flowers."

That's not all I need. "Come upstairs. Beth is still asleep, but I've got a pot of coffee going."

When we're in the dining room, he unpacks the grocery bag while I hunt up a vase. My mother always insisted you cut the stems sideways under running water and add aspirin, but guess what? Flowers don't get headaches, so I just stand them in the glass. On the center of the dining room table, they make the place look almost rustic. Well, rustic for an origami-covered table in the 4th floor apartment of a Brooklyn brownstone.

Hal looks up. "You got rid of one?" He pokes through the vase. "I'm sorry—it was supposed to be a dozen."

I laugh. "Maybe that's why she was so eager to sell them. We get her leftovers."

Inside there's this little stab, as if I'm not quite a dozen roses to Hal if I keep holding back that little bit of myself.

Hal mutters, "I'm an accountant, for crying out loud. You'd think I could count to twelve."

"It was sweet of you to get them." I move around the table to lean over him, and he hugs me. "Life is more fun when it's just a little imperfect."

"Makes you appreciate all the times they did count to twelve?" Hal says.

I wink. "And sometimes you get thirteen."

Speaking of imperfect, I need to be dressed in something better than a ratty t-shirt, so I excuse myself to transform into a presentable human. When I come out, Hal is putting pastries on the table.

My throat is tight as I take a seat. "You're too good to me."

"It's just cannoli." He looks up, concerned. "Are you okay? Was your mother insane yesterday?"

I'm having a hard time meeting his eyes. "Would you expect anything else?"

He looks hesitant, then says nothing. He finally comes up with, "Our family barbecues are a little less intense than yours."

Forcing myself to relax, I wrap both hands around my coffee cup. "It would be a challenge to be more intense."

I've met his parents once at an Easter sing thing where his sister was in the choir. There was a reception in the church basement afterward, which I spent most of helping Hal in the kitchen. His parents weren't horrified by me—or at least, they had the decorum to hide any disgust until after we parted ways.

I'm never sure how to act around his dad. I assumed he was an attorney because when I first met him, he was wearing an oxford shirt and discussing politics with Hal.[*]

---

[*] *In the typical New York City fashion, which is to say, the basis of the conversation is not "Is there corruption in our government?" but rather "is there government in our corruption?"*

Then this happened:

Mr. Baxter: So, Lee, what do you do for a living?

Lee: Uh, I'm, um, well, I'm a wage slave. How about you?

Mr. Baxter: {insert twenty-five minutes of the joys of plumbing, including but not limited to being the sole plumber responsible for sixty-seven bathrooms in one condo complex; the most bathrooms he's ever seen in one house (seven in a three-bedroom); the strangest thing he's ever found blocking a toilet (a cardigan sweater with two buttons missing); the hours (brutal); and disappointment that so few youngsters are going into plumbing because a lot of master plumbers are retiring and every human being alive needs to—}

Mrs. Baxter: Don, dear, have you tried the fruit punch?

So yeah, he's a master plumber. How cool is that? *Master Don Baxter, The Plumbing King.* I'm going to him on my knees the next time I want a career change, begging to be his apprentice. He also put this tiny ad in a local circular offering to winterize people's snow-blowers for fifty bucks, and within a week he was turning away clients. "I thought I'd get three little old ladies." He guffawed. "Instead, half of Nassau County wanted me."

This October, I am definitely placing one of those ads and seeing what happens.

Now Mrs. Baxter, she was a completely different breed of bird, and with those riveting blue eyes, it's obvious where Hal got his looks. She doesn't keep a ring in her back pocket to shove into Hal's hand before pushing him down on one knee, and therefore I have not brushed up on Google News to find bland topics of conversation.

Hal drives a beautiful Camry, and I have many talents. Witness: I am the worst passenger in the world.

You know that imaginary gas pedal your brain installs in the passenger side when you're at a crawl and you want to see what a Camry XLE can really do? I have it floored. I'm sure his car can do more than *this*. It's not that he doesn't speed (who doesn't?) but rather that he doesn't speed *enough*.

"Maybe I can drive on the ride home," I offer as we putter along at sixty-five.

He sounds mystified. "Maybe you'll want to crash into a tree after spending an afternoon with my parents?"

"Your car is kind of a fun ride." It's got a spunky engine for a four-banger. Put me behind the wheel and that car would whisper, *Drive me like you stole me*.

Bucky can't hear it. In fact, last month he claimed he heard it saying, "Come on—drive me like you have your grandma in the passenger seat and the baby Jesus in the back." But I can't hear that either, so we're at an impasse.

Hal puts on the jazz station.

I hit the "seek" button, and it changes to the classic rock station. "Who-all is going to be there?"

He pushes the station button again so we're back on jazz. "My sister and her husband, and I think two of my mother's friends. Dad's going to spend most of his time at the barbecue."

The back of the car is loaded with groceries so Hal can cook, and ostensibly, I'm to help him. When I "help" Hal, it's generally one of three things. I:

1) watch
2) wash the dishes
3) eat the food

Sometimes I set the table, but I would bet his mother has that under control.

And so here we are, in the car, listening to jazz (when I'm not changing the channel) and he ambles along the highway at a leisurely pace. Traffic is moving. I've had my coffee, and there are a dozen-minus-one roses waiting for me at home. All is right with the world.

Oh, wait, no. It's not. *Bucky?*

Inside: a response.

Are you okay?

Inside: he's fine; it sure is nice to be traveling this highway at a sane rate of speed for once.

I make a face. *I thought angels weren't supposed to be sarcastic.*

If it weren't for sarcasm, he replies, *I'm not sure we could routinely deal with humans at all. Please, sign me up for hours of watching you dig a hole for yourself and all your close personal relationships.*

Ouch. I glance at Hal, who hasn't spoken for a few minutes. *I'm sorry.*

Don't tell it to me. Tell it to God Almighty.

With a sigh, I stare out the window.

Hal says, "You thinking about yesterday?"

My heart pounds, and I stiffen.

"It won't be that bad today." He reaches for my hand. "My mom won't hassle you. She's got my sister to give her grandkids."

Oh—he meant about that. "My mom already has grandkids."

"And she won't rest until you produce a daughter. Am I right?"

I frown. "Are you psychic?"

His voice drops a notch. "And if you jump out the window, you'll fall. I can predict lots of things." He shakes his head "Did your mom really work you over yesterday?"

I look up. "My mother makes Charles Manson look like the poster-child of the Good Mental Health Society."

Hal says, "Does she think if she constantly nags you, you'll give in and marry the next guy you see?"

"She hopes so," I say.

Hal mutters, "It seems counterproductive to push."

That's the moment I realize—he really does want to get married. He just doesn't want to force me away.

My hands clasp the seat belt across my chest. Sixty-five is still a bit too fast to jump. All the same, I look out the side.

I could end this discussion here and now by telling him last night I went out with Francisco.

Instead the song changes and Hal tells me about the singer. It's just as good as Google News headlines, and the trivia carries us through to his parents' house.

I am not getting out of this car.

Somehow out here in Glen Cove, where I wouldn't be able to afford a house even at three times my salary, Hal's parents have a palace. There's lawn on *all four sides* of the house. They have a driveway! It's circular! They have a picket fence, and it's crawling with flowers, flowers, flowers. Hal didn't have to get me my Supermarket Almost-Dozen this morning—he could have brought me here and declared, "I planted these for you."

While I'm trying to screw my eyeballs back in their sockets, his mother sweeps down the front steps carrying a tray. "Come around to the back!"

I haven't unbuckled. "We've got to leave." My hands are shaking. "I'm completely outclassed."

Instead of doing the reasonable thing and driving away, Hal walks around the car and opens my door. (He has a key, so it'd be no use locking myself in). "Do I outclass you?"

"From minute one." I force myself to stand up out of his car.

"You'll do fine." He kisses me lightly. "My mom wants to impress you, that's all."

I've heard the "wants to impress" line before. That's what people say when you're invited for dinner and the family has a soup course in addition to their main meal. I refuse to believe they installed a circular driveway just to get on my good side.

On the deck out back, Hal's father holds a spatula beside a Martian space ship. There are two patio tables with umbrellas, the first with Hal's sister and husband, and a younger boy who looks somewhat like Hal except for being plugged into a hand-held game. At the other table is a couple the age of Hal's parents (younger than my mother, older than me) and a woman named Mrs. Smith who is old enough to be their mother. After introductions are made, it turns out that's exactly who she is, and the couple are friends of Hal's parents.

Hal has, bless him, stayed by my side. When his father calls, I trail Hal over to the launching pad.

This metal thing is not actually a Martian shuttlecraft: it's an outdoor kitchen. It won't launch because while the burners are putting out enough BTUs to help this thing achieve escape velocity, it's turned over the wrong way. Although come to think of it, facing the way it is, it may be pushing the Earth out of its orbit. It's daylight, so that will send us closer to the sun, meaning it must cook the food by raising the world's temperature five hundred degrees. Good thing I wore shorts.

"Isn't this great?" Mr. Baxter claps Hal on the shoulder as he ogles the machinery. "Picked it up at an end of the season sale last year for a song.* Look at this thing! It's got a FEATURE and a FEATURE and a FEATURE—"

I need to brush up on my Martian Spacecraft option packages. They sound fabulous.

"Is that a FEATURE?" Hal gasps, moving around the setup which is so large and shiny that spy satellites must pause overhead, either worried or envious.

"I love cooking outdoors," says Hal's father. "I don't know how you can stand living in that apartment, unable to get back to nature."

Hal must not have mentioned suspending the hibachi out his window to experience nature three stories up.

"It's kind of like being on the frontier." Mr. Baxter adjusts the knobs to shoot a flame so high that Bucky recalls witnessing the birth of the solar system. "Have a shrimp."

I find on the warming tray a school of shrimp big enough that you could slap each one in a bun and market it as a quarter-pounder. I don't care about being outclassed if it means I get to eat these things.

You want a bite? I ask Bucky.

Thanks, he replies. *Oh, wait, I forgot. Angels don't eat. Too bad for you.*

There's a dip served in a bread-bowl the size of a bowling ball. They've also arranged a plate of cheeses with differently-shaped knives for each. Over the next fifteen minutes, I will sample every cheese just to try each kind of knife.

I take a seat with the friends and their mother. They ask what I do for a living (which I deflect) and I learn the husband is a stock broker and his wife is an attorney; they have no children.

_____

* *Which song? "If I Had A Million Dollars" by the Barenaked Ladies?*

The elderly mother sits beside her daughter taking an occasional nibble of brie on a toast point. Dressed in a pink and white checkered sundress, she's got white hair in the obligatory perm, and while skinny she doesn't look bony. I say, "Are you enjoying the visit, Mrs. Smith?"

She glowers at me. "It's a black mark against humanity how they cancelled *Firefly*."

I swallow. "Pardon me?"

"The series was every bit as good as *Babylon 5*, but do you think the networks gave it a chance? They juggled it from time to time so you couldn't find the thing. They pre-empted it for football, advertised it during shows that had no crossover whatsoever with its audience—"

My jaw would be in my lap if I hadn't had it beaten into me as a kid that you never, never disrespect your elders.

"Now Kaylee, she was an engineer!" Mrs. Smith thunders. "Scotty was king, but Kaylee had an affinity for her machines and didn't spend her life reading technical journals."

I'm blinking. "Scotty—? Oh, you mean from *Star Trek*?"

"The one and only!" She rises from her chair and raises the arm not gripping her cane to shake her fist. "Geordi LaForge wasn't worthy to unsnap the collar of Scotty's jumpsuit, and yet *Next Gen* was on the air for seven seasons, four of which were positively lousy."

Hey, I grew up with that. "The first and second seasons were rocky, but the rest were top-notch."

"What?" She knocks me backward in my seat with the force of her fandom. "Half of season seven could be summed up in a telegram. *Let's tell a story about slavery—but instead we'll set it on Planet Zoron in the Outer Rim!* Sermons don't become SF just because you went to Saturn to preach them!"

She's pale. I hope her heart doesn't give out.

"The cancellation of *Firefly* rang the death-knell for decent SF programming! What the original *Battlestar Gallactica* couldn't do for making good SF a laughingstock, the network executives did out of hand. And instead? People eating live worms in order to be part of a tribe during a race across the desert and canceling the series only when every character has been in bed with all the characters they already have."

Hal has long since vanished, and Bucky is laughing into his hands. No help here.

Mrs. Smith shakes her bony fist as she roars louder than Mr. Baxter's gas grill. "I saw the golden age of Sci Fi! I saw *Amazing* when it first came out and read the old pulps. I heard *War of the Worlds* when it was relevant to the situation between England and India. We didn't need ten billion dollars in CGI effects because we stood on the precipice of tomorrow!"

Before I can reply, she adds, "And what do we have today? *Star Wars*! It isn't even science fiction!"

Now here I'm on good ground. Bucky had this rant at me ages ago, although I'll add that he did it with less intensity than a Category-5 hurricane. "Oh, Star Wars is just a western in space ships, and the prequel trilogy was an abomination. It would have been better if Jesus had returned to end the world so that waste of film never got recorded."

Mrs. Smith stops cold.

I continue, "The special effects were okay, but they only served to make the supposedly 'later' trilogy look crude and outdated."

I swallow a bite of spinach and artichoke dip. What else was it Bucky said? "Plus, there's the issue of Luke's character development—a whiny kid in the first movie, clearly Leia's junior by several years, but by *Jedi*, he's her twin? Very, very badly done. Poor planning."

Mrs. Smith settles back into the chair.

I put my elbows on the table and rest my chin in my hands for the killing blow. "If I didn't know better," I whisper, "I would be certain Lucas made the other five movies only for the money."

Mrs. Smith dabs her cheeks with a starched white handkerchief. "You understand," she weeps. "There's hope for the younger generation. At last, I can die in peace."

Five minutes later, having extricated myself from a sobbing Mrs. Smith, I escape to the kitchen where Hal and his mother are doing meal prep. *Bucky? Is she going to be okay?*

You've given her the greatest gift of her life. Bucky sits on a tall stool at the kitchen island, his chin on his folded hands. *She's handing the torch to another generation. Besides, you should have heard God laugh when she leaped out of that chair and you just about jumped out of your skin.*

So my purpose in life is to make God laugh, and I seem to have fulfilled it. It's better than making Him yell. I guess God can't roll His eyes. Whom would he be looking at if He did?

Hal's mother glances up, her eyes bright and her smile brighter. I want sunglasses. "You and Shirley's mother are getting along famously! I'm so glad. I was worried we wouldn't have any entertainment for her."

I nearly say that if they have *2001* on DVD, that might have tided her over, but instead I ask if I can help. They put me to work making the one thing I'm relatively sure I cannot corrupt: a salad. Doubtless I will slice the tomatoes with improper technique, but nevertheless, tomatoes will be sliced.

Hal's mother turns to me. "Did you have a nice visit with your mother yesterday?"

Now I don't really want to tell her what went down with my mother yesterday, do I? Nor do I particularly want to lie. "It was memorable."

While cooking, Hal shudders.

Hal's mother picks up a bowl. "Oh, you didn't have a good time, did you?"

She stands closer while I continue slicing tomatoes. "Is she the kind of person where everyone says she means well?" When I nod, she says, "It wouldn't help to say that she probably does mean well. But maybe she's like tofu. Everyone says it's good for you, but you don't want too much of it, and it doesn't usually taste too good on its own."

Hal says, "You have to get used to it, too."

I look up. "My mother or tofu?"

Mrs. Baxter says, "Have you ever prepared tofu?"

"I've eaten it."

"But not straight out of the package. It sounds like you need a soup to float her in, or maybe some stir-fry vegetables."

Hal mutters, "Chopped into very small pieces would help."

"Hey!" I exclaim, even as Mrs. Baxter says, "Sweetie, don't insult her. Even if Lee does it, even if the woman annoys you too, she's Lee's mother."

I sit back a bit on the stool and start cutting celery. "He's got a point."

"I raised him better than that." She puts a hand on Hal's shoulder. "You'll put up with her, won't you? For Lee's sake?"

He drawls out, "Yeah, Mom."

A moment after, Hal says, "Tofu isn't right. Tofu picks up the flavor of the things that surround it, and as far as I know, she hasn't changed a bit no matter what Lee has done."

His mother says, "So not a soup so much as a fruit salad?"

I drop my voice, "You calling my mother a fruit?"

Hal bursts out laughing.

His mother uses a mock-dreamy tone. "She's the starfruit in the fruit salad of life."

Before this afternoon, I never would have compared people to ingredients in a fruit salad. I want to be a grape. There are never enough grapes, and everybody loves them. Best of all, if you stick grapes in the freezer, they taste just like popsicles, but they're still fruit.

Mrs. Baxter says, "How do you get along with your father?"

"Perfectly." I beam. "He died when I was five, which conveniently short-circuited all those arguments we'd have had when I was a teenager."

She looks crestfallen. "I'm sorry. I wouldn't have asked."

I shrug. "Not a problem. But he can't step between me and my mom."

"Your brother helps," Hal puts in.

I nod. "And don't think Mom doesn't realize that. Yesterday was a mother-daughter-only lunch."

"I always liked those." Mrs. Baxter looks dreamy. "Watching Sheila grow up was like looking into a mirror and seeing myself if things had been different. I was able to see her potential, and it shone light on what mine had been, but it also highlighted the different choices we made."

Every conversation with Mrs. Baxter goes like this: if she tells you about an experience, she never describes the experience. She only tells you what it was like. *I went to the beach on the hottest day of the summer, and it was like stepping into an oven.* Or else, *We rented a subcompact, and sitting in the passenger seat was like sitting in a bucket.* Why would anyone think that way? Why not just say it was cramped? But to her, everything exists in terms of something else. *No thanks, Hal—I tried kim chee once, and it was like what happens when the dentist misses your gum with Novocain and your entire mouth goes numb for a moment, then hurts for hours.*

Then, once she's established the comparison, she draws conclusions on your original situation based on the way things work for the comparative. It's insane—if my mother is tofu, and tofu tastes better when it's mixed with other things, then my mother will be easier to take in larger groups. (She's right this time, but seriously.)

It makes more sense now why Hal went into accounting. Because the number five is not *like* anything. It's five.

So I turn to Hal. "This is the point where you're supposed to show me your childhood bedroom and make me misty-eyed with nostalgia."

"Sure." Hal points. "Take a left and walk down the hall twenty miles."

I frown.

"When I was a kid, we lived in a three bedroom New Englander out in Hicksville, next door to the fire station and ten feet from the main road."

"We moved here four years ago," Mrs. Baxter says.

"After my sister got out of college. Usually people downgrade their homes after the kids move out."

Mrs. Baxter looks out the window at Sheila and her little bundle. "I wanted room for my grandchildren."

"You can have the grand tour, if you like," Hal says, "but we're fresh out of nostalgia."

I do get the tour, though, and it lives up to the "grand" description. For starters, in the grand ballroom, there's a grand piano. ("Only a little," Mrs. Baxter says when I ask her if she plays. Yeah, I don't think a piano that big can do "only a little" anything.) They've got hardwood floors and cream-colored couches so soft you'll never stand again once you sit. There's also a dining room with a table Hal says opens to one hundred sixty-three inches. His mom ordered the special leaves so she could seat thirty at a dinner. And if she does that, so help him, Hal's cooking it.[*]

Upstairs, they have a master bedroom suite in one color scheme, then two guest bedroom suites in pastels, all of which have mini balconies. Each balcony is a jungle of potted plants. A ceiling fan spins over each bed, and fresh flowers stand in crystal vases in front of a mirror on both guest bedroom dressers. I expect to hear her demur that she hired an interior decorator, but instead she tells me the thought process behind each color scheme. *This room is like being on a tropic island in the Bahamas, with cool greens and blues.*

She shows me where the attic steps are but declines to take me up because the third floor belongs to Hal's kid brother, and he doesn't want adults snooping. "Strangely, he doesn't object when you go upstairs to do his laundry," Hal says.

Mrs. Baxter chuckles. "He's like an animal in its den, and he knows which hand feeds him."

I'd have gotten lost, but Hal's at my side to lead me back down. Bummer. *Please don't send a rescue party. I'm enjoying the cool blues and the white-noise fountain.*

Outside, another couple has arrived, and I help Mrs. Baxter set the buffet while Hal catches up with them.

I turn in time to hear them ragging on Hal because he's an accountant. Sounds like the new guy is a contractor and

---

[*] *If I ever host thirty people for dinner, I'm not going to be one of them.*

his wife is the contract manager for their business. She also operates the excavator. *Let me know when you're ready to do a real day's work! I'll show you how to operate a forklift.*

I'd want Hal to deck him, except I'd like to learn how to operate that forklift. But the way they go on, they must think they're Comedians Of The Year: *It must be so hard pushing numbers on a calculator all day.*

Then the new guy tells everyone about his new truck, and all the men insist Hal come admire it. ("You'd better see the thing that frightened your sedan when we pulled in!")

I take his hand for a walk around front. "Why don't you ask them who does their taxes?" I murmur.

"Because I'm the one who does them," Hal replies in an equally low tone, "and you'll have to trust that I'm getting paid for every joke at my expense."

I snicker.

Mr. Contractor has a brand new Ford 350 with an extended cab and doo-dads. I've seen the earlier models of course, but because he's got an in with the dealership, he's got the very first one of *next* year's model. It's a candy-apple red (sorry, it's probably something like Still-Beating-Heart-Crimson) and he's polished it to the point where the spy satellites, after pausing to look at the gas grill, will feast their electronic eye on this and go blind.

Satellite X-3-niner-7 to command control: I can die now. I have seen it all. Over and out.

Popping the hood, Mr. Contractor tells everyone about the new upgrades (yawn) and gets the appropriate oohs from Mr. Smith and Mr. Baxter.

He turns to Hal. "I could run you over on the LIE and not feel a thing."

Hal has his hands in his pockets. "I'm certain you could."

The contractor chucks him on the shoulder. "Do you even know what all these parts are?"

I say, "Of course he does. Ask him to find something."

Hal looks as if I've just volunteered him to perform cardiac surgery on his sister's baby.

Mr. Contractor maneuvers him in front of the engine. I get right up behind so his elbow is in my stomach.

"Okay," says Mr. Contractor. "Where's the air filter?"

With Hal's elbow in my hand, I nudge his arm. He points, and I guide his arm until he's pointing to the right place.

"Good one!" says Mr. Contractor. "How about the spark plugs."

I redirect Hal's arm again. He's struggling not to laugh.

"Now for a toughie," says Mr. Contractor. "Where's the A/C compressor clutch solenoid?"

As if Mr. Contractor could find that one himself. It takes me a minute to trace the system back to it, but then Hal's pointing at our quarry. The men all congratulate him on having useful knowledge as they slam the hood.

Mr. Baxter wipes a tear from his eye. "I'm so proud of you, son."

Hal smirks. "It wasn't anything." He adds, "Even Lee could have done it."

The food is ready, so we serve ourselves from the buffet area and then pay homage at the grill for wholesome meaty goodness. (They grilled whole ears of corn! You can grill corn on the cob! Why did I not know this?)

Mrs. Smith says to me, "So Lee, what do you do?"

"I do just about everything you'd expect a human being to do." I smile. "I tried defying the law of gravity once, but I wasn't determined enough."

She laughs. "I mean, what's your job?"

Well this isn't good. If I tell the truth, they're going straight back to mocking Hal.

And that's when Hal, mild-mannered Hal, Hal who hated when I lied to him, says, "She's an angelologist."

I glance at the grill and wonder if it will be less painful just to hurl myself into the gas jets.

He's wearing that same smirk as before, and his brilliant blue eyes are all but glowing. He might as well be saying, "Payback's a bear," but what he actually says is, "She studies angels."

Mrs. Smith sits up. "Like in *Ghostbusters*?"

I glare at Hal, but he just makes himself look cute. So instead I see how far he wants to take this. "*Ghostbusters* wants to drive ghosts away, but I trap-and-release the angels. I take their measurements, study them, tag them, and release them into the wild." My voice is this close to shaking, and I'm wondering when I'm going to crack. "In conjunction with Oxford University and universities in China and India, we're studying their migratory patterns and trying to get a handle on their numbers."

A sea of blank stares meets me. Mrs. Baxter frowns. "Without joking, have you ever seen an angel?"

I gesture idly. "You would be surprised at how many people have. I'd be shocked if at least four of us haven't had one experience where we realized afterward that an angel helped us."

Hal's sister sits forward, nodding. "I saw an object fall from a shelf toward the baby, only it changed its trajectory mid-fall and landed near her. And it didn't break."

I point to her. "That's exactly the kind of thing I'm talking about. You can't be said to have *seen* an angel, but you saw its effects. Almost everyone has at least one story of that variety."

Hal frowns. "You know, I don't think I have."

Thanks. Thanks so much for dropping me head-first into hot water and then turning it up to boiling.

But Mrs. Baxter shares with us a time her car skidded to a stop just before sliding into a ditch. Mrs. Contractor tells about the time she had a terrible dread about a customer, so she deliberately over-bid the project by tens of thousands of dollars. Later she found the customer had harassed the staff at another contractor and ultimately ended up suing them for spurious reasons.

"See," I say to Hal. "It can be subtle."

Hal shrugs. "I still don't think I've ever had an experience like that."

I give him the Death Stare, and he grins again so he looks really cute.

"You've just got a collection of stories," says Mr. Baxter. "That's not really very useful."

Hal says, "She also does comparative research from historical documents."

Ooh, he's good. Let's take a swing at that softball: "I compile information based on Biblical and apocryphal sources, with occasional cross-checks against new age material when I need a laugh."

Abruptly I realize even the gas grill has cooled off, listening. I'm about to make Mrs. Smith's knowledge of Star Trek look normal and well-balanced.

"It's important research," I say breezily. "Angelic strength is the ultimate in clean energy. Sennacherib's forces were driven away from Jerusalem when an angel wiped out thousands of his forces in a single night. Just one angel. Think about what all of them could do." I lean forward. "In Revelation, you have only a handful of angels harvesting people from the entire Earth, and again, you're talking about billions of humans and only a few angels doing it."

Hal's sister chuckles. "So for them, changing the trajectory of a falling book is nothing."

"It's probably less to them than you scratching your nose, yeah." I chuckle. "It's probably harder for them to deal with pig-headed human beings than it is to perform works that change nature or change energy."

"Surely we're not that bad," Hal says. "It's got to be like dealing with second-graders."

Bucky says preschoolers, but I'm not going to point that out.

"There's a culture gap, too," I continue. "Human people have parents. That gives us a history, a culture, and a heritage. All the things you see existed before you did, but all the angels were created together at the beginning of time, so nothing but God pre-existed them. Our forebears did the trailblazing for us, but angels had trail-blaze for themselves."

Mrs. Smith dabs her eyes. "That was wonderful. I never knew." She sniffs and adds, "I so wish that Mr. Smith were here to have heard you."

I feel hollow inside. "Has he passed on?"

She shakes her head sadly. "No, he's home fansubbing episodes of *Sanctuary* into Croatian, for our family back in the Old Country."

Eventually the day ends, and it was okay even though I haven't driven a forklift or piloted a rocket to the sun. Mrs. Smith has recapped all of *Star Trek: Enterprise* so I don't have to waste my time watching it (her words, not mine—I thought it sounded fun). Hal has his keys in his hand while he waits for his mother to box up leftovers for me to take home.

Music from a 3DS gets steadily louder as Hal's kid brother wanders into the kitchen, hooking the sliding glass door shut with one ankle while standing with his eyes glued to the screen. He shuffles to the table and takes a seat.

Hal says goodbye to everyone, including the brother, who doesn't respond. Mrs. Baxter puts her hand over the game, and the brother looks up to snarl, "Goodbye."

"The pleasure was all mine," Hal shoots back.

The kid glares up at me with the same expression of *I'm only doing this so Mom will give back my game* and starts to get up off the stool. I say, "No, really. Don't interrupt the important things on my account."

He grins, and for a moment his eyes sparkle just like Hal's. "Fine." He puts down the game and gives me a hug. "You're going to be a cool sister-in-law."

You know, I thought for once I could get away with not being pestered to pair-bond and spawn.

What was I supposed to say, other than "Thanks"? I could have said, "No, I won't," but that would sound more like "I'm not going to be cool," and I think I am. I'm already a cool sister-in-law to Corinne, and I didn't even need to be a wife first.

Regardless, now we're riding home. Hal says, "Thanks for the help with the Ford." Then he laughs out loud. "You just about died when I said you were an angelologist, but it was entirely worth it."

"Thank heaven they didn't ask about who pays an angelologist." I run my hands over the seat belt snug around my waist. "It sounds a lot better than *freak*."

"I never said you were a freak."

"You still aren't sure I can see Bucky."

"You wouldn't be in this car if I didn't think you were sane. I'm not really sure what to think about it, so I don't." He smiles at me. "Did you have a good time?"

I nod.

He turns back to the road. "I had never met Paul Smith's mother before. I'm terribly sorry she went off at you that way. I had no idea what to do that wouldn't make it worse."

"Are you crazy?" I burst out laughing. "That's the kind of old woman I want to become, and now I have a beacon! She gave me her email address." I fish through my belt pack for the business card I stuck in my wallet. "She's going to email me an invitation to her SF forum and a link to her *Last Starfighter* fanfiction."

He frowns. "She writes fanfiction?"

"Trust me," I say, "every girl writes fanfiction at some point."

"I thought fanfiction was evil."

"Trademark violation, yes. Evil, not necessarily." I laugh. "But really, she wasn't a problem."

There's a long silence, and then Hal says, slowly, "I'm glad you had a good time. They liked you. A lot."

They did tell me that: you could see it in how they treated me. Other than the brother's parting shot, no one mentioned marriage, but maybe they just assume it in this family with are four happily married couples on a deck along with one half of a couple in its sunset years; clearly the final couple is in its dawning phase, the glow only nipping above the horizon.

I should break it off with him. It's not just his expectations that are going to be shattered if we date for three years and nothing happens.

"Does Mr. Contractor always attack you that way?"

Hal shakes his head. "Sometimes, he's downright vicious. Did you know," he adds, "that a Real Man doesn't need reading glasses?"

I do a double take. "You don't wear reading glasses."

"Something he will not believe, since as everyone knows, all accountants wear glasses."

"Does he know that real men can count to twenty without removing their shoes?"

Hal shrugs. "I know the score. He's happy doing his job, and I'm happy doing mine. If I tried his job, I'd drive a nail through my foot, and if he tried mine, they'd have him in Federal prison within five months. It's just his way of ribbing me for not following my father's footsteps."

"I thought you looked up to your father." I frown. "You said he was your hero."

"He is." Hal touches my knee now that we're on the highway. "He's worked sixty-hour weeks for years to get my mother a home where she can plant a flower garden. All that, plus he volunteers in his church and forgets to bill the clients he knows can't afford to pay." He shrugs. "That's not running into a burning building to save a pair of kids, but I can look up to it anyhow."

"That's a different kind of being a hero." My voice blends into the engine because it's dropped so low. "In a lot of ways, slow and steady for thirty years has to be harder."

Chapter Twelve:

Months Of The Year

While I'm cashing out the customer, Max takes a call, then puts his hand over the receiver. "Lee, you ever work on a bus?"

As I staple the credit card receipt to the work order, I say, "It's that squeaky thing you see in the streets? Bigger than a car?"

Max tosses me the keys to the wrecker, then lifts his hand off the receiver. "Yeah, we got an expert on bus engines."

Another tidbit to add to my ever-growing resume. Outside, I yank open the wrecker's door and find myself facing the Shadow.

She's wearing jeans and a pink checkered shirt with the sleeves rolled up. She leans forward and looks me straight in the eyes. "Lee. Bucky is dying because of you."

She smells of roses, and her hair shimmers in the light, but when I inhale I can smell grease. I smell gasoline, and the weight of a toolbox drags down my arm.

I'm grounded. I'm right here, and I'm grounded.

"You're a liar," I say. There we go. She sits back, eyes sharp. "I don't listen to liars. Get out of the truck."

She grins. "I'm you, Lee. I'm a liar. You're a liar."

"You're Betrayal."

"And you're the Betrayer. We belong together. Tell me," she says, and abruptly I can taste a chocolate-almond shake and remember the smells of a Thai restaurant. "Tell me how you're different."

"Because I'm not trying to hurt anyone, and you're trying to hurt me."

"No." She reaches for me, and I back away. "I'm just selfish. I want you all for my own. And you want yourself all for your own. I think I've made my point."

She vanishes. In her place I see Bucky, doing a slow clap.

"That's it?" I say. "She's gone?"

"Not hardly." Bucky's mouth twitches. "I wish they disengaged that quickly. But you did good. Now go learn to fix a bus."

Ten minutes later, I'm edging the wrecker up onto the BQE looking for a bus broken down on the shoulder. You'd think the city of New York had contracts for this kind of thing, but apparently the authorities decided to call us instead.

"Bucky, is this even legal?"

It's a good thing Bucky is an angel, because in our suspension-free truck you need better-than-average hearing to detect any sound louder than a nuclear bomb. Instead I feel Bucky assuring me I should just do my job and not worry about the vagaries of the New York municipal government, a mystery into which angels long to look and understand, if only for the laugh value.

"I thought angels didn't want to give scandal."

It's wrong to laugh at evil, Bucky admits. *But when the only other choice is to scream in frustration, laughter is the better choice.*

Traffic slows to 98-year-old-man-with-walker speed, meaning we're in New York. No, actually, it means we're coming up on the bus alongside the road while dozens of drivers rubber-neck in hopes of glimpsing something truly awful.

Sure enough, twenty minutes of traffic later (half a mile) there's the bus off to the side, not blocking the highway with anything other than curiosity. I get up ahead of them with the wrecker and then pull over.

As I climb down from the cab, I meet the eyes of the uniformed men by the bus, and all of us blurt out the same rude word. They're aghast that I'm female.

I'm aghast because the guy looking into the engine is wearing a jumpsuit proclaiming "DEPARTMENT OF CORRECTIONS DETAINEE."

We have an awkward standoff. The men, it turns out, are prison guards, and the bus is transporting prisoners. They would rather have a prisoner look over the engine than a woman; the bus driver would rather have the woman do it. I'm willing to phone Max to send out someone with the proper equipment* but one of the Boys In Uniform realizes that's discrimination and might get them in trouble. One of them says, "I think I remember you from when I was a cop. Didn't you date Alex Murphy? But I thought you worked for the Census Bureau."

I force a smile. "Now why would you think that?"

The prisoner turns away from the engine. He has a light Korean accent. "It's the water pump."

I stick my head into the engine. "Man. He's right."

And thus I have made new friends in the criminal justice system, and I also have a new friend learning to navigate that same system from the inside. It turns out Chen earned the legal stinkeye because he knows how to hot-wire anything that moves. As I get greasy and think longingly of sunscreen, Chen regales me with the tale of a Corvette that yearned to transform into an F-15. Unfortunately for Chen, hot-wiring a car is not the same as

---

* *Why are you looking at the footnote? You know exactly what equipment I'm talking about.*

being rated to drive it at a-hundred-fifty-stupid miles per hour; but fortunately for him, it turns out the air bags worked.

Not as well as his guardian, Bucky says. *She called in prayer debts from every angel she'd ever encountered to save his life.* He snickers. *Me too.*

Chen tells me where, if I look very closely, I can find a Corvette-shaped imprint on a brick wall (or what's left of it) in Kew Gardens.

The security guys don't seem alarmed that Chen wants to help with the pump. Not as alarmed as they look when I suggest they put my handcuffed friend back on the bus. Hoping he won't cold-cock me, I work as quickly as possible, and once I'm sure it's going to hold, the guards ask Chen if he thinks it's safe.

New York's finest indeed.

Then it's back to Mack's with the hope that they'll at least pay him for today's adventures, plus a scrap of paper where Chen has scrawled his address so I can write him at Rikers Island.

"What do you think, Bucky?" I start the engine and shatter the relative silence of sitting alongside five thousand idling cars on the shoulder of the BQE. "Do you think he'd be a good marital prospect? I'd always have plenty of cars to drive."

No doubt. Maybe he'll come to Jesus in prison.

"Jesus is doing time?" I duck as Bucky hits me with a wing. "What kind of car does Jesus drive?"

Eyes sparkling, Bucky leans up close to me. "*What else? A* Fiat Lux."

"Boo!" I wave a hand at him as if scattering a cloud of gnats. "Angels shouldn't make puns."

He feigns a sulk. "God makes puns. There are lots of puns in the Bible." But there's that little grin distorting the corner of his mouth. "Anyhow, that's not mine. It's made the rounds of the choirs for decades now."

"Too bad it didn't get any funnier." The truck lurches as I pull off the shoulder. "Hey, as long as I have the tow truck, is there anywhere you'd like to go? Little old lady stranded alongside the highway with her car overheating?"

Bucky vanishes, and then, fit repayment for being a wiseacre, I find out that yes, there's an overheating car a mile ahead, and a nice person should drag it to Mack's.

In a week, Francisco has stuffed three letters in my mailbox. So much for not bothering me again in exchange for one last chance.

I don't know what to do. I see a letter and all the steel inside me goes soft until finally I buckle and open the envelope. Bucky appears to me every time and says, "Pitch it. You recognize the handwriting—just throw it away."

So the third one I drop in the recycling bin, wracked with guilt.

Let's have a tally, shall we? I can regret the following:

- leading on Francisco
- cheating on Hal
- bringing down the Shadow on Bucky's sweet head

Like a famished prisoner at the dessert bar, it all looks so good, it's hard to know where to start.

Okay, so first I'll feel guilty about Bucky, and then I'll work on the other two.

I could move to California. But I like my job, and it might be hard to find another mechanic who would take a chance on someone as obviously ill-equipped as I am. I could open my own shop, but that takes money, and Bucky wouldn't be happy if I cleared out the savings account just to run away. Francisco's been persistent enough that I'd need a legal name change, too. That would get my mother off my back. But I'd miss Randy and the rest of my family, and I'd need to bring Beth with me. That's getting unworkable.

I've already ruled out a restraining order. And unfortunately, we've seen self-discipline isn't going to cut it either.

"Bucky?" I ask as I turn on the lights. "What should I do?"

He gasps. "God asked you to ask me? What an honor!"

I fold my arms and rivet him with a Look. "No, really. What should I do?"

"You should pray about it, you goofball." He spreads his wings and glides to the window to gaze at the dead spider plant hanging there (oops.)

"I need to see your job description someday." I toss my backpack by the pantry door and head toward the living room. "I'm sure giving advice must be in there."

"There are seven oaths." Bucky sounds abruptly serious. "Discernment is your job. Helping you carry out what you discern is mine."

I pause. "Angels can take oaths?"

He calls after me, "I'm so glad you paid attention while reading Revelation."

"That book was tough. Lambs with seven eyes—eew." I wake up the computer and find an email from Hal, just checking in, and one from Mrs. Smith inviting me to a live chat with a genuine red-shirt from original Trek. Ooh, sign me up for that. Oops, deleted. Too much trouble to drag it back from the trash.

"Okay, talk. What's this oath the angels swear in Revelation." I grin at Bucky. "I want to read it and find a loophole."

"The guardian oath isn't in Revelation, silly." He folds his arms. "But an angel swearing an oath is in Revelation 10. The angel raises his right hand and swears by Him who lives forever and ever and who made the sea."

I chew on that a moment. "He raised his right hand? Angels don't have hands."

Eyebrows furrowed, Bucky raises his right hand.

"You tell me over and over that you're immaterial. Pure spirit means no body. That's not really a body." I fold a paper airplane and send it right through him. "So why did the angel do that?"

Bucky says, "What does this mean?" and kneels. Then he stands and salutes. "What's that? How about this?" He widens his eyes and holds up both hands.

"It's affected. That's my point."

"Not for humans is it affected. You tell truth with your bodies. You use body language to reinforce the words you're saying. When you're saying the Pledge of Allegiance, what do you do?"

"You stand," I say. "You put your hand over your heart. But an angel wouldn't do that."

"That's not where I'm going. Of course the angel in Revelation didn't need to raise his right hand. But he had taken a form so John could see him, and John needed to recognize it as an oath. Now tell me this: how do you know Hal loves you?"

I should burst out singing "The Shoop Shoop Song," but instead I say, "He spends time with me. He cooks for me."

Bucky says, "He holds your hand. He kisses you."

Oh, he did expect me to sing The Shoop Shoop Song. "I've held plenty of hands."

"Bear with me. When he squeezes your hand, he's telling you something, right?" When I nod, Bucky says, "Carry it forward. It was important the first time he kissed you, right? Because it felt good? Or because it meant something?"

This is kind of uncomfortable. "Your point?"

"My point is, you talk with your bodies. Remember when you promised me not to have sex with anyone until you were married? I wanted that because I didn't want you to make a false promise. What do you think sex says?"

My eyes widen. "I...okay, I have no idea."

"It says *I love you and have given you everything.*" He nods. "Clothes are off and you've let someone else access your body and your fertility. Inasmuch as you're doing that, you're allowing the person to touch your future."

I shiver. "I think you just put a finger, so to speak, on why I don't ever want to get married. I don't want to give someone everything." I fold my arms. "I've seen movies and TV, though. People *do* 'do it' just for fun."

"In which case they're saying *I'll use you and you can use me.*" Bucky shrugs. "Not quite the most inspiring message, no? And they've still got that pesky fertility thing to deal with somehow, so they're holding back all sorts of parts of themselves. Sex should be like an oath."

"You make it all sound so not-like-fun." I shudder. "I'd rather just cross my heart and hope to die."

I head back to the dining room and realize there's a package on the table. Francisco? No, worse than Francisco. It's from my mother.

Bucky takes one look and bursts out laughing.

"I hate you." My mother wraps packages so that the Marines couldn't break into them with their highly-sharpened swords. "What's she done this time?"

"I don't want to spoil your surprise."

"Hey, remember that thing about having no body?" I hurl the packet through his head, and he leans against the wall, laughing helplessly. When I retrieve it, I whack him again for good measure. As I trim off six layers of packing tape, I make cute eyes at him. "Come on, give me a hint?"

"There's no way you'd believe me even if I told you."

It's squishy, about the size of a DVD box set. Too small to be a wedding gown, thank goodness. Finally my scissors reveal a rainbow of seven colors. (Red, Orange, Yellow, Green, Blue, Indigo, and Criminy.)

"Underwear?" I turn it over and let out a yelp that leaves Bucky laughing even harder.

"Days of the week underwear?" My mother. They're my size, and sure, they're always useful, but... Oh, and they have little princesses on them. Why wouldn't they?

"I wouldn't have minded if the Post Office lost this," I murmur.

"How could they?" Bucky leans over my shoulder. "She put a tracking number on it."

With a gasp, I look at my phone. It's blinking with a voicemail. I bet she's left a message asking if I got anything special.

"I'm going to show her." I grimace. "I'm going to wear Tuesday on Friday."

"You wouldn't!" Bucky holds his hand over his heart, probably to show how serious he is. "Think of the consequences!"

"I'm afraid I already have given the matter all the consideration it requires.

"I'm afraid you haven't. If the days of the week aren't properly coordinated with your underwear, think of the problems that would ensue."

I sit at the table. "Bucky, educate me."

"My delight." Apparently he's forgotten that bit where he's not my spirit guide. "What would happen if you awoke in your ordinary fog and staggered to the bathroom, where you saw Sunday underwear, and then proceeded to sleep in? Only it was Wednesday and because of that you were late to work?"

"Think about it for a minute." I drum my fingertips against the table. "When I wake up on Monday, I'm going to be wearing Sunday anyhow."

Bucky recoils in horror. Then he makes a brave face and pulls himself together. "I'll awaken you at midnight to change."

"You will do no such thing."

"Your immortal soul is at stake here."

All right, now I can't keep a straight face any longer. Momentarily, neither can he.

Bucky manages to choke out, "You could change the night before."

"Would totally mess up my system. There's no way out."

Bucky rubs his temples. "Oh, the travails of a fallen world."

"We'll make it through together." I square my shoulders as if mustering my strength. "I couldn't ask for a more dedicated guardian."

He winks. "Don't I know it?"

I break up in giggles. "You know, they have days of the week underwear, but they don't have months of the year."

Bucky's eyes are wider than golf balls. "Well, in the Middle Ages, that would have been practical."

"Other than the rampant illiteracy thing."

Bucky rubs his chin. "If you were really fastidious, you could have hours of the day underwear. You know, noon, one, two..."

"Don't tell my mother. I'll have to bring a backpack full of them to work." I toss the package aloft and then snatch it from midair. "So, Goodwill or Sally-Ann?"

Bucky folds his arms. "Oh, so I'm back to being your spirit-guide, am I?"

"I thought I could trick you." I grin as I go for the phone. "But at the very least, my mother taught me always to say thank you for a gift."

As he vanishes, there's a light in Bucky's eyes that I haven't seen for weeks.

Chapter Thirteen:

Marriage is an act of despair

I'm picking up Avery in the Acura for our girl's afternoon out. I think this afternoon I'm teaching her to drive. Don't tell the police. Or my brother. Or my mother. Come to think of it, Bucky wasn't too pleased either. Better change the subject.

I flip on the radio and hear the opening chords of U2's "I Still Haven't Found What I'm Looking For." It's a good song, but a tad overplayed. It's a classic rock song, so those stations play it. Adults hear it and hearken back to their youth, so it ends up on the "adult pop" stations. It's not terribly hard, so it's also "soft rock." And yes, somehow although it offends my heart, it's now considered an "oldie." Just about the only stations that don't play it are the hip-hop and classical.

I don't feel like hearing it now, so I change channels.

WPLJ: "And I still....haven't found..."

Z100: "...what I'm looking for..."

WCBS: "still..."

105.5: "...what I'm..."

WLTW: "...And I..."

The Peak: "...what I'm..."

Q104: "...still...haven't..."

K-Joy: "...looking for."

I snap off the radio. "Bucky, quit that."

In my heart, I hear, *I didn't do it.*

I stiffen. "Oh gosh. You'd have used 'Don't Stop.'"

In the seat beside me, I find a crestfallen angel. "I wish I'd thought of it first."

"I love you anyhow."

He lifts up his head. "It probably doesn't count since one of those was the cover by John McVey, right?"

"You know what? I don't even want to know about inter-angel competitiveness." I plug in my iPod. "I'll play the *Rumours* album while you nurse your broken heart."

"You're all sweetness and light," Bucky mutters, and I feel him shift to the back seat as "Never Going Back" starts up. At a red light, I glance behind to find him playing acoustic guitar.

"Show-off."

"Yeah. Because this is so tough, a human could never master it."

"It took you a week."

"I didn't have a lot of time to practice, with all that warding-off-of-evil I have to do." Bucky's fingers fly over the strings as he finger-picks the riff in time with Lindsey Buckingham. "This is all sleight-of-hand anyhow. I was thinking when you get to Heaven, we could learn an instrument together."

I giggle. "Harps?"

"No, silly. Bagpipes."

"Absolutely not."

Stricken, Bucky stops playing. "Why not?"

"Because it's *Heaven,* that's why. God wouldn't allow bagpipes!"

He looks hurt. "If you're so smart, then what should musicians play in Heaven?"

"Violins." I point at him. "I want to learn violin."

"Done." Bucky returns to his guitar. "You do realize that in Heaven, violins don't make any sound until after *Suzuki Method Four*."

I frown. "Why?"

"Because God loves us."

Yeah. I heard what happened when Brennan picked up the violin. Heck, I heard what happened when I picked up the trumpet in grammar school. Bucky had a headache for six weeks, and next September, he encouraged me to take drama.

Before the end of the *Rumours* album we're at Avery's school, and she sprints to the car with her friend Jenny. It's still warm enough that they can wear their uniform shorts, and they've tied their jackets around their waists.

Avery sticks her head in the window. "Can you drive Jenny home?"

"And leave you here?" I say innocently.

"Aunt Lee!" She yanks open the back door and shoves her bag inside, then follows it. Jenny follows her. "It's not far."

I nod as I pull into traffic. "And are you going to give me directions, or will just any home suffice?"

They break out in giggles, and as I get to the light, Jenny says, "Go left," and that's easy, I only have to cut off a city bus to get into the left lane and sit with my blinker on while fifty passengers stare in loathing. Behind me there's much giggling and whispering. I might as well not be here.

Bucky gazes in the back seat. "Wow. The fond memories are overwhelming."

I wasn't that bad!

"No," Bucky deadpans. "Not at all."

I'm much maligned, I tell you.

After a dozen, *Oh, you should have turned theres*, Jenny gets off at a building she assures me is actually where she lives. Avery climbs into the front seat. I say, "Which do you want? Driving lesson or mini golf?"

My niece disappoints me. "Mini golf."

There's a cheesy, overcrowded outdoor place for that not far off the Belt. After the game, we buy popcorn lightly doused with a gallon of melted butter in the hopes of hiding its staleness, and as a chaser we pick up a cone of blue cotton candy bigger than your head. We may get permanently stuck to each other and to the picnic bench, but that's a small price to pay.

"I don't think we'll be able to do this anymore." Avery picks off a wad of blue spun sugar and shoves it into her mouth. "Jenny wants to do debate club, and that meets on Wednesdays."

"It doesn't have to be Wednesday." I take some for myself. "Tuesday?"

"School play. Tryouts are tomorrow. Thursdays too."

Fridays are out because, well, they're Fridays. That'd be pretty lame of me, and besides—

"Grandma warned me not to take up your Fridays, either," Avery adds. "She says Hal wants them."

"Oh, did she?" I shake my head. "You're family. Hal's a guy. He'd cope."

"Yeah, but he's your boyfriend."

I shudder. "He's not a boy, and he didn't lie on his couch playing sad songs every Friday night until I walked into his life."

Come to think of it, what did Hal do on Fridays before I met him? Maybe he did lie on the couch listening to sad songs. Maybe he played chess online. I could totally see Hal doing online chess the same way I can totally see me not. "There's Mondays."

Avery says, "What if you marry him?"

"I'll still be your aunt."

"But you know what I mean. You won't be able to take me mini-golfing or roller-blading. You'll have to be home."

"Doing what? Cooking?" I snicker. "Women don't hang around the house any longer looking pretty for the moment our husbands walk in the door."

Avery's looking glum. "But you change when you get married."

"Not like *that*." I chuckle. "Your father was the same person after he got married that he was before. Still my brother. Still just as irritating and smug." When Avery giggles, I say, "What would be the point of finding someone you loved enough to want to be with forever if you got married and the person immediately changed?"

Avery takes another gob of cotton candy. Her fingers are blue. "I read something once, about changing a guy if he did something you didn't like. You marry him and then you change him."

I wave the cotton candy stick at her, and she snags another piece. "No, no, no. Get that out of your head." I hand her a napkin. "The point isn't to find a passable guy and change him into a prince. A really good friend of mine told me the point is to hang in there so that when you get married, it's an act of despair."

Avery squawks "What?" even as Bucky inside me squawks, *What?*

"Don't get married until you have to admit to yourself, it absolutely cannot get any better than this."

Avery's eyes flare. "Is that why you're not married?"

I bet my tongue is blue. Avery's certainly is. "I'm an eternal optimist. It can always get better."

She laughs. "So Hal isn't the one? You can do better than that?"

I'm about to answer when I hesitate. "Well...no guy is perfect, but we're not perfect either. It's a matter of finding a guy whose neuroses match up with yours."

She stares in incomprehension.

"You've seen gears? How they have teeth that lock together?" I hand her the cone of cotton candy and lock my fingers together. "Like that. Well, your gears and the guy's have to interlock well enough that you can turn one another and keep the machinery running. The ways that you're a little off-beat have to match the ways he's off-beat. Your good points have to counterbalance his and your bad points have to have a balance too, and then you can work together. Forever, if necessary."

Avery gestures at me with the cotton candy. "That's so deep."

"Of course it's deep." I wink at her. "I'm a mechanic."

"So how do your gears mesh with Hal's?"

When you do a tune-up, there's this little printout you can analyze. I can't exactly clamp a bunch of electrodes on me and him, so I have to guess. "In low gear, we work together pretty well. And I guess we shift gears okay too, so we've got a good transmission. But I'm not sure about the higher gears or if the engine is rated for a hundred fifty thousand miles. Maybe it's one of those economy models that are designed to crap out after eighty thousand."

Avery laughs. "People aren't cars. They don't need oil changes."

"Hey, there's a lot in common between a good boyfriend and a good car!" Oops, are the people at the next table staring? Maybe they'll learn something. "They do run better with high octane stuff, and they need regular maintenance." I shrug. "Although I guess title isn't as easy to transfer, and insurance is harder to come by."

Avery exclaims, "You need a license for driving *and* for getting married!"

"You decide what features you want," I say. "You decide about performance, staying power, flash, storage space, safety. And then you need to comparison shop and get testimonials from people who've tried that model. By the time you're done test-driving, you'll know everything except what color the interior will be and the presets on the radio."

Avery takes the last bit of cotton candy. "When are you done test-driving?"

"Before your first long road trip," I say. I hope.

If life were a standardized test, today's question would read like this:

Bucky appears to be:
- *infuriated*
- *perplexed*
- *frustrated*
- *beyond confused*

"I never told you marriage is an act of despair!"

"You did so!" I'm driving home in the dark, and Bucky and I have had this go-around several times. "You told me not to settle."

"And in what language does 'don't settle for the first guy who comes along' turn into 'get married only as an act of pure desperation'?"

"You never explicitly said 'act of despair.'" I wave a hand at him. "But how else would you interpret not settling for someone when there could be someone better out there?"

A wave of frustration shoots through me, and I'm sure it's Bucky blowing off steam. "Okay, let's try this again. You need to set certain standards for a husband. It has to be someone who shares your basic values and someone who respects you. In your case, you decided early he had to have a sense of humor, had to have a certain chemistry with you, and had to be gainfully employed on a regular basis."

I smirk. "Knuckles not dragging the ground is also a plus."

"There are a lot of things you've added in over time, like the importance of family. But you're talking about setting the bar so high that no one could possibly meet it!"

"You could."

He yanks back toward the door. "Whoa!"

"I'm not in love with you. That'd be—eew." I grimace. "But you and I have a certain chemistry, and you have a sense of humor and a sense of honor, and you don't always take me too seriously, and you have a good work ethic."

Bucky sounds frazzled. "But that makes sense. I'm an angel, and God designed our souls to match up with each other."

"My point was, you meet my criteria."

There's silence. "You mean I really did ruin you for marriage?"

"You said it's okay not to get married, so how would that ruin me?" I shake my head. "You also say you can't read my thoughts, but you come pretty close sometimes."

"Apparently I read them a lot less than you think because I never saw you interpreting 'don't settle' as 'make sure you've exhausted every possibility first.'" Bucky's wings flex. "Okay, so talk to me about Hal. What could be better about him?"

"He's predictable."

"I'd say," Bucky says, "you and he have a certain chemistry. He has a sense of humor and a sense of honor. He doesn't always take you too seriously, and he has a decent work ethic."

The list sounds familiar. In case I'm exceptionally dense today, Bucky adds, "That's how you described me."

"He's more rigid."

"My point is, if you're looking for someone who's going to beat me, I'm not sure you're going to find him on the human side of the equation. I'm a higher-order being, and you can't get around that. But he's good enough."

"So…" I accelerate onto the Prospect Expressway. "You've just changed your advice from 'Make sure you can't get any better than this' to 'Good enough is okay.'"

"I'm not lightly pronouncing him 'good enough.'" Bucky's eyes gleam. "I would walk through fire for you, and it would break my heart to see you married to someone who didn't treasure you. More to the point, Hal fits *my* standards, and I don't have low standards when it comes to you."

We don't have a very long time on the Prospect Expressway before my exit. As we're pulling up the ramp, I finally say, "But it hasn't always been easy with him."

"Love is hard work. By definition."

I frown. "What good is that?"

"It's not easy for God to love us the way we are either. There's friction and misunderstanding and times when the gears should turn smoothly, only they don't. There are going to be fights and things said in anger. But it's not supposed to be easy." Bucky waits a beat, then adds, "Maybe this is the hard work that makes you fit for Heaven."

Beth is home, shellacking origami Christmas trees. The apartment has that special glitter-and-glue scent I've come to associate with her presence. Beside the trees are a number of drying cardboard and glitter projects in various states of drying: cutouts of feet, painted paper plates, and a painted pine cone.

I drop my jacket by the pantry door. "Why do you practice crafts you've done seven times already?"

"Because the eighth year, the kids are going to find a new way to mess it up. And I need to be able to describe the project in detail to the new teachers. Come here and help me out."

"Me?" When Beth taught me origami it culminated in a catastrophe of paper cuts, teary tissues, and her recommendation that I stick to changing tires.

"I need to see how a three-year-old would do this." She grins and hands me the camera. "Oh, and you can photograph all this stuff."

Oh, that I can do. I take pictures of the origami forest overgrowing our table, then unfold cardboard boxes, pack the trees in sets of five, label the outsides, and seal them. She'll sell them on Etsy when the Christmas rush begins.

After that, I hang out online, trade IMs with Hal, answer an email from my SF buddy ("Dear Mrs. Smith: I just finished your *Heroes* fanfic, and the slash pairing was definitely different than the ones I usually see") and then I head to bed where I thumb through *Car and Driver*. They're always good for a laugh, but tonight my eyes keep closing, and I keep having this persistent thought that Hal would want me to get up and floss my teeth.

"Lee!"

I start up from my pillow, heart racing. But there's no one with me. I fell asleep in my clothes and with the light on.

The next moment, Bucky is in front of me, urgent.

I blink. "Was that you?"

"Go downstairs. Now."

I'm out the apartment door before I wonder what I'm doing. "Wait—do I need my wallet or a jacket?"

"Just go!"

I don't even know if I'm heading out the front door or into the basement, but I sprint down the stairs. As I reach the second floor landing, I have a horrible thought: Mrs. Goretti needs me.

On the ground floor, I race to her door and knock repeatedly, calling her name. Bucky reminds me that I left my cell phone in my back pocket, so I dial. Through the door, I can hear her phone ringing, but no one answers.

"Unlock it," I tell him.

"Call 911," Bucky replies.

"But if you let me inside—"

"There's no time to mess around!" Bucky gets larger in my field of vision until I can't think of anything else. "Call!"

He may not have said the last, only put it into my heart. I call the emergency number.

I yell again through the door that Mrs. Goretti needs to hang on.

And then proceeds the strangest 911 call in the history of emergency response, because naturally the operator wants to know why I think we need help, and I can't very well say, "My guardian angel told me that Mrs. Goretti's guardian angel told him that she needs help."

I look at Bucky helplessly and just keep stammering to the brusque-sounding operator that my landlady needs help, that she's ill, that she has a heart condition, that she's not answering, that I'm scared. Bucky looks worried. *Please, God, make her take me seriously.* Bucky hates it when I lie, but I'll do it to save Mrs. Goretti's life and tell God to put it on my tab. I've lied for far less.

Except then the operator decides I'm incoherent not because I'm hiding the truth but because I'm terrified. She tells me help is on the way and to make sure the door is unlocked.

I run for the front door. "Bucky, so help me, unlock her apartment. She's going to go ballistic if the firemen take an axe to it."

"Totally discreet." Bucky folds his arms. "I'll just slide the deadbolt, the chain, the Master Lock and the knob lock, and you can tell everyone you left a bowl of milk for the lock-sprites."

My heart pounds as I unbolt the outer door and turn on the stair light. "Why bother waking me to help her if you're not going to get me in there?"

Bucky leans close. "Surely you remember the spare key for the parlor doors is behind the picture of her grandfather in the hallway?"

I turn toward him, livid. His eyes sparkle.

I dash inside. "She never said that."

"She must have." Bucky flies behind me. "How else would you know?"

"Maybe some wiseacre angel told me." I lift a gold-toned frame featuring a black and white portrait of the world's sternest individual, and a key the length of my pinky plinks to the carpet; the tape lost its stickiness decades ago. The cellophane finishes fluttering to the floor as I snatch up the key.

Brownstones were constructed for the grand effect. While Mrs. Goretti uses a normal door at the far end of the hallway (which opens directly into the kitchen) an unused set of French doors leads directly into a parlor at the front. She's going to use them now: for one thing, it'll be easier to get in a stretcher.

She's parked a cedar chest in front of the doors. With a groan, I slide it out of the way, then fit the key into the lock with hands that shake. The lock is more reluctant to move than a cedar chest on carpet. Hoping the key won't snap, I force it until the lock yields. The knob is loose after decades of rest, but the door clicks, and I slide it open enough to admit my body sideways.

I'm in.

"Mrs. Goretti!" I bang into a buffet she's got up against the other side. No matter; I slide that enough to slip past, then stumble through the parlor to reach Mrs. Goretti's bedroom.

Her light operates with a pull-chain. I flail for it until Bucky guides my hand. Light. At last.

Mrs. Goretti lies still. Grey. I rush to her side of the bed and grab her hands. "Help is coming. There's an ambulance. Hang in there."

Her eyelids don't even flutter. I fight panic.

Bucky draws close. *She's alive.*

Not very much.

That's why I got you.

Next thing I know someone's shouting on the street, and the paramedics have arrived.

Half an hour later, I'm in the ER at Methodist Hospital on Seventh Avenue and Sixth Street. No one fought me about this because I didn't ask permission. I just climbed into the ambulance with Mrs. Goretti and didn't bother climbing out again.

That gets me only so far, though. The nurses have said that due to HIPAA, blah blah blah, no information for me even though I'm standing right there as two ER docs work to stabilize Mrs. Goretti's heart.

Angels, fortunately, are not bound by HIPAA, and Bucky can tell me anything he feels like. "Of course," he admits sheepishly, "I'm not a doctor, so I can't make a definitive diagnosis—"

I crack up laughing. The nurses spare me a glance, and one pointedly asks if I need a cup of coffee. Yes, I do—desperately.

In the hallway finding coffee, I end up in a designated "cell phone use" area, and there's this cell phone in my back pocket, so I guess I'm required to use it. It's awful, but I do the worst possible thing: I phone Hal.

"Lee?" Then at a higher pitch, "What's wrong?"

"I'm at Methodist Hospital with Mrs. Goretti." I swallow. "There's no one else here with her. I don't want to leave, but—"

"Okay, give me a minute. What time is it?" I hear him mutter under his breath when he gets a glimpse at the time. "I can— I can be there in ten minutes. Where are you?"

"In the ER waiting area. At least, I will be. I'm in the hallway right now. But when you come, I'll make sure I'm there, and—"

"You're babbling." There's a gentle humor in his voice as he awakens. I can hear him moving around. "How bad is it?"

"It's her heart. The nurses won't tell me exactly what's going on, but Bucky says she had a heart attack. Her numbers are all over the place, and I'm not sure if they've reached any of her relatives yet. For that matter, I'm not sure anyone knows how to."

"I'm getting my shoes on. I'll be right over." You can see Hal's building from the hospital parking lot, so it will be about four minutes until he's here. "Are you going to be okay?"

I swallow. "I'm a big girl."

"Then why'd you call me at one o'clock in the morning, big girl?" He's amused. "I've got my jacket and my keys. Heading out the door. Buy me a cup of coffee for when I get there, okay?"

"Why not?" I smile vaguely. "It's free."

By the time Hal arrives, I've got Beth awake and on the phone, and she's heading downstairs to look for an address book or whether Mrs. Goretti has numbers programmed into her phone. I hand Hal a Styrofoam cup, but after I hang up with Beth, he puts it down and wraps me in a hug.

"Can we go back to see her?"

"They'll have to stop me." I rest my head on his shoulder. "She doesn't look good."

We weave our way through the ER doors and back to Mrs. Goretti's room. "Room" is a misnomer: it's a curtained-off area with every square inch of floor-space crowded by machines. An ash-white Mrs. Goretti wears a breathing mask, wired with more electrodes than I use for a tune-up.

Do you think fixing a heart is the same thing as fine-tuning the spark plugs? The heart has to pump in a rhythm; the spark plugs have to fire in a rhythm.

"You're getting punchy," Bucky says.

I rub my temples. "I need more coffee."

Hal hands me his cup. "Be my guest. This stuff is terrible."

"It's liquid caffeine."

"Yeah, but who brewed it? Moses?"

Bucky bursts out laughing. "It's the special Temple blend."

By reflex I repeat Bucky's wisecrack, and Hal gives a frown. "God can afford better coffee."

First Bucky, then me: "He likes it strong."

"That's omnipotence for you."

"It's why the blood of the martyrs cries out from under the altar in Revelation," Bucky says, which I relate. "They're annoyed at being woken up so early."

Hal smirks. "Well, this stuff could wake the dead, that's for sure."

My taste buds were slaughtered long since by the stuff Max brews, so I don't appreciate the finer points of roasting one's own coffee beans. At this moment, I care only about the caffeine hit.

Bucky's about to speak, but then he stops.

I raise my eyebrows. "Come on—you can't quit on me now."

"My next line got a little too rude for comfort." He shrugs. "You'd have laughed, but I'm not sure it would be worth seeing that look on God's face."

Hal says, "The angel said something?"

"I was repeating him. He backed out of giving me the world's snarkiest rejoinder." I glare at Bucky. "Some fun you are."

"Great—I'm trading jabs with an angel at one o'clock in the morning. Shoot me now." Hal leans against the foot of Mrs. Goretti's gurney. "I know a bit about medical numbers, by the way, and I don't like the ones I'm seeing."

I stroke Mrs. Goretti's limp hand. "Me neither. I wish the doctors would come back."

I don't want to leave her alone, but there's nothing we can do. We're not authorized to say yes or no to the doctors. She's not even aware we're here.

But Hal doesn't look angry that I woke him up for no reason. Instead, concern. It's so bright in here, too busy for whatever hour it is after midnight. Someone down the hall is shouting, and the loudspeaker blares a page every few minutes. Random-seeming beeps, blips, and alarms chatter forth from a variety of machines that ought to turn the techie in me green with envy.

Instead I wish the world would silence for a moment, just let Mrs. Goretti sleep and let me sit here with my worries and my kinda-sorta-boyfriend who isn't mad that he's losing sleep for me.

Hal disengages from me, then returns with a plastic chair. Sitting, I rest my head on the gurney beside Mrs. Goretti's pillow. The oxygen mask hisses.

Hal rubs my shoulders, but I can't relax. It wasn't even six months ago that I did this with Avery, when she overdosed on her mom's medication. Different hospital, but the same smells and tension and sounds and worries. Only they never left Avery alone like this. If I go, my landlady won't have anyone.

My phone blares a song by The Fold, and I fumble for it. "Beth?"

We're probably in a no-cell-phone zone. I don't care.

"I reached one of her granddaughters." Beth sounds efficient, not worn to the bone. Maybe it comes from teaching preschool, since preschool teachers always know everything. "She's going to get in contact with everyone."

"Everyone?" That's pretty cool. "There's this poly-branched phone tree covering millions of people, every one of them related to her even if you have to go back to Lorenzo de Medici?"

"You need sleep." Beth sighs. "Someone's coming to take over for you, but wake me up if you need me."

I can think of only one reason to wake her. "Sure."

"Excuse me?"

At the "door" of the emergency "room" there's a black-clothed man in a white dog collar. I blink for a moment until Hal's shaking the man's hand, and Hal says to me, I guess because I look as baffled as I feel, "Father Savin is a hospital chaplain."

The priest looks younger than me, which I didn't think could happen, but whatever. Through an exhausted haze I learn that in the past, Mrs. Goretti checked off "would like to see a Catholic priest" on her hospital record. The chaplain asks if my grandmother would still like that.

I shake my head. "I'm just her tenant."

The chaplain nods. "Then let's assume she hasn't changed her mind, shall we?"

He prays a sweet prayer, and something happens then that I've never seen before: Bucky joins him.

It's the fear or the exhaustion, but for some reason I can see what it means to pray. The prayer "gets big" in my head and suddenly it's everything I can think. Then while the priest recites, Bucky does something in counterpoint, wrapped around the prayer and through it, supporting it. Presenting it. It's as if he's wrapping it up like a gift and handing it over to God.

A warmth wraps around him, from him to Mrs. Goretti and then from him and her to someone else—maybe her guardian? It's a current from all of us outward, not upward as much as in and out, like breathing, like an interior crying that we can't even form properly but which between all of us is formed and flows back to its own source.

The priest puts a spicy-smelling oil on Mrs. Goretti's head. Then he asks if it would be okay if he prayed for us too. I'm bleary-eyed. Hal says yes for us both, but I don't feel the praying-thing again.

I'm dizzy. The priest leaves, and we're alone again in the ER.

Bucky glances at me, his eyes concerned. I probably shouldn't have seen what just happened. I'm glad I did, though.

Hal disappears for a few minutes and returns with a Snickers bar and more foul coffee. "This has protein," he says as he splits the bar in half. "It'll wake you up a bit."

Bucky eyes the coffee. "I have curious moments, but right now I'm glad I don't eat."

I repeat this to Hal, and he laughs out loud. "When we get to Heaven," Hal says in Bucky's general direction, "you have to drop by for dinner. I'll make you a meal you'll never forget."

"As long as I can forget some of the things Lee's eaten," Bucky says.

"Hey!" I throw an empty Styrofoam cup at him. "Not fair!"

"Knock-knock?" says a voice.

"Who's there?" I turn and there's a woman about my age with one of the nurses. Thank goodness—Mrs. Goretti's actual granddaughter has come to the hospital with an actual husband. In the next five minutes I hand off whatever actual information we've gleaned (both doctor-derived and Bucky-derived) and I get her phone number.

I kiss Mrs. Goretti on the forehead. "You have to get well. Who's going to make sure I'm eating if you don't?"

The granddaughter strokes her hair. "I'm glad to hear Grandma treats everyone the same."

And then, unceremoniously, Hal and I are out on the street in front of the hospital.

"If I didn't know your angel warrior would cut me in half for suggesting it," Hal says as we start walking, "I'd inform you that I long to sleep on my couch, which leaves a perfectly good bed available for you only a block from here."

I can't help it: I burst out laughing.

Hal sounds timid. "Which was the most ludicrous part of that statement?"

It's three in the morning. Anything sounds hilarious at three, including my great-grandmother's *Settlement Cook Book* ("The way to a man's heart? Hah!") but that sets me off worse.

Hal sounds hurt. "The idea of sleeping in the same apartment with me is amusing?"

I shake my head. "No, the idea of Bucky with a sword."

"Don't all angels have swords?"

I frown. "I don't think so."

"They fight in Revelation."

"There are angels with censers in Revelation. And lampstands."

Hal says, "They follow on horseback behind Christ waging war."

"Hey wow! I wonder if Bucky owns a horse. That would be so unbelievably cool!" He should have told me back when I was horse-obsessed, except I'd have pestered him until he brought it to Earth for a ride. And we didn't have a pasture in the apartment.

We're at the Clockworks, but Hal shakes his head. "I'll walk you home."

"So I can sleep on my couch?"

"I have these things called feet—I'll walk myself back. I can't leave you on the streets alone at three AM."

Oh, the perpetual New York City Night Life problem. You want to hang out after dark, but you also don't want to be killed on the streets. Decisions decisions. Beth and I worked out this solution when we lived several blocks apart, me with my mom and she with her dog. She'd hang out with me at my mom's until one AM. Then, ready for this?

- I would walk Beth to her studio apartment.
- Beth would leash the dog and escort me back to my mother's apartment.
- Beth would return to her apartment with the dog to protect her.

Beth never got mugged under this system, and the dog got plenty of exercise—as did Beth, come to think of it. When the dog died, Beth had no one to walk her home any longer, so she suggested we split rent together.

"I've got a sword-bearing, horseback-riding angel to keep me safe." I kiss him. "Go home. I've kept you awake long enough."

Hal kisses me back. "What if I call you a car service?"

"By the time it comes, I'd be home."

Hal hesitates.

Bucky says, "Tell him the coast is clear."

"Bucky says." I hug him. "Thank you for doing this for me. I'll call you tomorrow."

"After nine," he says as he returns the squeeze. "I suspect I'm going in late."

There's that hesitant kiss, the kiss-plus-another-kiss as he's unwilling to let me go. Then he heads inside as I walk up Seventh Avenue.

I love the city's permanent twilight, where the street lights keep it almost as bright as day, half as many people and a third the cars. All the shops are shut, but not all are dark. It's to deter criminals from breaking in, but I have no idea how that would work, if the criminals would just smash and grab with the lights to help them.

"Do you have a sword?" I murmur as I walk.

"Would it make a difference?" Bucky says. "You'll be heading back to Hal's in a heartbeat if I say, 'Actually, I'm the one with the censer'?"

I giggle. "It would definitely make a difference. Guys in uniform are gorgeous. If you have a sword, I bet you also have armor."

Bucky pauses, thinking.

"What about the horse thing?"

"I totally flunked horseback riding." Bucky gives a sigh. "I was fine when they walked, but then we got to trotting, and the whole thing just went crazy."

"Really?"

He laughs. "You're cute when you're exhausted."

"You're infuriating when I'm exhausted. Can I at least take care of your horse when we're in Heaven?"

"He's been out to pasture for the last thirty-one years. If you can catch him, be my guest."

I gasp with horror. "You fiend! You don't even go home to give him sugar cubes?"

"Apple slices are healthier."

We're quiet for a minute. As I cross the street, I say, "I can believe the horse easier than the sword."

"Really?" He sounds surprised. "I'd look cool with a sword."

In the next moment, he's got a broadsword in his hand. He wields it in a gentle arc, then whips it so it slices the motes hanging in the streetlamp glow.

"You do look cool. I just can't imagine you fighting."

Bucky says, "I fight for you. I fought the Shadow."

"With a sword?"

"With everything I have. If the only thing I had left was a two-pound piece of metal, yes. As it turns out, we have better weapons than swords."

I raise my eyebrows. "A Glock?"

"Better. You'll have to wait to find out." He parries and then thrusts against an imaginary opponent. "Maybe I'll keep this. It does look cool."

I'm warm inside. "What about armor?"

"Maybe tomorrow. I still need a scabbard." A belt with one appears at his hips, slung loosely over his jeans. "I wonder if Michael gives fencing lessons?"

"You need a foil for fencing, and then you'd just look like one of the Three Musketeers."

Bucky's eyes brighten so much they throw shadows. "They have feathers in their caps! I have plenty of feathers!"

I cock my head. "How about a cape? When you get your armor?"

"How would that work with wings, though?" He flares them, glances at his shoulders, and shakes his head. "It might get caught when I ride the horse."

By now we've reached home, so I let us inside. I replace Mrs. Goretti's key behind her grandfather's photo, then double-check that Beth locked all her doors. I trudge up three flights of creaking stairs so I can drop into bed and die.

There's a message on voicemail, left only fifteen minutes ago, and my heart sinks. Not already.

I push the button, and it's worse than a death notice.

"Hey, Lee—Francisco here." He sounds as chipper as if I haven't been doing everything short of homicide to avoid the sound of his voice. "Why aren't you home? Give me a call when you get a chance!"

Chapter Fourteen

It's the "Oh, crud" moment

The last thing I'd done before collapsing into bed was to text Max that he could have me in on time, or he could have me in awake; choose one. Since I'm paid hourly and since Max hates to re-do work we've messed up, he prefers we be alive and coherent, so I know what he'll decide.

All those things that seemed hilarious last night? Not funny this morning. Bucky is still wearing his sword, but I'll give him grief about it later.

It would horrify Hal that Beth brewed half a pot and then shut it off for me, leaving a note that I should chug it all. My microwave turns it hot again. It's better than the stuff last night.

Mrs. Goretti's granddaughter texted at five in the morning letting me know she's been moved into the Cardiac ICU, and this-number looked good but that-number was still fluctuating, and thanks again for staying with Grandma.

My Wheaties are getting soggy, but at least my landlady is alive. But geez, what do I do now that Francisco has my home number? How did he even get it?

Beth would get rid of him for me. At the very least, she can help me screen calls until he gets it through his head that really, when I say I'm not interested, I'm not interested. Maybe with her help I can get it through my own head, too.

The rest of Beth's coffee fits into a thermal mug, and I chug it on the way to the shop. By then I'm awake enough to change a tire.

Bucky spends time practicing with his new sword, and I can tell from the way he periodically looks to the side and corrects his stance that someone is giving him tips.

By the time I'm done, I've had two calls and three texts from Francisco. I have one from Hal, none from Mrs. Goretti's granddaughter. I leave them all unread.

Mr. Hartman and the Axlemobile are back at the top of my list. It's got its new axle. I've worked on the whole brake system. I've replaced the shredded front tires and the bent rims. I've also discovered some hidden damage: something hit and broke open the oil pan. That's next on the docket to replace.

I'm looking over the paperwork when I get a sudden urge to go make more coffee. The coffee maker is empty, and I really shouldn't drink any more if I want to sleep tonight, but I start scooping out new grounds.

Behind me, the Maxima explodes.

With a scream I drop the coffee, but the car's still there, suspended on the lift over a pile of detritus. Ari and Carlos have fled to the back wall, and Max runs into the garage, shouting, "What in blazes was that?"

I edge toward the car, then pull down my safety goggles in case something else goes. Sometimes when one part gets destabilized, especially with the suspension, another follows suit. I nudge the metal beneath the car with my steel-toed boot, then bend and take a closer look.

Ari comes up beside me. "Shock strut."

Max snorts. "It just snapped?"

Ari says, "I've seen that happen before when there's really bad body damage. I wish I knew what that kid did with this car. He has to have been chasing someone, or was being chased."

Carlos says, "Drag racing."

Ari adds, "Drugs, maybe?"

Max says, "Could have been. I saw the insurance report. Neighborhood that kid said it happened in is a known drug deal area."

"The spring kept that thing from flying out across the garage." I swallow hard. "Otherwise one of us would be dead."

"Or worse, filing for workman's comp." Max shakes his head. "I'll call Hartman. Let this thing rest a bit in case something else is going to blow. And for pete's sake, Lee, look at all that coffee you dropped! The stuff isn't free."

"Put it on Hartman's tab." I close my eyes. *And thank you, Bucky. You're the reason I was making coffee instead of standing under the car, right?*

I'll take the credit, he says, thrusting with his sword.

What did that kid do to cause this? I know you know. Angels talk.

Angels talk, Bucky says, *but we don't engage in character defamation or gossip. Just do your job and let Hartman do his.*

And thus with no further answers, I sweep up spilled coffee grounds and set up the new stuff. It's just after I've pushed the brew button that the sky falls. Out in the waiting area a woman starts shouting.

Max sticks his head into the garage. "Lee, get over here." He adds dryly, "With all the excitement, I forgot to tell you."

Startled, Bucky lowers his sword. I follow to the desk.

"You killed my battery." The woman slams her leather purse on the countertop so hard the row of keys takes momentary flight. "It's died three times, and it's your fault!"

I know I'm exhausted, but I can't place her at all. I turn to Max. "I don't remember an electrical job."

"Brake job," Max says.

Since when do those systems even interact? It'd be hard to mistake brake pads for battery leads.

"It was dead when I picked it up," the woman say. "You jumped it. I ran it fifteen minutes like you said," she snaps the last two words, "and as soon as I turned it off, the battery died again. I had to jump it again in the evening, and then jump it this morning to bring it back to you so you can fix what you destroyed!"

My brain is flailing with exhaustion. "I'm sure I didn't touch the electrical system." I pull up the file while Max watches over my shoulder. "I looked over the brakes Monday, ordered the part Monday afternoon, got the part Tuesday and had it installed Tuesday by close of business. You picked up the car yesterday."

"And it was dead," she repeats.

She's got a five-year-old Honda Accord with fifty thousand miles, a sweetheart that was working great until the brakes started squealing. Just maintenance stuff. I didn't mess with the electronics, but I did have to move the car around a bit because I discovered one of the rear calipers was jammed.

Hondas and Acuras have this quirk with the brakes. If the front brakes are squealing, or if you're replacing the front rotors, you cannot let that car out of the shop without inspecting the rear brakes.

It's something not even all Honda/Acura dealerships realize, but Max realized it long since (when he figured out it was an opportunity to make more money off one repair.) In some Hondas, the rear brakes and the front brakes get out of sync, leaving the front brakes to take the full weight of the vehicle whenever the car stops. A mechanic will glance at the rear brakes and verify that they're fine, and naturally they're fine—I'd be fine too if I lounged with a glass of frozen lemonade in my hand and ABBA on the stereo. The front brakes, meanwhile, work themselves into powder, eventually wearing down the rotors and the calipers, and finally the axle. Sometimes the CV boots will rupture. It's not a pretty repair.

My notes indicate that when I looked at the front brakes and saw the damage, I then spent an hour adjusting the back brakes so they were, you know, braking the car. Coordinating both sets of brakes to work in unison was harder than getting Fleetwood Mac to perform together.

But it's worth it. I like being the hero who saved two axles over the lifetime of the car.

When the owner came for pickup, I found the battery dead. So I jumped the battery and kept the engine running while I ran the customer's card and explained the repairs. It should have held the charge. Not holding the charge after three jumps equals a dead battery.

I don't need her to impart to me knowledge of which I'm already in possession, but she gives the litany: the car is only five years old; it's only got fifty thousand miles; the car worked fine the day before she brought it in; it's unlikely that the squealing of the brakes scared her precious electrons into fleeing for their lives; nor did the front-end shudder dislodge the protons from the wires; therefore, there's only one likely cause: my stupidity.

Max confirms or denies nothing. The woman thrusts me a status report from the Triple-A guy. It's full of numbers and blank circles—but you know, how much of a graph do you need to indicate "Dead"?

Max follows me outside to the vehicle, which predictably died again. I'd have to jump it in order to get it inside, but it's a nice day. I'll just do it out here.

"I didn't touch the electrical system."

Max grunts. "You certainly didn't bill for it."

I pop the hood and check the leads. After three jumps, if one of the wires was loose, you'd think they'd have noticed, but it's worth a check.

I carry the battery inside to test it on the charger. I've seen carpet tacks with more life in them.

I'm living every mechanic's nightmare. It's the "Oh, crud" moment when something goes wrong that's entirely unrelated to anything you touched: you changed the oil, and the rear tire goes flat. You replaced a headlamp, and the transmission goes wonky.

As a professional, I want to tell the owner it's a horrible coincidence. I could insist until the day I die that her battery was probably on its last bit of juice, that five years is all you can expect from a battery. I could have the Angel of Automotive Death* floating at my side to say he reaped the electrons with his sharp sickle, and she still wouldn't believe me. The problem happened while the car was under my care. Therefore, it is my fault.

She might even pay for a new battery without protest. But she'd know. She'd never trust me again.

When Beth still owned the Sheltie, she brought him to have a tooth extracted. By that evening, the Sheltie was huddled in the back of the closet, panting like crazy and ears hot to the touch. I stole my mom's car to bring them back to the vet, and Beth insisted they'd caused an infection; the vet insisted he hadn't. His protests sounded lame as I stood behind her, arms folded, while Beth argued right in the vet's face. He kept the dog for three nights on intravenous antibiotics, not charging her, but all the while he swore it was just an opportunistic infection, nothing he'd done. I never believed him.

---

* *The Angel of Automotive Death drives a menthol-green 1972 Dodge Dart, the only car with an engine he cannot kill. He says it keeps him humble.*

Fortunately, a battery is not a living thing. You can recharge a battery much easier than you can recharge a Sheltie*. The replacement will take ten minutes.

The question is...

"Who pays?"

Max stands at my side, arms folded, looking as forbidding as I must have when defending the honor of Beth's Sheltie. He stays, frowning as I get a new battery out of the parts closet. It fits right into the car. When I turn the key, the engine flares into life with a reassuring thrum.

"You're a good baby." I pat the dash. "You didn't mean to give us all that trouble."

Max remains in the garage door, watching with a completely flat expression.

My phone vibrates. I don't bother checking to see who's calling on the grounds that I'd like to keep my job.

Bucky? Was this my fault?

I don't see anything deceptive about the way—

You know what I mean! Asking an angel if you made a mistake sometimes yields an ontological discussion about the state of your soul. *If I killed her battery doing the repair, then I need to pony up the cash.*

No answer. Terrific. I can't postpone doom any longer, so I shut the engine and head back to Max.

"Comp it."

It's all he says. He disappears into his office.

I trudge back to the desk. "I've replaced the battery," I tell the woman, handing over the key. "You're free to go."

She doesn't thank me. We may well have lost this customer anyhow, something Max despises. It could have been a scam. She could have been waiting for a repair and

---

* *Golden Retrievers are a different deal entirely. A distracted glance in a Golden's general direction recharges it for five weeks.*

then swapped out her brother-in-law's old beat-up battery for her own and claimed we killed it. Most likely her battery had been dying for months, only she never noticed the gradual increase in time it took to start the ignition. I'll never know.

My phone vibrates again. Boy, I'm popular. And boy, am I antisocial too, as once again I allow my voicemail to feel the thrill of a job well-done, something I won't feel again for a while.

I close out her file and, disliking a long wait before a beheading, head into Max's office.

He won't even look at me. He keeps typing. I take a seat.

"Do I pay you to sit around?" But Max also isn't much for the preamble, so he glares up. "That was entirely your fault."

I stiffen in the chair. "I didn't touch her electrical system!"

"Of course you didn't! You fixed the brakes and did a darn good job, and she's never going to remember that because her battery decided to die while the car was parked in the shop."

But— "So how is that my fault?"

"As soon as you realized her battery was dead, you needed to throw it on the charger and leave it there for five hours." Max's voice is brittle as ice. I wish he were shouting because it would match the fire in his eyes. "Think like a customer for once. What would the customer rather hear? *Oh, I messed up your car?* Or, *Whoops, on final check we found one more thing, so the car isn't ready?* Either way, she's got to make another trip. Either way, she's going to be pissed off. So better to have her angry because we're doing our job than angry because we didn't."

My heart pounds. "But—"

"Don't go all goody-goody on me." Max focuses back at the computer screen. The conversation is effectively over, except he adds, "It would have lasted five more days, maybe a month since it's summer. She'd never have been able to make the connection stick. Except now she's going to tell everyone we messed her up. We lose seventy bucks for a battery, we lose the next repair for her, and we lose her friends. You can get back to work now."

I'm shaking as I take the next ticket. There's an oil change sitting on the counter, so I grab that. No one's in the waiting room. No one to see me swipe the tears from my eyes.

Figuring it can't get any worse, I pull out my phone and check the caller ID. One is a call from Beth, right at her break time. The fact that she called then means she's checking to see if I've had an update on Mrs. Goretti, not because she's got one for me. The other one is my mother, and right now, I don't know if I can face her.

On the other hand, didn't I just say I preferred a rapid beheading? Oh, choices, choices...

Sometimes you've got to figure the day simply can't tank any worse. I mean, we start at midnight with my landlady fielding a cold-call from Death and then Francisco tracking me to my home phone and me in Max's doghouse. Short of a nuclear conflagration, how much worse could today get?

Let's find out!

Mom's voicemail doesn't give any information except it's not an emergency and I can call her back "whenever." So far, so good. It's when she calls me with "You have a date tonight with the temporary chef at the nursing home" that I start thinking about call blocking and a legal name change.

Given that Max wants my head on a plate, and I'd usually break for coffee some time in the morning anyhow,

I give my mom a call at the nursing home where she's an administrator. She picks up before the second ring, professional and confident. She'd administrate my life just as efficiently as the nursing schedule if I gave her a chance.

She gets right to the point. "Avery and Jenny are trying out for the high school performance of *A Streetcar Named Desire.*"

I gasp. "I was in that in high school!"

How cool is that? My mom not only remembered what play I did in high school, but she thinks I can give Avery tips about the roles! I wonder if she and I will have the same one?

"Yes, and for heaven's sake," my mother snaps, "don't go talking to her about it."

I blink. "Why?"

"Isn't it obvious?"

I don't usually ask obvious questions, like "Is gravity still working?" or "Do you still hate the way I turned out?" so no, it really wasn't obvious to me, and it still isn't. But maybe my mother always thought my acting stank on toast. She always came to my performances, even when my role was too small to be listed in the program.

But yeah, if I tell Avery about a really cool thing the director did for our performance, I guess she'll join a biker gang, take up fire-eating, and never get married. I guess that's what's supposed to be obvious.

I can act really well, believe it or not. For a while, I could play-act just about any occupation in New York other than 'auto mechanic,' as Hal will tell you. (Come to think of it, that's a good reason to marry him: I don't want to have to tell another boyfriend what I do for a living. Bucky would have to give me honesty lessons all over again.)

Being on stage was fun, and I loved it, but the thing I loved even more than that was working the lights or the sound equipment.

Mom says, "She's got to be herself. You'll let her alone?"

Automotive repair is contagious, and in a perfect world Avery's "herself" would perforce involve pink nail polish. "Yeah, yeah. Whatever." I yawn.

"Are you okay?"

I give myself a mental shake. "Mrs. Goretti went into the hospital with a heart attack last night, and I stayed until her granddaughter arrived."

Just like that, Mom-mode changes into Medical-mode. HIPAA violation or not, I answer what of her questions I can.

"Well, it sounds good for now," my mother says. "It would be a disaster if she died."

My heart sinks. "I'd miss her."

"And if she dies, they'll sell the house! You and Beth will need to find a new place, and you'll have to move away from Hal! Plus, the new lease will probably be for a year, and Hal might not wait that long."

Eval Knievel didn't make leaps like the mental leap Mom just made. "Are you suggesting I urge Mrs. Goretti not to die so I can get married on a better schedule?"

Mom goes on as if that would be the most natural thing in the world. "No, no, of course not. But Beth can't swing the rent there alone, right? Maybe Hal could move in with you. That would work. But with a new landlord, there would be all sorts of issues."

She's insane.

Then my mother has a brilliant idea. "Maybe you can live with me for a few months."

I would sooner go live in my Mustang and have Hal bring me a sandwich every night. Maybe my mother hears me thinking it, because she's already on her next mental leap. "Is there a chance Hal could buy the brownstone?"

No one has that much money. Mrs. Goretti bought this brownstone for fifteen thousand dollars back when Park Slope was a working class neighborhood and immigrants all lived a few blocks from their families. Back then you could walk into the Italian deli and pick up a loaf of fresh bread for tonight's manicotti* and chat in Napolitano with the clerk about his mother-in-law's fight with your neighbor's sister. It's the same fantasy world where I'm going to turn into a princess bride.

There's only one useful response: I tell her my break is over, and I sit shaking.

Still, that wasn't as bad as dealing with Max, so I sort through the rest of my voicemail while Bucky polishes his sword for the eighth time. Results: Francisco still thinks he's the hottest thing in two shoes, and Hal wants to know if I'm okay. Guess which one I call back?

"Baxter."

"I need an accountant," I say in a dusky voice.

He laughs. "What a coincidence. I need a mechanic. What's up?"

"Returning your call." I start the engine on the oil change vehicle and shift it into gear with the cell phone jammed between my shoulder and my ear. I'd never drive this way on the streets because Bucky would sheathe that sword in my head, but I'm only pulling into the garage. "How are you?"

"Tired. I'm working from home."

I'd love to work from home, but you can't get a sedan up three flights of steps.

---

* *Mrs. Goretti says "mon-ee-goth." It's just her dialect of Italian, the same way she says "muut-za-dell" instead of mozzarella.*

He says, "Any word on Mrs. Goretti?"

"None yet. I was going to drop by on my lunch break." For purposes of not sullying my mother's reputation, I refrain from saying my mother wanted to schedule her death so we could book a convenient wedding.

"I could join you." There's a pause. "I'll bring lunch."

Hooboy, this ought to be good. "You have gourmet peanut butter?"

"I only make Fluffernutters on seven-grain whole wheat bread, yeah." He sounds distracted, and I think I hear typing. "Give me a call and I'll meet you in the cardiac ICU."

"Sounds good." I swallow. "Thanks so much for coming with me last night."

"Not a big deal. I love you."

I don't know if he meant that to sound like cause-effect, but it certainly did: that it *would* have been a big deal if any other of his friends had asked. "I love you too." My voice rasps. "Bye."

I've got the car in the garage, so I text Beth that I haven't had any updates. At which point, I'm free to change some oil.

At the end of the job, Max's wife Allison comes into the garage. "Lee, you got a minute?"

I look up, startled. "Max sent *you* to fire me?"

"You're not being fired." She comes up alongside the car. "I'm more in the smooth-things-over committee anyhow. You had no reason to think the battery wouldn't hold a charge. Max is looking at the write-off, but I don't want you to leave us for another garage."

"I'm chasing away your customers."

"Not as many as you bring in, or I *would* be firing your sorry behind." She folds her arms and chuckles. "Ari heard Max go off the rails, so he called me at home. You look awful, by the way."

"Lack of sleep."

"Get a nap on your lunch break." She glances at the clock. "There's a customer waiting for a state inspection. Since this one's a drop, leave it here and take the other."

"We're done." I've been checking fluids all the while she's been talking to me, so I slam the hood. "If you'll ticket this one out, I'll grab the keys on the inspection."

She agrees, then says, "No hard feelings."

That's the thing about working in a garage: I'm surrounded by so much testosterone that I needed to learn a different language. And I'm not talking about all the technical terms; those were fun. It's the way guys apologize without ever apologizing. Carlos or Ari would never come up to me and say, "Boy, was he unfair! You okay?" (Tim wouldn't because it would require human speech.) So instead they call Allison and say, "Max flew off the handle at Lee—will you get him under control already?"

Allison may or may not tell Max that he's been a bonehead. Max may feel bad that he went ballistic, but I'd drop dead on the garage floor if Max were to say, "Hey, Lee? I was a total jerk to you before. I'm sorry."

No, he'd just find some stealth method of making it up to me. It'll be him offering to buy lunch or him finding an extra screwdriver or offering to take my Saturday shift. And from that, I'm to understand he's making things right. It's like dealing with another species.

Now Bucky really is another species, but you know what? The dude knows how to apologize.* I mean, he also tries to make things right on the rare occasions he messes up, but when he's wrong he says it and then asks me to forgive him. Maybe that's because he knows I can't exactly fire him.

---

* *For example, "I'm really sorry I called you 'Dude.' I should have said Angel Dude."*

I wonder if marriage gives that kind of security. Maybe it used to, but nowadays people start out their marriages by saying "And if it doesn't work out..." and of course everyone knows marriages where eventually there was a blow-up to end them all. If it's a church wedding then you make vows before God, but unless you know for sure what you're vowing, and you know the other person knows it, then how is that any security? What if you can't do the thing you promised?

There are no married couples I can ask. Maybe Randy, but not really. He's married, so of course he'd say it's worth the risk of regrets or worth risking failure.

And I really can't ask Bucky. He bound himself to me by oath, and more incomprehensibly, he begged God for it. I never asked him what it was like to wait all that time on a promise God made one bright day in a prairie and trusting that whatever person God set aside for him, it would be the best person possible.

But I can't ask if he regrets oathing himself to someone when we'd both know the person he regretted being bound to was me. So how else is he going to answer?

When I'm done with the state inspection (it's a brand-new Sienna, so I expect no problems and find none) it's time for lunch. I affix the new stickers, sign off, charge the customer, and return the key.

My text to Hal: "I'm on my way."

His reply: "I'll be there."

It's not the world's deepest conversation, but it's the same as a quick squeeze of his hand when I'm nervous. It's like he's saying "I'm here, and I'm on your side."

Even when I'm wrong, he's on my side.

The hospital stands about half a mile from Mack's, so I'm there in ten minutes. Another five gets me to Mrs. Goretti in the cardiac ICU. She's awake.

She's *awake*? Crud. Now what do I do?

"Uh, hi," I should have brought flowers and probably should have a card. I think cultured people bring those things.

Instead, since I'm empty-handed, I take her hand, and she just holds it. Cultured people are supposed to say get-well things too, so I ask how she's feeling.

Oh, I'm totally fine, Lee! That's why I'm hooked up to five machines and have all these tubes in my arms and nose.

Instead she has pity on me. Her voice is a whisper, but she says she's all right.

I grab a chair and sit by the head of her bed where it will be easier to hear her breathy words over the bustle of health being dispensed to the needy. She's got a cannula to shoot oxygen into her nose, and the head of her bed is already raised a bit, but she asks me to raise it further. I'm a mechanic, so sure — I can't bring flowers, but I can get her to a 35 degree incline, and then I readjust her white blanket around her shoulders because I also used to be a nurse. These are both useful skills.

I force a smile. "You scared me last night."

She whispers, slowly, "How did you know?"

My eyes flare, and for a moment nothing emerges.

"You needed help," I manage. "You were having a heart attack."

"I didn't call you." That's a statement, not a question.

"I used your key to get in." This, at least, is perfectly true. "The one behind your grandfather's picture, that you keep for emergencies. The paramedics came, and Beth locked up for us. She called your granddaughter."

Hal's arrival saves my bacon. He's so easy with her, so affable. He doesn't look shaken even though she's grey and without that bright concern in her eyes.

"Are they feeding you here?" Hal asks.

Of course! Food — you can always ask about food.

She whispers, "The food is terrible," and I laugh because Mrs. Goretti makes the world's best tomato sauce (she calls it gravy) and sometimes she'll invite me and Beth just because she thinks we don't eat enough.

Hal leans forward. "I'll smuggle you in a pizza."

She smiles weakly.

She's always liked Hal, although she's never truly forgiven him for feeding me omelettes for dinner the first time he visited. "So refined," she always says, and Hal knows just the right amount of deference and good humor to keep things light around her. He does it now, as if he's stopping into her kitchen before taking me to the movies.

Then our visiting minutes are over, and the nurse tells us to leave. Hal says goodbye, but Mrs. Goretti grabs my hand. "One more thing. The house."

"I'm keeping an eye on everything." I squeeze her fingers. "Your apartment is locked up. I'll bring in the mail and take out the trash, and if you're here for a few more days, I'll get into your fridge and see if anything's spoiling . Don't worry about a thing."

She gives me her left hand. "Take my ring. If I die here, no one will ever see it again."

I use some lotion to slip off her wedding band and the diamond ring nestled alongside.

I show her the safe place I put it in my wallet. "I'll leave it in your apartment."

"No." She swallows. "They'll break in and steal it. You keep it until I'm home." Then she stares at her hand, and her voice is hollow. "Tony put that on me in 1946."

"And it never came off?" I'm startled. "You should keep wearing it."

"They'll take it." Then she looks up, and I start: she's got tears in her eyes. "I miss him."

Now I've got tears in mine too. She's been a widow since 1996.

I say, "Just don't see him anytime soon."

"I saw him last night." Her eyes are really glistening now, and I hand her a tissue. "He came to me and smiled, and he didn't say anything. But he was here. He stayed."

Are those goosebumps on my arm? No, I think they're better described as goosemountains?

She musters a smile. "Don't mind me. I'm an old woman. You go with Hal. He's good for you."

With Hal's goodbye kiss still warm on my lips, I head back toward work. "Do dead people visit us?" I ask Bucky.

Bucky fingers his sword handle. It's got to be killing him that I took him out of the garage for lunch because he couldn't exactly practice his parries against the IV poles. "You're asking because Mrs. Goretti dreamed about her husband when she thought she was dying?"

Once again, Bucky seizes the Gold Medal in the Olympic category of "Perceiving the Obvious."

He shrugs. "What do you think?"

"If I knew what I thought, would I be asking you?"

"You do that all the time." He snickers. "Do you remember anything from the Bible?"

Oh, sure, pick now to quiz me on whether I remember anything from endless Sunday school classes. "Well, Saul saw Samuel after he was dead, but Saul had some witchy help."

"Yeah, I missed it if your landlady set up a magic circle." Bucky gestures in a circle. "What else?"

I stop for a Don't Walk sign, an oddity in New York but there is, as it turns out, a Ryder truck bearing down on the intersection. "No, I'm drawing a blank."

"Lazarus the beggar." I'm glad he clarified that, otherwise I'd have thought he meant Lazarus the Formerly Dead Guy Who Shouldn't Count As A Ghost. "When the rich man asked if Lazarus could go speak to his brothers, Abraham said no because the brothers wouldn't believe Lazarus, not because it wasn't possible."

Oh, now I remember that one. "Doesn't he say there's a big hole like the Grand Canyon?"

"Between Heaven and Hell." How do you GPS different eternal dimensions? "It's not between Heaven and Earth."

"Makes no sense." Someone stares at me because I'm talking to myself, so I start walking again. "There's an abyss between Heaven and Hell, so Lazarus can't go *there*. But clearly there isn't one between Heaven and Earth, because angels cross it." Bucky nods. "And there isn't one between Hell and Earth because you get demons like the Shadow." I raise my eyebrows. "Someone needs to figure out how to use a bus transfer. You go from Heaven to Earth and then Earth to Hell."

Bucky touches my hair. "You ask too many questions."

"You're the one who asks too many questions! I just wanted to know if Mr. Goretti really came to see his wife and you started quizzing me about ghosts in the Bible."

Bucky gets right in front of me, eyes gleaming. I stop in my tracks. "Why would it matter if he had?"

Because I'm curious. Because it's astonishing that someone running loose in Heaven for two decades would still care about someone left behind on Earth. Because my own father died twenty-plus years ago, and it would be neat to think he lectures God that He'd better be looking out for me.

But I don't know if I'd want him to show up. For one thing, I haven't put away my laundry. And he'd die if he saw those stupid days-of-the-week underwear on the kitchen table

"Have you ever met my father?" I ask Bucky. "Since he died?"

"Your father is still your father." Bucky touches my cheek. "Location and distance didn't change that. He promised to take care of you forever, and forever means *forever.*"

"What is this, tautology theater?" We're back at Mack's, and I'm probably going to get my head handed to me again. Maybe I should run. I never promised Max my fealty.

And then I realize: I just got my answer. Mrs. Goretti misses her husband. Half a century ago she oathed herself to a man, and she's still glad she did it.

Chapter Fifteen

I know someone who knows someone who once conquered Europe

Beth and I actually see one another the next morning so we exchange updates on our landlady. By the time Beth visited her, Mrs. Goretti had been moved to a semi-private room. Naturally Beth thought to bring her flowers.

"I signed your name to the card." Beth sounds amused. "I knew you'd never have thought of it on your own."

"Gee, thanks." We're drinking "live" coffee today, stuff that's just been brewed. Beth is wearing a sweatshirt the kids must love because it's got rainbows all over it. Based on the crafts we did two weeks ago, the three year olds are studying light diffraction, only they think they're being colorful. "She gave me her wedding ring."

"She said. You know why she thought for sure the nurses would steal her rings, right?" Beth opens her hands. "Because they're not white."

Beth is Filipino. Mrs. Goretti seems to have forgotten that and will frequently tell Beth things that are rather, er, old-world in their origin. If I call her on those comments, Mrs. Goretti will scoff: Beth isn't one of *those*. She's Beth. I should be ashamed of even implying such a thing.

"I hope that's not it."

"Her cardiologist is Indian. The hospitalist is Pakistani, and I can't begin to guess at the nationality of the pulmonologist who visited just before I left, except that she has to be from somewhere in Africa."

I pour more coffee. "It's the American dream: anyone from any country can come here, and based only on his or her merits, find a way to overcharge for services."

Beth laughs out loud. Only Heaven is going to be more diverse than New York, and that's because it's drawing from all of time as well. What the Holy Spirit did at Pentecost is completely understandable in natural terms when you walk through any subway car. It's amazing and wonderful, and to be honest, I don't understand how anyone can live in New York for longer than a month and remain prejudiced.

Beth finishes up her cereal. "When Mrs. Goretti came over from Italy, didn't everyone hate Italians?"

"Spread the joy. After two generations, no one even notices."

"And speaking of two generations," Beth says, "who's this guy Francisco who called five times yesterday?"

I cringe. "Have I mentioned I picked up a stalker?"

Beth listens sagely to the whole sordid story, then says, "Okay, now I have a confession to make, and I hope you don't mind. But I think you're the world's biggest idiot."

I reach for a pad and a pen. "I'll add your name to the list."

"I hope I'm not keeping company with Hal's name there. I took the liberty of blocking your paramour's calls." Beth glares at me. "And the flowers I brought Mrs. Goretti? They were kind of a regift. He left them on the front door."

My eyes bug.

"Look, I like Hal a lot." Her voice picks up ice. Actually, her voice may just be an ice pick. "You lost him once by being stupid, and now you're going to do it again. Flirting with some other guy is beyond moronic, especially someone as self-absorbed as this one. Tell Frankie-dude to take a hike. Until you do, Mrs. Goretti is going to have a steady supply of flowers, and you can't guarantee I'll always intercept them."

I swallow. "What do I do?"

"Tell him firmly, finally, no. Then block his calls, block his texts, block his emails and IMs and any other way he contacts you."

Yes, she's a preschool teacher. Yes, she sounds like one now. I think I'd prefer the ice pick. "And how do I block the front steps?"

"Get out a restraining order if you have to. Mace him. Mafia hit. I don't care what you do." Beth stands, taking her cereal bowl to the sink. "Get rid of this guy."

And now that she's done, she gets ready to leave for the day. I muster up, "Pizza and movies tonight?" and she agrees as if she hasn't just torn off my head.

This is a lovely start. I head downstairs, terrified I'll find Francisco with a confetti parade. Nothing — which only makes me nervous. What worse thing is going to happen today?

Bucky appears beside me. "Look," he says, opening his hands. "A uniform!"

Bracing myself, I turn.

Remember I said all guys look good in uniforms? All of them? I want to add "all angels" to that category. I actually squeak as I stop on the steps to gawk.

He deflates, crestfallen. "You don't like it?"

Let's start from the bottom: he's wearing black boots that are polished to a shine. The boots are over silver-grey pants, and he's wearing a similar silver-blue shirt beneath a breastplate of silver and black. On his hands he's wearing gauntlets, also black and highly-polished, and so help me, Bucky has a cape. It's long and gorgeous and a midnight blue so deep it sucks the light out of the sky. I'm so struck by the cape that I don't notice at first he's wearing a scabbard with his sword.

"You're amazing," I whisper. "Where'd you come up with that?"

Bucky pulls himself together, still hesitant. "I know someone who knows someone who once conquered Europe. You really like it?" I nod, and Bucky shines brighter. "I wasn't sure about the silver and blue, but he told me it worked."

Whoever it was, the guy outdid himself.

I muster up, "You got the cape, too."

"You wanted me to try." Bucky turns so I can see how the cape nestles between his wings, which he's keeping a little more raised than usual.

I smile at him. "You're gorgeous."

"Don't I know it?" He steps closer. "Let's get going. I don't want to make you late for work, and I know you're already nervous."

Today turns out to be much easier than Thursday, thank goodness. Max avoids me, which makes me want to jump-scare him whenever he steps out of his cave, but when he's away from me Max banters with Carlos, and Ari is singing along with the radio while he replaces a muffler. It sounds almost as good as the video Mrs. Smith emailed me about last night, the song "My Heart Will Go On" sung by none other than The Transformers' Starscream.

Francisco phones twice, but voicemail gets it both times. I should give it to Max. Max would put the fear of Max into him, and that would be the end of the matter. But it might also be the end of me, and I enjoy my regular paychecks.

My mother, thank goodness, doesn't call. God must know I've had enough. Instead I text Hal that Bucky has a sword now, so he'd better behave himself when he comes over for pizza.

At lunch, I visit Mrs. Goretti. "Thank you, dear, for the flowers. You're such a sweetheart."

Just for the record, Francisco got me nice ones. I think they're tulips? "Oh, it was nothing."

Mrs. Goretti is looking more like a human and less like a chameleon trying to camouflage itself with the cotton sheets. She turns off the TV as I take a seat. "It's not my program," she tells me. That's a relief. I forget which program is hers, but she does follow one, and I suspect she wouldn't have bothered talking if I'd come when it was on because otherwise she'd never know if Judy was Elisha's half-sister or actually her mother. I wonder if Mrs. Smith has a program? If so, she's watching to find out if J'di is Ellyzha's clone or actually a replica from an alternate universe.

How is life? "The food here is awful," she tells me. "The nurses are terrible. My doctor doesn't speak English, but he put me on ten new medications!" And that's all awesome. She's herself again. I can assure my mother that changing my lease won't be an issue if Hal and I decide to pair-bond.

"Look." She slides open a drawer in the bedside table and hands me a folded white plastic bag the size of a paperback novel. I take the thing, confused. "Open it," she says.

I start unfolding it, and the thing keeps going, unfolding and unfolding again, and then some more—and when it's four feet long by four feet wide and I can still unfold it again, I stop, horrified.

"I asked the nurse if it was a body bag." Mrs. Goretti gives a mischievous smile. "She told me no, everyone has one of those. What for? For putting a sandwich to take home?" The thing has unfolded to eight feet, and I catch myself in a nervous giggle. "How dumb do they think I am? They thought I was going to die."

I say, "Well, I'm glad you're not. I still have to give back your wedding rings."

"Hold onto them a little longer," she says. "I'm going to see if I can get the doctor to kick me out of here tonight."

By the time I get back to the garage, Francisco has attempted to phone me again. I keep forgetting to block his calls. I'll do it now.

That's when Max barks, "Lee! Get over here!"

Maybe I'll do it later.

Friday is as good a day to be fired as any. It'd actually make it easier, like a long weekend, so without even taking off my jacket, I go to where Max is standing over an old car.

When I say "old," by the way, I'm talking about a car of my vintage. This vehicle drove the Interboro before it was the Jackie Robinson Parkway. It witnessed the inauguration of Ronald Reagan. This vehicle might have seen the first inauguration of Mayor Koch!

Max says to me, "Did you ever re-arc the brake shoes on a set of drum brakes?"

I shake my head.

"Well, you may need to someday. Come here and I'll show you."

And with me taking note of everything I can, Max walks me through the fixing of a part he probably worked on for the first time in high school shop class.

And that, you see, is how Max says he's sorry. But really, if it involves grease and a bit of trivia I never knew about before, I'm okay with it.

Pizza night! Beth looks exhausted, so of course Hal says she can choose the toppings, and Beth says anything goes. It's a fight in reverse. I cannot win.

So once again, I order for everyone. Beth pulls out a movie she borrowed from the library and gives us the low-down on Mrs. Goretti. This afternoon she got there in time to hear Mrs. Goretti's daughter bellowing at a doctor about some kind of surgery, with Mrs. Goretti torn between her urge to "not be a burden" on her children and her fear that the surgery they suggested could result in a stroke or life on a respirator. The doctors, naturally, were ~~bullying~~ encouraging her to have the surgery. The daughter was adamant that since her mother wanted nothing at all to do with a stroke, the surgery option was off the table permanently.

Beth said, "Apparently the doctors jumped Mrs. Goretti at five o'clock in the morning to obtain her signature on the paperwork to go ahead with the surgery."

I flinched. "That's ugly!"

"No kidding." Beth deflates. "From now on, our landlady has a twenty-four hour guard consisting of family members, and I'm betting they're armed. No question at all about the dangerous."

"Geez." I trace my finger on the tabletop. "My dad died in a house fire. Literally overnight. I think that's the way to go."

Hal puts a hand on mine. "We don't get to pick. I'd rather have time to say goodbye."

Can you imagine? *Um...so...goodbye...forever.* Yeah, someone push me in front of a train.

"You can pick what you *don't* want," Beth says, "and I think having a doctor-induced stroke due to surgery you don't want is one of those things. So before I left, I made her promise me she wouldn't sign anything without her daughter in the room. And then I made her promise she would keep her promise to me." She grins. "I told her she had to, since you and I promised to keep the steps swept in the fall and shoveled in the wintertime, and how we test the smoke detectors in the hallway every month."

Ah-heh. Yeah. That brings to mind a beloved conversation with Bucky: *"It's the third of the month, Lee. Do you know what that means? It means that tomorrow, you'll be four days late on testing the smoke detectors."* I say 'beloved' because we've had it a lot.

When Beth and I checked out this apartment years ago, Mrs. Goretti disliked us instantly. In. Stant. Ly. She was down in her apartment telling the realtor no, no, and Hell no while Beth and I in the foyer had a newspaper across our laps discussing where to go next. We needed a place we could afford, and once you ruled out "rat-infested" and "shared toilet facilities in hallway," there wasn't really a whole heck of a lot of choice. So Beth went back into Mrs. Goretti's apartment to ask what was the problem.

It turned out there was no problem. I suspect I know what was said, but by the time I came into the kitchen, Beth was showing Mrs. Goretti pictures of her then-boyfriend, and Mrs. Goretti was asking if we wanted to have coffee.

Beth can sweet-talk meat out of the mouth of a starving lion, you see. Or a lease from an old-world landlady. Next I delivered the coup de grace by changing three light-bulbs and tightening the hinges on a cabinet door before she had the coffee on the table, and we signed the lease before the realtor was out the door. Good thing doctors are lousy with screwdrivers.

Beth's eyes narrow. "Anyhow, I told her that since we'd been so good to her, she had to keep her promise to us. She has no choice. Now she can hide behind me when they badger her — assuming they even get past her kith and kin."

I mutter, "Her quite-possibly-armed kith and kin."

Hal sounds chipper. "Lovely world where we have to protect ourselves from the people we're paying to help us."

"She wants to go home." Beth shakes her head. "I don't blame her."

And yet Bucky clearly wanted me to set all this in motion. Very strange.

If I ever have a heart attack, I think to Bucky, *I want you to go track down Lindsey Buckingham's guardian angel and ask him for a guitar lesson. Take like four hours to get back.*

Of course, Bucky replies. *Because the guardian of someone in her final hours has nothing better to do than spend time practicing that cool guitar riff.*

Maybe if you can arrange for me to be hit by a comet, that's the way to go.

Duly noted, Bucky says in a tone of voice that means, "I'm going to obliterate this conversation from my memory in case someday I might accidentally think you were serious."

And because we live in a world rife with philosophical and ontological questions, that's when the doorbell rings to announce our pizza. I grab my wallet, and forty creaky steps later there's the guy from Pino's on the other side of the glass doors. He likes me: I tip really well, so he's put my name up beside the telephone at Pino's to ensure the manager knows that not only do we get a toasty-hot pizza fifteen minutes after ordering, but also that no one else is allowed to deliver to us. Ever.

Always, always be kind to your pizza guy.

I hand over the money, and he makes small talk as he hands over the pie. Then he says, "You want to catch a movie sometime?"

What? When did I ever give him the idea I'd tip him *that* way?

He slips me a piece of paper. "My treat. You're cute, and I want to stop meeting just this way." He grins boyishly. "We'd look good together."

I giggle nervously. He's cute, with short black hair and dark eyes, and based on a White Page's worth of experience, I can tell we'd have fun together. "Do you avoid the women that might make you look bad?"

He smiles again with a friendly unconcern so different from the gloom I left behind upstairs. "I'm going to pale in comparison beside you."

Because I look like a runway star? "Would ripped jeans and a stained t-shirt help?"

"You'd still be the most gorgeous woman in the place."

I tilt my head and wink. "This wouldn't matter in a dark theater."

He steps a little closer. "I'd know."

Okay, enough's enough. "I have a boyfriend."

He replies, "I don't mind."

And while I'm unable to run because I'm holding a pizza box, he kisses me.

It's the strangest moment, that instant I'm standing there not knowing what to do. Instead of screaming or shoving the pizza back in his face, I stammer goodbye and lock myself inside. I've still got his phone number in my hand. I should have handed it back. I should have told him hell no.

This is crazy. Where are all these guys coming from? Why don't any of them care that I'm already attached?

I mean, I'm not really *attached*-attached. It wouldn't be adultery if I did go off and have coffee with the pizza guy. It'd just be fun. Nothing more. Fun. Fun in the way talking about death is not fun.

My mouth is still tingling. The guy had a nice cologne, too. He must have been ready for me to order. Because we're so predictable nowadays that he knew Hal would have me calling every Friday night. But *he's* spunky and spontaneous.

That's when the stairwell goes dark.

I stop on the steps, rooted in place. Did the power just go out? That stinks.

I wait a moment, but the lights don't come back. Nor does Beth appear at the top of the stairwell with a flashlight.

I edge toward the wall, except it isn't where I expect it, and when I shift my weight, there's no groan from the steps. There's no sound whatsoever.

My heart hammers. *Bucky?* No answer. *Bucky—help me! God?* Fortunately I'm used to God not replying, so I've got some balance back when He doesn't. *God, what's going on? Where am I?*

I can't feel the heat of the pizza box in my hands. Blackness and silence dominate the world, and I'm in trouble. I'm an idiot. I've invited the Shadow back.

Worse, maybe I'm completely encased in the Shadow right now. Trapped inside her.

I can't breathe. What if I can't get out again? What if not even my prayers can get out? She's all around me and she's here because I invited her, flirted with the pizza guy and because of that was flirting with her; I listened to what she had to say and now I can't hear anything at all.

God, I'm scared. I close my eyes because it's the same scene with them open or shut. *God, what do I do? Help me. Help Bucky. Don't let her tie him up again. This is my fault, not his. I'm sorry. I didn't want to hurt him.*

Will God throw you a rope when you've done something stupid to yourself? But He should at least throw one to Bucky.

She slithers around me in the darkness the way an eel glides in cold water around its prey, always itself in silence, but both predator and prey knowing the location of the other and awaiting the moment of the strike.

My eyes sting. I want Bucky. I want my mother. I want Hal.

"Hey, Lee?"

A voice shatters the paralysis. I look up, and the world has light. The pizza box is hot in my hand, and I know where the rest of my body is. "Hal?"

My voice came out really shrill. "You okay?" He peers over the third-floor landing. "You look rattled."

I want to say no. I want to tell him a demon came after me, but there's no way he'd understand, so I say, "No, I— I'm coming up." And I force myself to take a step even though I'm dizzy. A familiar creak sounds under my weight. Another step. I get to the landing, and Hal takes the box.

When I reach the apartment, Beth is setting up the movie in the living room. I don't remember what we're watching, and I don't care. Hal carries the pizza to eat in front of the TV, and I vanish into the bathroom. I scare myself again by looking in the mirror.

Yeah, if Hal didn't recognize stark terror, I have only Mrs. Goretti's fifteen-watt bulbs to thank. God, help me. I've never been so scared in my life.

I still have the pizza guy's paper crushed in my hand. It's nothing extraordinary, only "David, 768-3440." I flush it.

Some color's coming back, but I still look like death warmed over (or death put through the microwave for thirty seconds on power five.) It'll have to do.

Then, my heart hammering, I say, *Bucky? Are you okay?*

Now I am.

Terrific. Every time I act like an idiot, he takes a bullet. *I'm sorry.*

You need to quit being sorry and shape up.

This is two people in one day who've ripped my head off over me being stupid. You really would think I'd learn from this, except for the fact that I'm stupid.

I can't do this on my own. I'm never going to be able to stick with the honesty and the fidelity thing. There's no way I could marry Hal. I need to tell him what's been going on.

Bucky puts a question mark in my head.

I'm going to tell Hal.

The question mark turns into an exclamation point, and then I can see Bucky standing beside me looking outraged. "You absolutely are not going to tell Hal!"

"But he deserves to know!"

"Why? Because it'll make you feel better to tell him? Don't even try to glorify it that way. You want someone to let you off the hook."

Bucky moves closer, and his voice drops. "Here's the deal: if you dump him, just dump him. Don't tell him you've met someone more exciting, someone cuter, someone who is something he isn't and never will be. Just give him the dignity of a clean break-up and no reason to believe you've been messing around behind his back."

"But—" I squint. "Aren't you always all over me about being honest?"

"Of course I want you to be honest, but that doesn't mean you need to tell him every single thing that occurs to you. In fact, especially if it's going to hurt him, then I have to ask what your motive is in telling him."

And again, the only thing that comes into my head is that Hal deserves to know.

"You'd only be telling him because you want to relieve the stress you're feeling. You flirt with other guys because at that moment, you're only thinking about yourself. You tell Hal and you're still thinking only about yourself."

My mouth twitches. "What about forgiveness?"

"Do him the biggest favor you can," Bucky snaps, "and don't give him a reason to forgive you. Let Hal believe you got rid of him on account of who you are, not because of some other guy."

I look back into the mirror. I'm quiet for a long time.

They're going to wonder if I'm sick. Well, I am sick. There's something wrong with me if I can't stick to my guns. I can be honest about that at least.

I whisper, "So I shouldn't tell him about Francisco? Or the pizza guy?"

Bucky rubs his temples. "I'm glad you listen to me sometimes."

"Should I call back the pizza guy?" I just flushed his number, but Bucky will remember it. "Tell him no? Maybe we should never get pizza again. But then I'll have to explain."

"Calm down. Next week, have Hal pick up the pizza, and that'll send a message." Bucky folds his arms. "If Hal is still around next week. Otherwise, next week order pizza, and when it's delivered, tell the guy when and where you'd like to meet."

I swallow hard, then turn off the light and leave the bathroom.

In the living room, they've gotten through the opening splash screens and have it paused. "Look," Hal says brightly. "Paramount! We'd never have guessed, except they already put that on the screen five times, five different ways."

I take a seat beside Hal with my head on his shoulder. He just gives me a sideways squeeze. Beth starts the movie, and for a moment, I can forget everything.

Chapter Sixteen

God loves me, so He wouldn't send me to France.

I awaken to the alarm and roll sideways to hit the snooze button when a sword slices between me and it. I yank backward with a gasp.

Standing alongside the bed, wearing a hat and full pirate regalia, is Bucky wielding a cutlass. "Avast, me hearties! No snooze alarm for ye this mornin'! It be a fine day and ye best be getting ta work!"

"Bucky," I stammer, "so help me, what on Earth is going on?"

"Dinna ken, lass? Today be Saturday, September 19th! Talk Like A Pirate Day!"

I collapse back onto my pillow.

"Today we'll be honoring yer piratical heritage. Ahoy there, Matey! Smartly, now! It be time to man the deck and hoist the sails!"

I raise my head. "Captain Bucky? Is that...a parrot on your shoulder?"

He nods enthusiastically.

The parrot chirps, "Halleluiah! Halleluiah!"

Today is going to be a long day. Very long.

I take a gander...I mean, a good look at Bucky's outfit while brewing coffee, or at least attempting to do so. He is wearing—and I say this trying to keep a straight face but nearly unable to—breeches, boots, a silk blouse that billows at the sleeves, and a tricorn hat. A black patch covers the eye opposite the shoulder where the parrot sits. At his side he's wearing the aforementioned cutlass, and he's frequently holding a telescope. I'm not sure how long I can go before I burst out into gales of laughter that are, take your pick:

- the point of it all, as he's trying to make me laugh
- going to hurt his feelings beyond belief because for some reason he's really into this.

I pour corn flakes into a bowl, and Bucky says something about a bung hole and weevils. A quick search of the bowl reveals no weevils, so hoping for the best, I pour in my milk and struggle not to laugh the milk out of my nose when Bucky peers out the window with his spyglass. He glances back, and I pretend to be coughing. At last I pour coffee into my poor beleaguered brain.

Having thus caffeinated myself, I now understand: this is a great idea! This will be fun! Beth teaches preschool, so she must have pirate regalia in the apartment. I too will dress as a pirate and say things like "ahoy there, Matey" and "Arr, that there transmission be needing about six hours of work. Here be yer written estimate, ye scurvy dog!" Max will love this. I am sure to get September 19th as a paid holiday every year for the rest of my life, unless he forces me to walk the plank.

Anyhow, it serves him right for making me work a Saturday shift. So there.

Sure enough, when Beth awakens, I learn she owns hoop earrings big enough to be bracelets, plus the jackpot: an eye-patch. I rummage in my drawers until I find a bandana to tie around my head. Beth's closet yields a blouse with poofy sleeves and a long satin scarf for a sash, and then it's just a matter of my tall black boots and black pants. Not even Long John Silver is this ready for Talk Like A Pirate Day, Matey.

As I walk to work (actually, Bucky swaggers) I phone Hal and growl into his voicemail that today be Talk Like A Pirate Day; mayhap he should be docking his schooner in friendlier waters this afternoon, and I'll be waiting for him in the crow's nest. Or something—it's been a long time since I read the Horatio Hornblower books, and they didn't even have pirates. I did watch *Pirates of the Caribbean*, though, and I make a mean Jack Sparrow. People stare at me, and I "Arr" at them and ask what they be lookin' at. It's a beautiful morning.

Max gets one look and orders me to change into coveralls and for the love of Pete to wash my face, so reluctantly, I do. Bucky and the parrot, however, are rocking their gear. *Halleluiah! Halleluiah!*[*] I can't even imagine what the other angels are thinking, but hey, maybe they're all doing it? It's possible there's an entire city of angels right now saying "Shiver my timbers, but ye be committing too many sins! Belay that, or God will send ye to Davey Jones' locker!"

"Strike the colors, Matey," Bucky says. "It be time for grub."

"Arr," I say, wrestling with a bolt that mistakenly believes it holds together the entire Earth, and by gum it will not allow us all to perish by a dastardly act of cowardice like, say, loosening. "Let me finish this brake job, Cap'n Bucky, or I'll be keelhaulin' you."

---

[*] *You're going to ask, "Where'd he get the parrot?" but for that matter, where'd he get the cutlass or the tricorn hat?*

Flapping its wings, the parrot squawks, "Arr! Save your soul! Save your soul!"

"Avast," Bucky murmurs, rubbing the parrot's head, and there's a gentility about his eyes, as the bird butts his chin with its head and his fingers smooth the tiny feathers.

Wishing I had a parrot, I turn back to the World's Most Stubborn Bolt. "I know you don't have to be a guy to do this job, but sometimes I'd like a guy's muscles."

To be specific, I'd like Bill's muscles. If I arm-wrestled Hal, I think I'd win.

But that's neither here nor there. If the bolt isn't coming loose now, clearly it's not going anywhere during lunch either, so I leave the car on the lift.

Allison is sitting out by the computer. "Max told me you were dressed like a pirate today. I didn't believe him."

"Arr." I clock out, then grin. "Honoring my piratical heritage."

Her eyes narrow as she enters something into the computer. "Trust me, I'm married to a pirate. You, Lee, are no pirate."

She's got something there. New Yorkers have perfected corporate corruption because getting around the laws has become its own second set of laws, and in some ways, it makes life a lot more efficient. For example, if you want to tear down a building, you need a permit to do so. In many cities, you apply for the permit, pay the fee, and then tear down the building. How quaint. Many times, this takes months, assuming you can get the permit at all.

In New York, the contractor assesses the old building for his plans and accidentally knocks out a weight-bearing wall such that the building is unsafe, and now it's only responsible to take it down, since you don't want it to fall. Since the building is already down, the contractor begins construction. The paperwork to demolish the old structure ambles its way through the system at a leisurely crawl while the new structure grows. At some point, the city government will issue a fine for demolishing a building without a permit, which the contractor cheerfully pays because they built the fine into the estimate. The certificate for demolition comes through about five days before the building receives its final certificate of occupancy. In terms of efficiency, you can't beat that with a shovel.

Maybe that's why Bucky wanted me to embrace this holiday in its fullness: it's actually a step up.

Out on the street, I look semi-normal, but I try to think like a pirate. Pirates eat fish, right? So I pick up sushi from a corner store and a bottle of cherry-lime rickey soda (limeys, right?.) I feel fully piratical as I head to the hospital.

Mrs. Goretti is looking terrific, and Beth wasn't joking about the armed guard: five people crowd the room. Someone brought decent food, so I don't feel bad eating mine. She is naturally upset that I'm eating raw fish ("They couldn't even cook it for you?") and offers me her hospital-provided "lunch." There is much laughter as one of her relations raises a plastic lid to reveal the world's smallest, flattest hamburger and a tablespoon of corn that looks as if it were run through a dehydrator three or four times. A young boy taps the roll on the plate with a satisfying "tok!".

"Any weevils?" I ask, in honor of Talk Like A Pirate Day. "If you soak the roll in the weak tea for an hour or two, you might not break your teeth."

"There's certainly enough weak tea around here," mutters someone who may be a granddaughter.

For some reason, and I can't figure out why, Mrs. Goretti prefers to eat her daughter-in-law's baked ziti. No hospital room has ever smelled this good, by the way. There's a distinct aura of basil and tomato.

"Where's Hal?" she says.

"I think he's out on the Island with his family." Possibly that's what he told me. I was still frazzled when the movie ended, and knowing I needed to work today, he pretty much just kissed me and took off for home.

"He's so refined," Mrs. Goretti says, and it makes me smile. "When I get home, have him come downstairs and I'll show him how to make fresh pasta."

Hal would pay three hundred dollars an hour to learn the kinds of things Mrs. Goretti would teach him for free. If she allowed him, he'd install a video camera in her ceiling and leave it running for eight weeks, then painstakingly transcribe every detail.

Instead of turning a cartwheel, I modulate down to, "Thanks, he'd like that." I tilt my head. "Any idea when that will be?"

"I'm going home tonight," she says. "How about tomorrow?"

There's a huge round of protests from her family, that **no** she is not cooking tonight, regardless, and everyone will turn out in shifts to make sure she's well-fed and taking it easy. Yeah, right. You can see in Mrs. Goretti's eyes that no prisoner in Alcatraz wanted to be free as badly as she does right now.

I want to be like her when I grow up.

Before I leave she takes my hand and thanks me. One of her relations walks me to the elevator and also thanks me for "everything" (whereas I have no idea if I've done anything at all.) I'm halfway back to the shop when I remember I still have her wedding rings, so I'll just bring them back tonight.

That's a first, a pirate returning booty.

I wonder if I can find a black flag with a skull and crossbones (do they call that a Jolly Roger, or is that something else?) but then again why would lawless non-patriated seafarers have a flag in the first place? "Hi! We're pirates, and we're here to kill you!" Now if I were a pirate, I'd just keep a bunch of flags lying around and then run up a flag no one finds threatening. "Hey, look, it's the Swiss! Maybe they've got chocolate." Then you get up close and wallop the tar out of their ship.

Although that would sink it, and you can't plunder something once it's a mile under water. Maybe I wouldn't have been a good pirate after all.

Think about the intelligence you needed to operate one of those ships! Anyone can learn to drive a car: point the wheels in the right direction, look at the traffic, step on the gas, and you're moving. Those ships have like fifty sails, though, and if I remember right from the *Master and Commander* movie, each one had a different name. There were mainsails, topsails, mizzen sails, ten-percent-off sales, and they were all in different places, and you had to have them arranged just right or the ship wouldn't move or would tilt over. I guess too much sail meant too much resistance, but not enough meant you didn't catch the air to move, and then how did you turn?

"I want to learn to sail," I say to Bucky.

Is it my imagination, or did he just get a shade paler? He musters himself, squares his wings, and says, "You'll wear a life jacket?"

"Anything to make you happy." I grin. "Think about it—all those sails? The clean power?"

"You getting blown a thousand miles away because you think it's fun to set sail in a hurricane?" Bucky's hand tightens on his cutlass. "Looking forward to it."

"Doesn't Genesis say something about the breath of God moving over the waters?"

Bucky says, "Genesis isn't a weather forecast. You'll end up in France."

I shrug. "You can speak French."

"Je peux. Je ne veux pas."

I beam. "That sounds like total agreement to me! Sign me up. Besides, the 'breath of God' would be the Holy Spirit, right? You said God loves me, so He wouldn't send me to France."

"I have it on good authority that God loves a lot of people even though they're in France." Bucky shrugs. "God makes the wind blow, but where you go with it is kind of your own decision. As long as you're moving, you're doing what ships do."

I say, "So I've got my 'go back to work' sail open and that's where I'm headed."

Bucky says, "You might consider opening your 'fidelity' sail before the Shadow comes after you again."

I say, "I'd rather keep chugging along under the 'single vocation' sail for a while more. Think about it: if I open the 'getting married' sail, then there needs to be another ship right next to mine moving with exactly the same sails open, otherwise we'd crash into each other. That wouldn't be any fun at all. And what if not all ships have the same sails? How do you operate two ships in unison like that?"

Bucky says, "Don't give me that. You'd be first in line to drive in the Presidential motorcade, and that's got only a foot or two between the bumpers."

My eyes light up. "You can sign up for that?"

"No." Bucky huffs. "No. You can't."

"Darn." I'm back at the garage now. "But I don't have a Marriage Sail either, so no Bridal Motorcade for me."

Instead of a sailboat, I have a car waiting for me on the lift. But the breeze is gusting, and it'll be cool if it blows me somewhere.

It's three PM and it's dead here, so Max tells me to leave. (Why keep me on the clock when I'm not bringing in any cash?).

Hal left a message: he wants to know when I'm off work, so I call, then wash up, then clock out. Another fun day at Mack's Auto.

I meet him in the waiting area, and since no one is around I wrap my arms around him, and he kisses me. He smells like Old Spice, and it's good. He murmurs, "I thought you were talking like a pirate today."

"Max was mean," I whisper against his neck. "He made me be a land lubber."

"Totally not fair." My accountant sighs. "Do you want to go exploring?"

Need he ask? In his car I replace my hoop earrings and my scarf-sash.

He says, "So did you work on a Cutlass today?"

"Ack! Not fair!" I fold my arms. "Bucky! Why didn't you think of that?"

No response. Angelic shame?

Hal snickers. I pout at Hal. "Well, since you were so mean, maybe I won't tell you Mrs. Goretti offered to teach you how to make some of her family recipes."

The car lurches as Hal's foot slams the gas. "What? Really?"

"Hey, careful! I don't want to be in the room next to hers."

"You're right, I bet they don't have a stove in there." His eyes are bright. "That makes today worthwhile."

By the time we pull up in a space on Fourth Avenue, somewhere near Twentieth Street, I think Hal's six inches taller. He's thinking about veal scaloppini and homemade ravioli.

"You realize the secret is in the butter," he tells me as he comes around to where I'm waiting on my side of the car. "It gives sauces that nice thickness and texture, plus that little extra creaminess.

"I didn't realize it was a secret at all." I take his hand. "Where are we going, Matey? Or is that a secret too?"

He takes me to a store I cannot at first classify. At all. I want to say it's a salvage shop, except the things in the window are simply random. And some are old. Others aren't.

He shifts his weight. "I couldn't quite bring myself to go in." He swallows. "But since you're dressed like a pirate, what's the worst that can happen?"

The store's name means nothing to me: Gomes & Co. I guess they're not big into PR.

"Well." I put my hands on my hips. "I don't have a cutlass or a blunderbuss, and pirates aren't known for being great bodyguards, but I'll protect you."

He chuckles, and I realize he's really nervous. What have I gotten us into?

Well, no time like the present. Bucky hasn't emitted a scream of horror, so I can't imagine it's all bad. That would be part of his job, to warn me if I were about to walk into the gates of Hell.

Instead we walk into the gates of Dust. The lighting is dismal, the aisles cramped, and a slightly-older-than-middle-aged Latino woman sits behind a wooden counter with a cash register, a black rotary phone, and a copy of *El Diario*. I nod at her with a noncommittal greeting. Without expression she glances up, then glares back at the newspaper.

I love the ambiance and welcome. When I get halfway up the first narrow aisle, I get it: we're in either a pawn shop or an antique store, but whatever this is, it's an *adventure*.

Here I am, the Great Pirate Singer, embarking on a treasure hunt! Ahoy! Because here laid out in front of me I can see bits and pieces of Brooklyn life from the past quarter century. Just at a glance, I find coffee tables, lamps, blenders, books, roller skates, vases, ceramic figures (tons of those—one more tchotchke and the place will explode), baskets, glassware, garden implements, AM radios tall as a Shetland pony, blankets, jars, vinyl records, and in one corner, one very alive and very irritated longhaired black cat.

Whenever someone dies, they empty her house into this shop. When a starving actor returns to Iowa, the unmoved contents of the apartment gravitate here to rest.

"Hal," I whisper, jumping in place, "this is marvelous!"

There's a jewelry case with horrible castoff costume jewelry, and beside it are electronics that may or may not work. There's a monitor from an Apple IIE, and beside that are seven keyboards piled on top of one another. A box with miles of cable. Someone's china pattern. Fisher Price toys from the late seventies (I had an A-frame house just like that!) and action figures with not too many limbs missing. Books on shelves covered with three solid inches of dust. Every time I turn and refocus my eyes, there's more to be found, and all this bounty, in a store not wider than twenty feet and deeper than sixty, to be explored only by me and Hal and that chatty woman at the register.

A couple of times I look for a price, but why bother? Things here are cheap. Well, they ought to be. It's a lot of garbage, and I'm not sure how they turn a profit. But it's glorious with old logos and heavy plastic and all of it thrust onto shelves or into any floor space where enough of a footprint remained available to set it.

I lose track of Hal for fifteen minutes in the clutter. I find a cache of tools: stainless steel by Glory, and heavy in my hands. I'll need a box for these.

When I feel a touch on my arm, I jump, but it's only Hal again. I've plundered a few more finds: long strands of beads for Beth, who will take them apart for craft projects, plus a book I remember reading when I was twelve and also a mug with a Mustang logo.

"Come here," he whispers. Intrigued, I follow. From his tone of voice, he might have located Jimmy Hoffa's final resting place.

"What's that?" I indicate the metal implement in his hand.

"The reason I came," he says. "But first, you've got to see this."

Whatever tool that is looks pretty neat, but Hal's being coy, so he leads me like the Pied Piper to the back corner where bookshelves wall us in. It's a good thing Mrs. Goretti trained me all these years with her fifteen-watt bulbs.

Hal gestures to one shelf. "Cookbooks."

We kneel because the proper shelf is at knee-height, and it's crammed. The first says, simply, *A World Of Good Foods.* "What's the big deal?"

"Lee!" His voice has a cajoling note. "Just look at this stuff! *The Temp-Tone Cookbook.*" He opens it and shows me: "Cooking with stainless steel! Stainless Steel is used today in hospitals, industry, the space program...and now you can *cook* with stainless steel too!"

I stifle a laugh at the picture of a rocket launching, implying that we're cooking in the space-age. "What the heck?"

"See?" He flips back to the front. "Copyright 1962! Think what a bright future we all had back then, when marvel of marvels, the average person could *cook* using stainless steel."

Hal pulls out a wine guide and flips through. "See, peasant women harvesting grapes with their hair back in babushkas..." He turns the page, then drops his voice an octave into a documentary-announcer's drawl. "But here, the actual *drinking* of wine is for stodgy white men wearing black suits."

I'm giggling helplessly as he goes for the next. "Ooh, *The Tupperware Cookbook*. Eighty-six meals you can cook using resealable plastic goodness."

"Where'd they get all this stuff?"

"We're not in Barnes and Noble." Hal snickers. "If you haven't noticed, even Goodwill didn't want these. Oh, wait, what was I saying? Here's *The Exciting And Versatile World of Microwave Cooking*. Copyright 1982, the heyday of microwave cooking." He opens randomly. "Microwave lasagna, anyone? Hey, and it tells you how to warm your wine."

"But only if you're a stodgy old man in a black suit."

"That would explain the joyless faces those guys were making." Hal replaces that. "Here's a good one: *No, Salt, No Sugar, No Fat*."

I add, "No taste."

"No thanks." He puts it back. "That's conveniently located beside *Crisco's Favorite Family Foods*. Otherwise known as cooking with lard. No recipes in this book contain fewer than a thousand calories per serving, guaranteed."

"This one's still shrink-wrapped," I say. "*The New Joys of Jell-O*."

"They must have had two copies." Hal beams. "I can't imagine leaving that gem unopened on my shelf! I wonder if they can beat my mom's recipe for Spam and Spanish Olive Jell-O Salad."

For a moment I pause. Then I say, "No. You're joking."

"You'll just have to wonder." His eyes are sparkling with the same zest that caught my attention last January and hasn't let it go ever since. "I'll ask her to make it for you."

"Your mother would never!"

"My mother is a saint," Hal says, "but even I know her limits. Don't even suggest such a thing."

I lean near. "If you made it, people would beg for seconds."

He kisses me among the graveyard of horrid cookbooks. I should suggest Spam Jell-O more often. "So what else is here?"

With a mischievous smile, Hal pulls out two books. "Hey, the zucchini cookbook. I could have used this about two months ago when my mom's garden was in full swing."

I frown. "Zucchini Jell-O?"

"If you'd suggested it back then, I'd have done it. Didn't you notice a plethora of zucchini bread and zucchini dishes coming your way? I ran out of ways to get the stuff out of my house fast enough. Mom leaves paper bags full of zucchini on people's doorsteps. My father threatens to give boxes to people who don't pay their bills, and then they pay. I haul Zucchini Everything to work and leave it in the break room, and after a couple of weeks, just as the zucchini season peaks, no one wants them any longer. It's awful."

It would never occur to Hal to discard perfectly edible food. Too much of something becomes a challenge, but his mother's garden must have brought him to his knees this year. "Poor you."

"Every summer, farmers pray for rain and I pray for drought. I'm outnumbered." He takes the next book. "Ah, here's a good one: *The Food Value of The Banana.*" He opens the slim paper cover to reveal...no interior. It's only the cover. "As I suspected," he intones. "Delicious and otherwise useless." He replaces that on the shelf. "Let's see—*The Fabulous Fructose Recipe Cookbook, The Blender Cookbook*—I'll live without that one, somehow. In fact, somehow I'll manage without all these."

When he turns back to me, I kiss him again, and we're there for a couple of minutes until I hear a pointed throat-clearing from the front of the store and realize the counter lady can see us through the mirror mounted on the ceiling.

My cheeks flame red. Hal sits back and continues going through cookbooks as if nothing just happened, but he looks flustered too. She's going to throw us out of here for being indecent and I won't get my stainless steel pliers.

"Maybe I need to keep looking," I say.

"I won't be much longer." Hal won't meet my eyes. "I found the thing I was looking for."

I nearly turn back to ask him what on earth he was looking for in this wreckage, but then I think of the counter lady sitting at the front door like Cerberus at the gates of Hell, and discretion becomes the better part of curiosity. I put some distance between us and browse the shelves.

You could have warned me about that mirror, I send toward Bucky.

Like it would have made a difference, Bucky replies.

Any angels in this store? The kind I can buy, I add. It's been a while since I've gone angel-hunting, and this shop is the perfect place to find one-of-a-kind angel figurines, books, wind chimes, and Christmas ornaments. I've had great luck at antique shops, although sometimes the prices there are as insane as if they were trying to pay back the R&D expenses of an actual time machine.

Bucky says, *I haven't found anything you can't live without.*

For a moment I'm worried: Bucky usually likes to go angel-hunting with me just to find the awful ones. Like Hal and I were doing with the cookbooks, in fact.

And as I think that, I shiver: is Bucky jealous of Hal?

This is all so confusing. I'm not going to think about it any longer; I'll just keep looking around on the shelves for something cool until Hal's sufficiently recovered his balance to buy his tool and get out of here.

Standing on a shelf taller than my head, I find a model sailing ship as long as my forearm. I nudge the solid wood into my arms, then set it on a clear spot on a shelf closer to eye-level. It's mounted on a base that seems to have once had a name plate. Best of all, when I tug on some of the string rigging, the sails themselves move up and down.

The ship is missing one of the largest sails, but other than that, it's perfect. Or she's perfect. Ships were always "she," right, like sports cars?

I bet the sail that's missing is the Marriage Sail. Maybe it's a sign. Maybe I should be thrilled that I don't ever have to get married. Maybe it's just a junky model of a sailing ship and I should be glad it's missing something so I can get it for half price.

"What do you have there?" Hal has come up behind me without me hearing.

I show him, and he makes an admiring noise. I point out the missing sail without mentioning that it's the Marriage Sail, and he studies the model for a few seconds before unhooking one of the threads from a wooden mast the size of a toothpick, and the sail unfurls from seemingly nowhere.

"See?" he says. "Perfect."

Uh-oh. I hope that wasn't a sign after all.

Up at the front, Hal pays for everything, maybe out of gratitude that I escorted him into the shop at grave personal risk in order for him to get that tool thing. He's also buying a generic-looking binder-style cookbook. I'm glad he at least found something in all that mess.

The woman does little more than grunt a price at us before shoving everything into a plastic Pathmark bag. I rescue the ship before she tries to cram it in as well, figuring it does no good to find your Marriage Sail if the masts are all busted.

Outside I end up blinking, counting my blessings I don't have a seizure because of the sudden influx of clear light and the dust-free bus exhaust. I point to Hal's tool. "It's still Pirate Day. Is that for playing Captain Hook?"

He bursts out laughing. "Almost."

Hal lets me into the front seat, then goes around to his side while I buckle in and fiddle with the ship's sails. I wonder if it would actually sail in Uncle Mickey's swimming pool. Maybe I can fill the tub with hot bubbly water, climb in, and play with my toy.

I must have a silly grin, because Hal says, "I'm glad you found something there that made the whole trip worthwhile."

"From now on, I'm visiting there once a quarter." I run my fingertips over the hull. "Okay, so spill. How'd you find that place? And how did you know they'd have a Captain Hook costume?"

"I was making an experiment at home, a honey bread," Hal says. "I screwed it up. I had the dough in the KitchenAid mixer, and I'd made it so thick that the bread hook snapped."

For the life of me, he looks like a knight confessing he blunted his sword on the scales of a dragon. He pulls into traffic and then ends up idling fifteen feet away waiting for the light.

"I went on eBay to see what replacement attachments were going for, and on a lark, I asked it to locate stores in Brooklyn. This place has so-so feedback, but all of it was for slow shipping and bad communication."

I cannot, *cannot*, imagine why. "Ah! But if you came down in person, you didn't have to worry about shipping or emailing the seller. Got it."

"And you got a working pirate ship, complete with tiny pirates. Or are they termites?" Hal smirks. "You find the strangest things."

"That was the strangest store."

We're heading uphill again, and for a moment he looks exhausted. "I'll drive you home. It's been a long day."

Oh, that explains the experimental bread. "Your boss is on the warpath?"

"You have no idea. She phoned eight times while I was in the shower. Three times on my home phone, four times on the cell, and she even called my mother's house to look for me. I'm lucky she didn't call *your* mother. That's in addition to three text messages and two emails." Hal raises his eyes to Heaven. "Apparently we had a crisis no one could have predicted, say, yesterday. Nor solved on Monday. Or even at eight thirty this morning. When I got her on the phone, she was irate that I wasn't immediately available. The problem took an hour to fix, or it would have if she hadn't kept calling me every five minutes."

"You need to quit."

"After a while, I effectively did. I started making bread, but that's when the bread hook snapped." Hal's eyes are so piercing right now that I could fashion a harpoon and take out Moby Dick. "I kneaded the rest by hand and let it rise while I looked for the replacement part. She kept calling, and I'd tell her I didn't have it done yet, then hang up and go back to making bread."

I'm filled with awe. "And I thought I was piratical!"

"Please. This is unpaid overtime. She's lucky I did anything for her at all." Hal turns at Sixth Avenue, and miraculously, there's a space he can pull into. "Nothing I did today couldn't have waited. Eventually I took the phone off the hook and finished up in five minutes, emailed her that it was done, and walked away from the apartment without my cell phone."

"You need a new job."

"I need a new boss. I keep hoping she'll give herself a heart attack."

When he shuts off the engine, I debate reminding him that he was only going to drop me off, but I don't want him to go. So why remind him? I'm not five steps from the car when I register the crowd around my doorstep.

Actually, Bucky would get on my case for that, so... it's not exactly a crowd, and it's not in front of *my* doorstep. It's five people, and they're in front of Mrs. Goretti's doorstep, which is tucked into an alcove beneath the brownstone steps.

Oh, wow! She's home! They're bringing her home!

I shove the ship into Hal's arms and trot up to them. "Do you need help getting in?" I unlock the cast-iron gate that has a key-locked deadbolt on both sides and then stand back so her relatives can guide her shakily down the three steps.

They insist on putting her in bed; she complains that she wants to be at her kitchen table. Eventually everyone settles on letting her set up in bed. I talk to the relatives for a bit about how good it is she's home, etc., then more small talk about how we'll check on her, them saying Beth and I are good tenants to look after their mother.

Hal stays at my elbow, and that's when I remember. "Oh! I still have your wedding rings!" I grab the plastic bag and the ship from Hal. "Be right back!"

I bolt up all three flights of steps to the apartment, avoiding a teensie cringe when I remember getting swallowed by evil and then spit back out. I'm out of breath, but hey, it gets me moving faster.

I'm reaching into the sock drawer when I have a moment of horror: they aren't there.

"Of course they're there." Bucky sounds bored. "Don't panic. Reach further back."

I guess he could tell what I was thinking by the way my heart lurched up to two hundred beats per minute, but he's right: the rings are there, just pushed back further than I thought I'd left them.

"Hey, Captain Hook, don't disappear yet. What happened in that store?"

Bucky frowns. "What happened? You got caught smooching your boyfriend among the stacks of merchandise, and the genteel proprietor frowned on such behavior."

"Yeah, yeah." I gesture idly. "Tell God to put it on my tab."

"𝕴 𝖆𝖑𝖗𝖊𝖆𝖉𝖞 𝖍𝖆𝖛𝖊."

Shrieking, I jump and pivot to face Bucky, who's doubled over laughing. When I throw a ball of socks at him, he manages to gasp, "I bet you didn't know I could do that with my voice."

"I'm going to kill you." I swallow. "What I *was* going to ask you until you nearly put me in the hospital was why you went all scarce on me before."

Bucky's mischievous eyes change to a blank look.

"You backed out of angel-hunting."

"I wanted to get out of that store. So cluttered." Bucky shivers. "The detritus of mis-spent lives, on sale for three-ninety-nine plus tax."

Okay. I can deal with making Bucky miserable. I do that all the time.

Bucky squints. "If the place had been demon-infested, at least more than normal, I'd have alerted you."

"I thought you were jealous." Bucky's blank look returns. "Of Hal. Because we were laughing about cookbooks the same way you and I laugh about angel statues."

He raises his wings and his eyebrows. "I've got a short list of people you're allowed to laugh with?"

"Not to the best of my knowledge, no. But—" I shrug. "It's okay. As long as you're okay with that."

Of course, if he wasn't okay with that, he might still demur. I mean, we've established that angels and people don't marry each other. I'd see a movie like *City of Angels* or *Wings of Desire* and he'd be muttering insults at the screen, rolling his eyes, or openly astonished.

"It's more plausible for you to fall in love with Avery," Bucky said to me about ten years ago (when Avery was, for the record, four years old.)

"But you do love me," I replied, and he replied, "And you love Avery. Randy loves you. God loves me. They're talking romance. I'm talking something fifty times more powerful and infinitely more permanent."

I return to the hallway. "What would happen if you didn't like the guy I wanted to marry? Or the guy's guardian? You would have to spend a lot of time together."

"I'd pray about it."

That's a loaded statement. "Pray for me to break up with him?"

"Pray to like the guy, or the guardian. That's not an issue right now. But keep in mind that if you ever have children, it's the same thing. I might not personally mesh with the baby's guardian, but I wouldn't demand you make an adoption plan for the baby."

I bite my lip. "If I had a baby, would I suddenly see two of you?"

Bucky laughs. "If you're pregnant, you'll know. Trust me."

Uh-oh. "You'll come with a lily and get down on one knee saying, 'Rejoice, O highly flaky woman'?"

He points at me. "I'll have to remember that. But to get back to reality, when I was assigned, I had no idea in advance who your siblings and parents would be, and I was going to be spending a lot of time with them too. In fact," he adds, "your mother's guardian was in charge of my initial training."

"Lucky you. I hope my mom's guardian is easier to get along with than my mom." I kinda-sorta don't want to go back down the stairs again. That darkness. I'm pretty sure I'm safe, but...well, I can't live up here forever. Although maybe I can have groceries delivered.

He runs a hand over my hair as I lock the door, like ruffling it except without the ruffling part. "It's just something the mother's guardian does."

"Oh, so I'll know I'm expecting when you start turning your head five times an hour and saying, 'See, Fred? That's another example of how they screw up. And this is how you hit them in the head with a frying pan afterward.'"

Bucky says, "You never respond well to the frying pan. I'd recommend a rolling pin."

"Ouch!"

"Then in that case, I'd recommend avoiding sin."

I stick out my tongue at him as I start down the stairs. The steps may not be perfectly safe, but hey, what is? It'll be an adventure. "That's neat. You had an apprenticeship!"

"I shadowed another guardian too." Bucky takes flight to follow me down. "A century ago, in another country. It was exciting, knowing you were just around the corner, trying to guess what you'd be like based on the kind of person I was shadowing."

I pause. "That person... Okay, I'll bite. Was it a pirate?"

Bucky laughs out loud. "Not even close!"

"Then why the fascination with Talk Like A Pirate Day?"

He leans close to me, rests his hands on my shoulders (they tingle) and says, "Pirates had swords. They had sailing ships. What's not to love?"

"Murder." I fold my arms. "Theft. Kidnapping. Nautical terrorism. I'm pretty sure if I were doing those things, you'd deliver me an epic scolding with nary an 'arr' in sight."

"Well, yes, I suppose more than a couple of them failed to make Heaven." Bucky's shoulder slump. "But you look cute as a pirate. You should wear hoop earrings more often."

"Remember I said before I was going to kill you? I'm really going to kill you now." Then, I chuckle. "I never thought about that before, who trains guardians."

"The same people who train parents. Don't worry about it. You have a wedding ring to deliver." As I walk, he adds, "No one trains wives, either. You pick it up from watching the wives and mothers around you."

I smirk. "Nowadays we have advice columnists and talking heads on CNN."

"Dear Abbiel," Bucky intones. *"I've never written you before, but I have a problem with my charge. She's a wise-acre."*

"Dear Guardian," I reply. "Roll your eyes and be patient with her. She'll get a clue someday."

He laughs.

Back downstairs, Mrs. Goretti has prevailed on the Goretti hoard: she's sitting at her table where she belongs. "Thank you!" she exclaims as slips her rings back on. Hal looks absolutely bemused by the uproar only five of her relatives can create. They all talk loud and they're all opinionated, so the conversation flies fast and thick as rain in a hurricane. I take my position behind Hal, who stands. "You want a seat?"

"Don't bother," I say.

Hal kisses me on the cheek and moves toward the door. Let's see, can I read his mind? I think it says, "This was fun, but I'm done."

"I like him, Lee," Mrs. Goretti says loudly.

Hal's eyes widen. They probably haven't widened as much as mine have.

"He reminds me of Tony," she adds. "So polite. You two need to get married."

"I'll put it on the list of things to do." I smile easily. "It's all your fault we're not married. I still have three months on my lease."

She waves a hand. "Beth needs to get married too. She has that nice young man here all the time."

"In your condition it would be a pain for you to screen new tenants." I back toward the door until Hal is right behind me, but he doesn't budge so I can flee. "Call me if you need anything."

"Lee." Her voice drops in pitch, and she stares right at me. "Don't be ridiculous. He's a perfect gentleman. I've seen everything: lock him down."

I nod, and then I push back past Hal.

In the hallway, Hal says, "I think you took my bread hook upstairs."

"Oh, right. It was in the bag." We head up, silent. I muster up, "I'm sorry about that."

"Don't be sorry. You don't control what people say."

Everyone's right: I can't string him on forever. He's going to want a commitment, and it's not something I can give.

In my kitchen, I unload the junk-shop's Path-Mark bag. As a truth-in-advertising thing, they could have used a garbage bag. "Oh, you found a cookbook!"

Hal chuckles. "Open it."

Inside I and find a generic set of cards, yellowed, clipped in a binder-style notebook. Units of conversion, roasting times for a chicken of so-many pounds, instructions for different cuts of meat.

"Keep going."

I flip a few more pages, and there's handwriting.

"That's worth its weight in gold." Hal folds his arms. "Old-world recipes copied out firsthand by an old-world cook, someone who fed these things to her family on a regular basis and knew what worked, what you could substitute, and all the work-arounds for the way you'd do things in a normal kitchen of the 1950s.

I keep paging through. Most of the recipes sound German. The handwriting is tall and loopy, very even. And then, in the middle of pages filled with index cards, there's a hand-written letter. *Dear Sophie,* in that same loopy handwriting, with a date of July 8th, 1957.

"Did you see this?" I grab Hal's arm. "So cool!"

I've been unsure how to reply to your previous letter, so please forgive me the delay in responding.

For some reason, the letter makes this someone's cookbook far more than someone's personal recipes ever could. I read the letter and find that the writer is quitting her job, that she has to take three buses to her jobsite and she gets written up for every lateness even when there's snow but they send her home early when there isn't enough work to do. So many details, just a life embedded in the middle of a woman's daily menus.

How many meals did this woman cook for her family over the course of a lifetime? Me, I'll make do with raw pasta if that's what I've got time for. But if you think of a woman cooking three hundred sixty-five meals a year for two or three decades... That's practically heroic. They'd be screaming it was cruel and unusual punishment if some judge sentenced a murderer with, "I want you to cook seven thousand dinners." But one day at a time, this woman did.

At some point, the letter breaks off, before there's a signature. We don't even know her name.

"How did that get there?"

Hal shrugs. "There aren't any names. Don't think I didn't already look."

Bucky?

Hal looks surprised. "Why does it matter? I assume it got donated."

"Because—" I bite my lip. "Why would you get rid of hand-written recipes like this?"

Bucky's appeared on the table, running his hand over the binder rings. "I can investigate if you like," he said, "but maybe she never had children. Maybe her husband remarried and the new wife wanted it gone."

I flip through again, some pages empty, some having recipes tacked down onto pages with only flimsy pieces of scotch tape that long since lost their stick. But it's someone's history that ended up donated to a junk shop. A life lived in detail and then discarded.

I ask, "Why didn't anyone want this?"

Bucky said, "Maybe she never rooted herself down so people would."

It's just so different from what's going on downstairs right now, on the bottom floor, where Mrs. Goretti's children and grandchildren are crammed around her table mocking the doctors. This book is silence and loneliness.

Chapter Seventeen

Cooking the books as well as the cookies

My Mustang lives on Garfield Place between Fifth and Sixth Avenues, in a place that is, quite literally, just a garage: three cinderblock walls, one wooden door which raises to admit the vehicle, and a roof. It locks, but because that wouldn't be enough, there is also a ten-foot-high wrought iron fence around the property, topped with coiled razor wire. If you manage to get through all that, you have one more obstacle: a garage door weighing two thousand pounds. Automatic garage door opener? You're looking at her.

And this, my friends—this is where I am spending all day Sunday. Why? Because so help me, I deserve it.

My windowless garage is as dark as the inside of King Tut's tomb, so I installed fluorescent fixtures on chains as soon as I could drive hooks into the ceiling. On the back wall I've installed a pegboard where I hang my tools. If a thief ever succeeds in breaking into the place, he's going to have a hard time deciding between the car or the tools. But he'll also have to contend with the place's owner: an eighty-nine-year-old who carries a shotgun and longs for his Army career to make a glorious return. Sergeant-Major GloryDays lets me use the utility sink out behind the garage and maybe the bathroom in his house if I ask nicely, but he audits the squares of toilet paper to make sure he doesn't need to raise the rent.

I could back the Mustang into the garage and work in the daylight, but that leads to two things. First, I gather an audience, some of whom feel compelled to deliver commentary about the shape of my backside. And second, it makes my fluorescents feel sad. I paid for the lights. I'm using them.

And so, with lights contentedly glowing to illuminate the engine and Chilton's open on the workbench to illuminate my brain, I get to work.

As soon as I start, my phone rings. After I let it go to voicemail, it rings again. Again, voicemail. This is my time with my car. Deal with it. Even if it's an emergency, what am I going to do?

Hey, Lee! Thank heaven you answered your phone. The house was on fire, but as soon as I heard your voice, the whole thing extinguished. Talk to you later!

Next thing, I hear Hal shout, "Lee? You alive back there?"

I glare around the raised hood of the car. I've got to wipe off my hands and trek to the sidewalk to unlock the gate, then lock it at his back. I don't say, "Exactly what about this situation tells you I'm craving a visit?" I substitute the more socially acceptable, "What's up?"

I don't wait for a response. I just head back to my car.

He follows me holding an insulated bag, black vinyl. "Beth told me you were working on the car, so I figured I'd see if you wanted lunch."

"I just got here."

"It's twelve-thirty." I gasp and he laughs. "I figured you'd gotten lost in time, and I can't allow you to starve to death. You might not have noticed until well after midnight."

After a check of my cell phone reveals he's correct that three hours have passed, I go over in my head all the things I've done to the engine and yeah, he's probably right.

Avoiding my oily rags, Hal opens lunch on the work table. "I hope you don't mind seeing another human being."

Now that I'm back in reality, I'm kind of hungry after all. I clean off my hands as best as I can, then scrub down with handiwipes until I'm presentable enough to eat. "That's sweet of you. You're probably right that I wouldn't have eaten until dinner."

He hands me a turkey and lettuce sandwich on a cream cheese bagel, which I have to admit is something I wouldn't have tried with a thirty-foot pole before he insisted it tasted good last April. Sitting on the trunk of my car, we split a thermos of coffee (hazelnut crème, and yes, he used real cream) and then fresh-baked chocolate chip cookies. "I'm sure the church coffee hour folks won't notice a half-dozen missing," he adds with his eyes glinting in mischief.

I pause. "Do they count them?"

"I'm the accountant. They trust me to count them."

Making my eyes wide, I push him away from me. "Embezzlement!"

"White collar crime is the worst," he says. "It's easiest to spot the crumbs on a white collar."

I shake my head. "You're cooking the books as well as the cookies!"

He feigns a worried look. "Maybe you'll accept a bribe to keep quiet about my nefarious plan?"

I lean forward. "You know my price."

He kisses me, and for a little while I lose track of time again. He puts his hands in my hair, and I wrap my arms around him.

Hal concludes that if only he'd known, he'd have brought me lunch earlier, so I laugh and kiss him once more.

A passer-by yells that we need to get a room, which embarrasses Hal and makes me throw my arms around him to kiss him again.

He gentles me away from him. "We probably should cool it. Can I watch you work for a while?"

So we clean up the lunch containers and I give him a brief tour of what engines used to look like before black-box systems overtook the automotive world. "Today we're having a tune-up. I adjusted the idle speed already, but now I need to replace the choke because she's begun stalling before she warms up."

I lean over the engine. "This is the choke."

He gets directly behind me and wraps his arms around my waist, breathing against my neck.

I get goosebumps. "And, um, that's the bi-coiled spring that expands when it gets hot to keep the, um, choke open."

"Keep talking," he whispers. "Don't mind me."

"Yeah, I, um, don't normally work this way." With his hands on my hips, he's pressed right against me.

"Good," he whispers. "Let me be the first."

He kisses me lightly from my shoulders up my neck to right beneath my ear. I tilt back my head, and he kisses my throat. He wraps his arms around my waist and keeps me against his hips. He's right here, the scent of him and the feel of him making my head swim.

Did we attract an audience before? We're at the back of the garage with the hood up, otherwise we'd really be attracting an audience, and they wouldn't be telling us to get a room. They'd be taking video, and Hal's elderly fan-friend would be compiling a soundtrack from anime theme songs. I drop my wrench onto the engine and face him, and there's a lot of kissing, and there's some touching, and there's more kissing. He's probably got grease on him now. I don't think that's his primary concern. At some point there's hands and nuzzling and clothing shifted around, and his hands fumbling at my bra strap.

"We ought to cool it," I whisper.

"No, we shouldn't," he whispers back. "This is just fine."

I swallow hard. "Do more than that and you're going to need a condom."

He whispers, "I'd have a baby with you."

He kisses me hard, harder, edges me back against the quarter panel. There's the back seat of the car just feet from us, and he's all over me. *I'd have a baby with you.* My heart's pounding, and I'm scared but at the same time I'm not thinking. A baby. It's an adventure. Sex is a few minutes, but a baby is forever and ever.

He says, "How does the back seat sound?"

It sounds awesome. It sounds scary. But the more he keeps kissing me, the more it sounds like a great idea.

He reaches around me for the door handle, and I close my eyes. "Wait."

He puts his hands in my hair. "Wait?"

"Wait. Please." My throat tightens, and I shake my head. "Give me a minute."

I put my face into his shoulder and try to breathe, and he holds me.

I'd have a baby with you.

That's not just him having some fun. He's serious. He's talking about everything. He wants my *everything*.

He kisses me on the neck and then runs his hand again through my hair. He kisses my closed eyes, and then his hands are back again under my shirt. He wants me in that car. He's been clear all along. He wants me.

And I want...this minute? Just this once? What's the harm? Lots of people have sex. This isn't Victorian England and it's not a fantasy novel where sex forms unbreakable bonds. Or is it?

He fingers the button of my jeans. "Is this okay?"

Is this okay?

It's fine. It's yes. It's wonderful. It's scary. I close my eyes.

And in my mind, I see Bucky. Eyes dark, piercing. Watching me break a promise I made to him.

I push back from Hal and shake my head. "No. It's not. Please—please stop. You can't stay like this. Just go."

I didn't actually see Bucky. But now I'm seeing Hal, and he looks angry. "Really?" Offended. "Just go?" Upset. "Just like that?"

Bucky appears, and that's two people glaring at me.

Hal reaches toward me.

Bucky fires a glare at him and snaps, "She said no!"

Hal jumps backward.

"Please!" I turn to Hal. "I need time. I need to think."

He puts his hand on my wrist. "How long do you need? You're going to think forever and it's never going to resolve."

"But I don't want to decide it this way." I swallow. "Not like this. It's all following the wrong way around."

Bucky's armored, and he's wielding his sword. I've never seen him this way. He's not defending me. He's offended.

Hal doesn't look much less offended, but he's steeling himself. "Fine. You know what? Call me when you're done thinking, if that ever happens." His voice sounds flat. He slips through the garage gate, and then Bucky and I are alone.

Even after Hal is out of the garage, Bucky doesn't relax. He stands, arms folded, chin down, glaring at me with a ferocity I haven't seen since... I don't know since when.

I fasten my clothes back together. Then I sit on the concrete floor, my back against the cinderblock wall, and hug my knees to my chest.

The silence stretches like a pizza dough, wider and longer but always thinner, me expecting at any moment that it's finally going to part from itself in the center where it's gotten too thin to stretch any further.

I can't begin to predict how long this is going to go on. "Bucky, I'm sorry."

"I have no idea what to do with you." His voice is rife with disgust. "Absolutely none."

"I didn't expect him to do that."

"What did you expect? He's a man. You're a perpetual tease. He's going to yield eventually."

I look up. "Am I the keeper of his conscience?"

"Yes. To the extent that you're the one causing him to violate it, yes." Bucky takes a deep breath. "The answer to *Am I my brother's keeper?* is not a resounding no. Of course you're supposed to take care of each other."

I tuck my chin. "I'm sorry."

"I'm not sure you should apologize for things you aren't sorry for." His head raises even as I draw breath to protest. "Don't tell me you're sorry when the only thing you're sorry for is having gotten in over your head. You're not sorry for wanting to break your promise to me. You're not sorry for leading him on. As far as you're concerned, you're using him for a good time, and that's fine with you."

I frown. "Is it using someone if he's having a good time too?"

"If he believed you were never going to marry him," Bucky says, "would he continue dating you?"

I flinch.

"Then you're dating under false pretenses."

"I told him I'm not ready for marriage."

"*Not ready* is not the same thing as *German shepherds will bark a full performance of* Aida *before I consent to marry anyone.*" Bucky settles to the floor in front of me, keeping his wings high. "The temptation is going to increase the more often the two of you dance with the physical attraction." He shakes his head. "He's going to push for a commitment in every way he can. You're at a crossroads here. You need to figure out what you want."

With a roll of my eyes, I mutter, "I thought I had figured out what I want."

"I'll clarify." Bucky sits forward and looks earnest. "You need to figure out what you want that isn't going to turn you into a serial user with a heart of ice."

I don't want to break up with Hal. But neither do I want to break up with, effectively, every other male on the planet.

Without answering, I get up to start putting away my tools. The carburetor needs to be put back together, so I take care of that, and then I do one more thing, and before long I'm back up to my elbows in engine parts. Bucky vanishes again.

Maybe he assumes I'm thinking. Either that or he knows me well enough to realize thinking is the last thing I want to do.

I work until I run out of things to work on, and then I start on the laundry list I never got around to taking care of. There's a screw I meant to tighten in the door frame. There's that squeak in the rear seat. When I find myself checking the pressure in the spare tire, I look outside and see the light slanted, the shadows long. I'm starving. I don't want to leave. But I can't stay all night.

So after putting away my tools and shutting the hood, I lock up the garage, lock the wrought iron gate, and trudge up the hill toward my apartment.

I need to figure out what I want to do. What I want to do that doesn't turn me into a horrible person.

Because getting married doesn't automatically make you a great person either. It would prevent me from using Hal in one way while effectively opening the door on an entirely new world of nastiness. I can't commit adultery until the minute I'm married, for example. What would the Shadow become if I had the option of breaking not a boyfriend's heart, but a husband's? What about scorn? What about boredom?

No, that's not what I want, either. I want it my way. All the time. A boyfriend when I want company and no boyfriend when I want to do my own thing.

I slip my hands into my jean pockets and find a crescent wrench and a nut I forgot to put away. Not a big deal, but it that's how distracted I was. Tools need to go where they belong. Leaving them lying around is just not professional.

I hate this. It's all Hal's fault. I could deal with my mother breathing down my neck. It's his breath down my neck that's changing everything. I've got a great job, a great apartment, a great life—why am I even considering monkeying with all this? Because Hal's funny and sweet and detailed but flexible and because he makes me feel safe and sometimes he lets me bring out the kid in him. Because he says he loves me and I don't want to disappoint him. Because I love him too, and I don't want to be disappointed.

I hate him. I wish I'd never looked into his eyes and wanted to look at them again. I wish I'd never brought brownies to the coffee hour and met him last January. Then I'd be out shooting pool with Francisco and seeing movies with the pizza guy, and I'd never have met the Shadow, and I wouldn't be on my way back to my apartment to take a long shower and hope it melts me like ungelled Jell-O and washes me down the drain.

And who knows?—maybe there's a message on the voicemail saying *Lee, you're a cocktease and there's no way I can deal with that avenging angel of yours. Have a nice life.*

There won't be. It's never that easy. If there's a message, bet me it says, *Lee, give me a call when you get back. I kind of want to talk with you, if it's okay.*

Before I talk to anyone, though, I want to stand in the shower, steam billowing around me and obscuring the mirrors and fogging the doorknob and the metal handle on the toilet. For once, I have no idea what's about to happen, and it's not more exciting this way.

Chapter Eighteen

Relationships are bulky things

There is, as it turns out, a message on my voicemail: *Lee, I shouldn't have gotten angry at you. Give me a call when you get back. We need to talk.*

I take my shower. I pray. I hear nothing from either God or Bucky. I toast two frozen waffles and dub them dinner. I call Hal. He promises he won't touch me if I come over, but he wants to see me at his apartment. So now here I am, walking to Seventh Avenue.

I haven't spoken to Bucky since he told me to figure things out. Anything I say will be met with "Have you thought it through?" and if I ask his advice, I'm going to get a snide remark about oh, did my cellular prayer connection run out of minutes *again*, and who needs that?

Despite my silence, I get a prompt from him.

I shove my hands in my pockets. "What?"

Do I want to hear a story?

"Not if it ends with the prince and the princess living happily ever after."

I don't care if other people on the street hear me talking to myself. We're in New York. I'd have to be shouting in three different languages before heads turned.

Inside I feel Bucky indicate the story doesn't necessarily end with "happily ever after."

I incline my head and open my hands.

Back a long time ago, before Eden, before God made the Earth, God made the Heavens and the morning stars, all the angels in one gush of love. In my heart, it's the ferocity of water blasting from an open fire hydrant on a scorching July afternoon, cold and clean, white-frothed and welcome even as it's unexpected and perhaps unnecessary.

I can't help it: I'm smiling.

Next, a song; it's a union and a recognition, joy and fascination, the discovery of oneself as existing at all even as one realizes that the other voices are other selves, the realization that oneself has a name and is singular and is loved for that singularity. Amazement, a pledge, a raising of the eyes to see what it is that poured one forth like water into the silent dryness of a previously empty creation—then even further amazement to meet the eyes of the One who has done the pouring-forth, the laughter—

Without breaking stride, I find myself beaming with the unbridled delight of Bucky being born.

Unbidden, details swirl in my mind. I can't see them because I don't think Bucky *saw* them himself; more that I recognize personalities and presences, facets of character. Impressions of sounds and colors, of a song unbroken from the start of time, of a rushing like wind. It all passes through me too quickly to name, too much to remember between one step and the next. I stop, overwhelmed.

Sorry, Bucky sends.

Don't be. I never asked Bucky what it's like to process the world without aid of your senses.

As I resume walking, Bucky unfolds the next part of the story. It's a question mark.

Puzzled, I frown while waiting for the light to change so I can cross Sixth Avenue toward Seventh.

Bucky repeats the sense of the question mark.

I need more help than that.

There's a sense of Bucky struggling to put it into words. It was a test, but not quite posed as a test. More like a sifting. *Afterward, we called it the Winnowing.* I get a sense of trying to figure out what floats and what sinks, or rather what is willing to fly and what falls.

Yeah, that helped. *I still don't understand.*

After a third attempt at giving me the question with impressions, Bucky sends a burst of words: *Will you love me?* And following that, *Yes.*

"Okay," I say slowly.

Next, a sense of the angels all arranged in spheres, connected one with another and all at attention toward the Creator at the center. The connections hold them like a web, both vertical and horizontal, uniting them to one another and making them known even as they knew.

Another burst of words: *Will you help one another?*

The assent that follows this question is more tentative, but still strong. For the first time I sense a hierarchy: many of the other creatures exist with not all the powers of oneself, not the same clear perception. Clearly they will need help to become like oneself...but also, it's possible to gaze closer to the center to behold greater creatures, creatures possessing more joy or more splendor, and they are expected to issue their help downward as well.

I fold my arms uncomfortably. *That doesn't seem right.*

Like it or not, all angels are not created equal any more than all humans are created equal in their intelligence, ability, understanding, and circumstances. It's possible to sort us and rank us.

I shiver. *But God loves us all.*

I never said He doesn't. Bucky chuckles. *Were you there? If so, I don't have to finish this story.*

What follows is a very forceful question mark. It carries a feeling of dismay, confusion, and wrongness.

I don't understand again.

Bucky doesn't answer at first. There's only that sense of a universe inverted, the rose of the angels turned inside out.

I wait. He feels shaken, almost disbelieving.

What happened, Bucky?

Whatever it is, it rivets him with a fear of what could have been. Worse still, at the base of it all, he's got an unanswered question of why God would have asked this question in the first place.

Bucky?

Then comes a story within the story: God intends to create something else, something beneath the very lowest of the lowest order of angels (of which I realize with a shock, Bucky is a member—he's a member of the ninth of the nine orders!). God's going to create Matter.

From the angels: a sense of fascination. I can imagine Bucky being delighted by anything God might have decided to do, and I smile as I anticipate his first reaction to my future existence.

But instead he sends a negative. I wait it out.

I have no idea how much time passes in this story, but I feel galaxies created, angels playing with subatomic particles and gravity wells. But later, something else: matter that reacts to other matter. Matter that self-replicates.

Life. God created life.

Now from Bucky I read a sense similar to mine on finding out Corinne was pregnant with Avery, or how I used to feel with my hands pressed against the glass at the pet store window, smiling at the kittens as they tumbled.

And later— How much time passed between those second and third questions? I can't tell, only I get a sense of change, of species come and gone and the universe transforming. *And then He said— He said He would* breathe Himself into these creatures to make them like us, to give them free will and self-awareness and intelligence. But that meant—

Bucky shivers inside me, a tension that leaves my stomach queasy. My fingertips go numb.

But that meant the Eternal would be trapped in the changeable, and that the immortal would be clogged with decay, and for what? Compared to the angels, these beings would be blind, deaf, paralyzed, dependent.

My throat tightens.

But He still expected us to love the bits of Him where He was buried in all that. Those little shreds of Him would be crippled. He wouldn't be— It was completely and absolutely wrong, only He was asking, and—

"But if God wanted it," I whisper.

But to give animals the gift of moral decision-making— It would almost have been palatable if He'd given it to galaxies, or even stars, tremendous creations all the angels already found beautiful. But to bestow it on self-replicating meat on a nondescript rock orbiting a small star...? Shouldn't something that wonderful be in a place of value? Shouldn't it last forever?

He's shaken.

And after all that—how many of those ensouled animals would live their entire lives without recognizing the gift God gave them in letting them choose who they wanted to become? Or even realze that they could choose between good and evil? And how many times would that gift be wasted because the souls don't recognize that what God gave in that one first holy Breath is the most precious thing of all?

A car alarm sounds from a couple of blocks away. "Stop," I whisper. I'm nauseated and I want to run, but where can I run? "Don't tell me anymore. I don't want you to feel like this—"

But the point is, Bucky insists, *we'd already promised to love Him forever. We'd promised to help one another, to help those less than ourselves. And what He was asking now was to love pieces of Him in this crippled condition, to help Him as if He were helpless.*

I stumble. I'm dizzy. It's coming from him.

And I asked myself— I had to ask, am I going to hold to my first and second promises? I didn't want to. I wanted to refuse, to say God should be at the top of creation and not lying scattered around the bottom. He should be stronger and smarter than all the things He made, not stupider and weaker. God should take care of me, not me of Him.

Bucky gathers himself. *But what it came down to was that I promised the first two times, and that's the only thing that made me say yes the third time.*

"But not all of them did," I whisper.

Within me, a heartbreaking hollow.

I get a sense of a shrieking protest, disgust with order turned upside-down, a question of God's own sanity and His right to rule over His own creations if He was only going to bestow an incalculable gift on something so disgusting. And Revelation is right: a war does break out in Heaven, but first a war broke out within each individual angel, and that was the bloodiest battlefield in all eternity.

My voice is thready. "I'm so sorry."

We're across the street from Hal's place now, and I'm waiting to cross Seventh Avenue. A bus belches out a cloud of exhaust thick enough to walk on.

Why was Bucky telling me this? Why now?

I frame the question with my lips, not voicing it while surrounded by other pedestrians.

I wanted you to know before you see Hal. He pauses. *I wanted to make sure you knew what you've been entrusted with: the freedom to form your Self, your*

Identity. That's what the Shadow wants to destroy. If she can destroy that, then she spits in the face of God.

I'm cold. But it makes sense.

You need to know the value of a promise. How keeping a promise sometimes can make the impossible very much a possibility. And equally, sometimes breaking a promise can destroy the thing you wanted in the first place.

Three minutes later. Outside the Clockworks, I'm still not quite ready to press the button so Hal can buzz me in.

I turn my thoughts toward Bucky. *Why am I even here? What are we supposed to talk about?*

Bucky's voice in my head says, *If you marry Hal today, you can have sex tonight.*

I roll my eyes. *Don't you normally take a longer-term view of things than that?* Then I pause. *We could have sex tomorrow night, too.*

See? Bucky replies. *You should think through all the possibilities.*

Hmm. Maybe I should walk around the block to figure out what I want to happen when we meet.

Maybe I should have gotten my act together quicker, because the door opens and Hal startles when he sees me. "Oh—good timing. I figured I'd wait for you out here."

"Yeah, well—" I offer a smile. "Here I am."

He ushers me inside. He didn't want to talk with me in the café we go to sometimes for dessert. Whatever this is going to be, it's Serious and Relationship-Changing.

We're silent in the elevator.

I've always loved dating, but I realized quickly it's different to be in a Relationship. Relationships are bulky things to be hefted awkwardly between two people, like a portage with a canoe over your head. If a date doesn't work out, you call and cancel the next one. You can't call and cancel a relationship. *Hi, it's me. You know, I checked my calendar, and that relationship isn't going to work out. Yeah, bummer. Later!*

We're nearly at his door before he takes my hand and squeezes. Timidly, I return it.

As soon as we're in his condo, he clicks the door quietly, and without looking away from the lock, says, "Are you angry at me?"

"No." Why would he think that? "Are you angry at me?"

"Not anymore." He turns. "I made decaf."

Of course he made decaf. He also has the rest of the cookies (don't say *of course*—at this point, I wouldn't) so I pull up a stool to the island and watch him pour steaming blackness into cups, then sugar and milk the way I like it. He hands my mug to me and keeps his in front of him. He doesn't take a seat.

Someone has to say something, and I'm tired of fiddling with the paper napkin. "I played it back in my head, and I realized you saw Bucky."

"I didn't see anything." Frowning, Hal looks up. "But I felt something."

I cradle the cup in my palms. "So you finally had an experience of an angel."

"One I could have done without. It still keeps ringing in my head."

"You did kind of pop the top on a can of Angry Guardian."

"I'd never have guessed." Staring at his hands, he says, "I'm sorry about before. You seemed willing, and I let myself get carried away, but you had every right to say no."

I disengage one hand from my mug to touch his fingertips. We endure a long silence, an awkwardness between us that hasn't been there since February.

I swallow. "I love you."

He looks up with a pain I haven't seen in an equally long time.

It's come to this, then, hasn't it? "I love you," I repeat softer, because in the next moment, he's going to take steps to ensure he never has to hear me say it again. But I don't want that to happen. I've been dumped before. But not like this.

Hal says, "Lie to me."

My eyebrows go up. "Lie to you?"

He nods. "Please. Just lie to me."

I have no idea what he wants me to say. Although maybe he wants me to remind him what a jerk I was so he has justification to dump me. It's the least I can do for him. "Um... I work as a physical trainer?"

He smiles as if I've surprised him. "Go on."

Okay, so it's a guessing game. "I didn't like meeting your parents?"

He nods.

That wasn't the magic phrase either. He has something in mind, and I don't feel like wasting our remaining hours attempting telepathy. *Bucky, what does he want?*

I suspect he wants you to lie to him.

Thanks ever *so much.*

I turn my attention back to Hal. "What do you want me to tell you?"

He looks down. "I just wanted you to lie to me."

Oh. *Oh.*

He just wants to hear me say it.

I've reduced the napkin to a thousand shredlets that might continue inhabiting this kitchen longer than I will.

My heart is beating so fast it hurts. "There's no way on Earth I could marry you."

He looks up, shocked.

My cheeks heat up, but there's no way to hide my face. "I haven't been bothered by the question every time someone brings it up. I haven't even given it a second thought."

He's looking rattled. My voice trembles. "Your turn. Lie to me."

"I hate cooking for you." As he speaks, his eyes sharpen in intensity. "Things can continue as they are indefinitely for all I care. I don't despise your mother."

I sit back. "What?"

His eyes have a coldness I've seen only once before. "Because she hasn't driven you into a corner. Sometimes I especially love you because you haven't allowed her to define your life."

Before he can go on, I blurt, "There's no way I can see myself married to you."

He stops in his tracks long enough for me to add, "I want to run around forever."

"Are you kidding?" He's put down his coffee cup. "I'm confused. Are we still lying to each other?"

About to reply, I realize there's really no way to answer that question honestly, and I break up giggling.

Brow furrowed, he steps closer to me. "It would never work."

Biting my lip, I stare at the coffee. "It would be extremely easy."

"I've hated the last seven months," Hal whispers, "and there's every reason to assume we'd both hate the rest of our lives together the same way."

Shaking my head, I say, "I can't... Sometimes... Crud, I don't know how to reverse this."

Hal says, "Straight-up, then."

I fish in my pocket, past the crescent wrench to the nut at the bottom. It's pretty large; I take his hand and put it on his ring finger. "Would you marry someone who can't stick with the same long distance company for six months?"

When I finally meet his eyes, he's beaming. It hurts. I have no idea what I'm doing.

He says, "I don't have—oh, wait." A nearby drawer yields a set of measuring spoons. He winds off the ring that holds them all together and slips it on my left hand. "Would you marry a guy who thinks Friday night will always be pizza night?"

It's like I'm a train on a track. I nod. He hugs me for a long time while I sit on the stool, my face buried in his shoulder.

When he lets me go, I give him a sad look. "Aren't you supposed to kiss someone after you propose?"

"Only if you haven't promised her annoyed guardian that you won't."

Inside: a chuckle.

"He releases you from that—"

I don't get the last word out before Hal seals the deal with a kiss. And like that, we're engaged.

Chapter Nineteen

A poofy gown with a train three miles long

Personal days. They never made sense to me, since technically whenever you're *sick* it's also *personal*. Companies don't offer group sick days for the whole legal department to have a cough. Regardless, Hal takes a personal day. I just call Max and tell him he may, *may*, see me after noon if he's lucky. And I meet Hal for breakfast at a delightful café that's delighted to overcharge us for croissants.

I look like five miles of rough road because I didn't get a lot of continuous sleep. Hal, on the other hand, looks thrilled to see me, and he can't keep his hand off mine the whole time.

We're engaged. It's our secret.

"I took off the 'ring,'" he says while we're waiting in line for caffeine and carbs smothered in fat. "I hope you don't mind."

I'm still wearing mine. "I didn't think it was a permanent fixture."

He squeezes my hand. "I have to get you something real."

"Please, don't. Think what I do with my hands all day." I shiver. "Gold plus electricity means five hundred degrees in about half a second."

He looks puzzled. "You need something."

"We need to talk." But then it's our turn to order and we don't say anything else.

I should be deciding between a chocolate or cinnamon croissant, but instead I keep wondering if this is really happening, if I'm at breakfast with a future-husband, or if this is all just a big game of pretend.

From opposite ends of the counter, though we're shooting looks at one another with hidden smiles. We're engaged. It's our secret. No one notices the spoon ring on my finger, or if they do, they must think it's just me having no fashion sense. They'd be right.

We eat our breakfast while walking through Prospect Park.

I have a great idea. "We should buy you a bike. We can go biking together." It's easier to think about biking together than living together, paying the bills together. "When was the last time you owned a bike?"

"College," he says. "Not since."

I don't reply.

"You're having second thoughts?" Hal says softly.

"I'm actually dreading having to tell my mother. She's going to be a living nightmare." He squeezes my hand. "She's going to steamroll every aspect of planning. She already tried to book us a reception site and picked out my maid of honor."

"You're hardly going to be a bridezilla." Hal chuckles. "She might as well let you decide on your own attendants."

"I just want it done soon. Every minute between when we tell her and when we get married is going to be torture."

Hal shrugs. "So don't tell her."

I stop in my tracks.

"Why does your mother need to know? We're paying for the wedding ourselves, so tell her on the morning of. Maybe the week before so she can clear her calendar."

Hal's eyes are mischievous in the autumn sunlight. "Let her hassle you about getting engaged while we work out details like when, where, what you're wearing—"

I groan. "Oh, man. Dress shopping. She's going to want a poofy gown with a train three miles long." I gasp. "No, wait. I bet she has her own wedding gown preserved and she expects me to wear."

Hal leans close. "Bet me she wants to wear it herself."

I burst out laughing.

We walk the curving pathways toward a playpark. Kids shriek as they run. I pause at the chain link fence and watch the mothers on the park benches.

"Here's the deal." Hal sounds just like the guy you'd want doing your taxes: rock-steady and totally not worried about limousines. "If you want, we can be married by a JP by close of business tomorrow."

I blink. "That's a bit fast."

"It's also a bit unsatisfying." He shakes his head. "That's the most practical, least satisfying option. On the opposite extreme is the two-year engagement culminating in the Big White Wedding at a cathedral, complete with two limousines, twelve attendants, and a string quartet during our five-hour reception."

"That's also a bit unsatisfying." I shake my head. "Let's do something different."

"See, I knew you'd say that." Hal pulls out his iPhone. "I have an idea."

I gasp. "A friend of mine sent a Christmas card last year saying she got married on a cruise ship. We could do that."

"We could—"

"Or Vegas!" I bounce on my toes. "We could fly to Vegas and get married by an Elvis impersonator singing *You Ain't Nothing But A Hound Dog!*"

"That too," Hal says, "but I was thinking—"

"Skydiving!" I'm all ashiver. "There's this place where they teach you to jump out of an airplane and a minister marries you on the way down."

Hal watches me with a worried look. "Are you quite all right in the head?"

I think you'd better listen, Bucky says. *I've looked at his iPhone, and you'll be interested in what he's got there.*

"You're double-teaming me," I mutter.

Hal breaks into a grin. "Oh, Bucky agrees skydiving is out of the question?"

Actually, I love skydiving, but I'm immaterial, so I don't have to worry about the skills of the parachute-packer.

Hush. I squint at Hal. "Okay, tell me your idea of immeasurable brilliance."

And oh gosh, is it ever brilliant.

As far as ideas go, Hal's is going to get me in five times more trouble with my mother than eloping to be married by an Elvis impersonator while skydiving onto a Caribbean cruise liner.

Deadline: two weeks.

Modus Operandi: bait and switch.

Cost: Very little.

Overhead: Not so much.

Surprise factor: Tremendous.

Bucky: Approves.

In all actuality, I'm stressing more than I have to. I tell myself that several times a minute while I sit, ramrod-straight, at the edge of my chair in the priest's office at the rectory. I clutch my travel mug of coffee as if it's my only lifeline before plummeting over the side of the Grand Canyon.

"Relax a bit." Hal touches my arm, and I jump. "You've seen Father Dan. He's unlikely to kill us."

That almost wouldn't be too bad. For one thing, it would completely solve the whole issue of me having second thoughts. I might even be considered a martyr. On the other hand, it would mean I'd never go ice fishing, and that would be a shame.

Father Dan comes into the office. "Relax," he tells me immediately. Hal hands him a plate of his homemade cookies, with proper thank-yous from the priest, who then insists I eat one. "You need some chocolate."

Father Dan says, "So, what's going on?"

Hal says, "Yesterday we got engaged, and we want to talk to you about getting married."

I'm sure it's a good sign that my vision blacked out when Hal said that, right? It indicates I'm a blushing bride.

The priest offers a beaming congratulations, and then Hal says, "We were wondering if you could do it two weeks from now."

Father Dan's eyebrows raise. "Are you getting married because of an unexpected pregnancy?"

I startle myself by laughing out loud. "No! We're not even— No!"

Hal grins. "We want to do this as a surprise. Gather her family and mine, and then bring everyone upstairs and have a wedding."

Father Dan leans back in his chair. "They disapprove?"

Despite jumping to all the obvious conclusions, he's batting negative one thousand. "Oh, they approve. My mother is going to be a bit...aggressive."

Father Dan chuckles. "It would be highly irregular to waive the normal waiting period and the standard premarital counseling. Planning the wedding is actually the first way a couple stakes out their individuality from their families of origin. How bad could it—"

Then he stops. He stops cold.

Is it my imagination, or are the good Father's hands trembling? He opens a desk drawer and takes out a day planner (actually he drops it twice) then flips back pages until he whitens. His voice rasps, "Lee Singer? Is your given name actually *Juliet* Singer?"

We both nod.

"I understand," he whispers. "Your mother called in mid-July and we...talked. You want this done in two weeks?"

I guess I owe my mother a debt of thanks. Again.

The short form is this: Hal wants to invite both our families to the church hall for a lunch or dinner. After the meal, surprise! We get married.

"And I won't have to talk to your mother again?" ventures a tremulous Father Dan.

Hal mutters, "Not unless you administer last rites because she dies of shock," and I swat him on the arm saying, "No, no, you won't have to talk to her."

The priest pulls out a stack of forms and clicks a pen. "Then let's get this started."

As it turns out, we have a couple of assignments, and the priest is going to waive a few requirements. We're supposed to have premarital counseling: he cancels his next appointment so he can do that right now. Hal will have to obtain a copy of his baptismal certificate. We won't have our names printed in the bulletin. Father Dan calls it a "Church elopement." Hal calls it "a surprise wedding."

And now for our premarital counseling, conducted by an unmarried celibate because that's the way pretty much everything goes in my life. He starts with, "There are no right or wrong answers."

Of course there aren't. That's why so many marriages suffer a head-on crash that totals both vehicles and ends in a six-foot high stack of paperwork.

Why are you getting married?

Neither of us answers at first. Father Dan looks up and I say, "I lost a bet?" even as Hal says, "Fraternity hazing."

"Really bad drug interactions?" I suggest.

Hal says, "Tax benefits. Loads of them."

"And it's cheaper than enrolling in the Witness Protection Program."

The priest snickers. "You two deserve each other. Why are you getting married in the Church?"

I say, "Because if you're not making a promise like that in front of God, then you're just signing a contract, and what's the point?"

"Good answer." Ah, no right or wrong answers, but apparently you can have good and bad ones. Or funny ones. He says to me, "Do you know what you'll have to agree to in order to have a Catholic marriage?"

I say, "Do I have to become Catholic?"

He shakes his head. "We'd love to have you, but no. Your children have to be raised Catholic, though, and you have to be open to children. Also, you can't go into the marriage intending to get divorced if things don't work out."

My brow furrows. "Does it count as having children if I'm the one who's immature?"

The priest spells it out then: "No artificial birth control."

Oh! Well, this is going to get interesting in a hurry. Hal says, "Um...not everyone does that."

I shake my head. "If we're doing this, we're all in. Fifty kids, here we come!"

"You don't have to have fifty kids." Father Dan hands me pink pamphlet that says "Natural Family Planning" and has a picture of a couple rocking tasteful late-seventies haircuts. Inside, though, they substitute the script font for charts, graphs, and statistical analyses.

"Oh my gosh," I whisper. "These are uterine specs!"

Father Dan looks aghast.

Hal says, "You just gave her a new machine to learn about, and she's living in it. Ignore her."

"No, look at this," I say. "Estrogen...progesterone... Luteinizing hormone and follicular-stimulating hormone and a bunch of other bits! Why didn't anyone ever tell me this stuff?"

Hal squeezes my hand. "Later."

Father Dan says, "What's the purpose of marriage?"

Hal says, "Companionship? Children?"

Still paging through my pamphlet, I say, "The salvation of our souls."

Hal breaks off and stares. "Really?"

Father Dan makes a mark on his info sheet. "Are you sure you don't want to become Catholic?"

Hal chuckles. "Where'd you pick that up?"

"Bucky told me." Then I start giggling.

Hal gives my arm a squeeze. "No fair cheating."

"Not now, you goober." I take his hand in my two and clasp it tight. "He said that's why it's a nontrivial thing."

You've learned well, Grasshopper.

I stifle a laugh. The priest keeps talking, but I can feel what Bucky's telling me: that we're okay. That this is okay, and while it might not be easy, we've got all the help we need right here, right in our families, right in our hearts, because while I have my hand in Hal's, we both have our free hands in God's hands, and nothing can break that circle.

Just before we leave, Father Dan hands us a pair of booklets one for Hal, one for me, in tasteful colors to match our genders. "I'm supposed to give you these information guidelines for marrying couples."

Oh—they're manuals! Like Chilton's for a husband. But how do they know what model guy I have? I mean, there are a lot of different kinds of guys out there.* How do they know if Hal is a stable, realistic guy, or a thrill-seeker or a dreamer with his head in the clouds? Shouldn't there be a different kind of manual for every kind of guy there is?

And who knows, maybe there is a different manual for every guy; it's in the heart of one woman somewhere on Earth, and the key is finding the person whose specs you have written inside.

And now I can't escape the planning. Hal forces me to have lunch with him at the jazz bistro while he lists everything we need so we can pull off our scheme. We have eleven days to plan, and on the twelfth day, it had better all come together.

"Don't worry about the details," the priest told Hal when he started to ask too many questions. "As long as at the end of the day you're married, it was a success."

Married? I wanted to scream. I'm going to be *married?*

Hal wants to talk about food, and I only can sit here weaving my fingers into a basket because I'm going to get *married.*

On the list there are things he needs to do, things I need to do, and things we need to do together. At the bottom of the page, he has written out questions we need to decide. The first is which car we're going to keep (no!) and where we're going to live (me moving in with him) and

---

* *Believe me, if you'll believe anyone.*

whether we're going to rope anyone else into the planning phase. Things like how we're going to get people to attend this wedding without letting it slip.

"Vegas is sounding better." My voice breaks. "It doesn't have to be an Elvis impersonator."

Hal jots down something about rolls.

"We could see the shows. We don't have to play the slot machines although really, when you think about it, isn't it insane to begin your marriage in a place where people gamble? Wouldn't you want your marriage to be a sure thing, not a gamble?"

He looks up. "I think you need more coffee. You're not tense enough."

I'm flagging the waitress before I realize he was probably joking.

You are kind of anxious, Bucky sends.

Why shouldn't I be anxious? I'm talking with Hal about *getting married*—getting married *to him*—and Bucky wants me to be calm?

The waitress pours coffee right to the top so it's in danger of sloshing over the sides as my hands tremble. "What about a pirate theme? I can do pirates."

"Here." He pulls off a sheet of paper from the pad and angles it around so we're both looking at it cross-wise. "We need to decide on a guest list. Once we have that, we can invite them so they actually show up, and we'll know how much food to prepare."

Nice practical details there. "Pretty much my mother, my brothers and their families."

"Plus Beth, and if Beth comes, Stuart comes too." He's making notes. "On my side, my mother and father, my sister and her family, and my brother."

"Date for him?" I say.

"Even if he's dating someone, that's not a social unit, trust me." He snickers. "Besides, if we say, 'and bring a guest for the pest,' they'll know something's up."

He calculates, and we're at twenty-five people.

"Oh!" I sit up. "My Uncle Mickey and Aunt Mary."

He grins as he jots them down. "Not a problem."

I frown. "Do I need someone to walk me down the aisle?"

Still writing, he shrugs. "Have Bucky do it. I don't even know if we'll have an aisle. Oh, you know, we'll have to invite Father Dan, or at least have enough food for him."

Bucky puts into my head, *You didn't invite me.*

You're a social unit with me. Or so you keep saying.

And that, my friends, is our guest list. Hal adds me and him into the head count (I hope I'm not a no-show—that would be embarrassing) and we've got thirty people.

Armed with a number, Hal compiles a menu with the ease of someone who knows exactly what thirty people consume. According to him, lasagna would be easy, chicken florentine would be easy, we could toss together a salad, we'll have a mountain of Italian bread, plus this many bottles of soda and juice and a couple of flats of bottled water. It's astonishing how quickly he dreams up appetizers and sides that can be prepared ahead of time and heated in the church kitchen.

"We're going to be doing a lot of running around." I rub my chin. "Maybe we should have it catered."

Aghast, Hal looks up. "No!"

And I can't help it—I break up in giggles because even if we flew over a French chef with a five-star *Michelin Guide* rating, he's reacted exactly as I would have if he suggested an oil change at Jiffy Lube. So I sit back to let him plan the food.

While he's tinkering with the menu, I pull over the list of things to do. In order to get married, we have to:

- get a marriage license
- get wedding rings
- move some of my stuff to his condo
- talk to the Clockworks about parking my Acura
- pick out readings for the wedding
- print announcements to send afterward
- possibly get a picture taken to include with announcements

Where does he get these ideas? Is that what you do when your family has money and isn't afraid to spend it? On the other hand, maybe I've never seen wedding announcements because no one I know has ever eloped.

Eloped. Wow. I'm going to get married.

"You wrote 'rings.'" I tap the list. "You want one too?"

He nods.

"I'll take a couple hours for lunch and meet you in Manhattan."

"Let's get the license at the same time." He sits back. "It would ruin the surprise if you show up to this thing with an overnight bag, so we'll move you for real afterward. Until your lease is up, you can bring things piecemeal."

Beth needs to look for a roommate, but three months should be enough time to find someone.

I look at his personal list of things to take care of. "You're renting a tuxedo?" I grin. "Chicks dig guys in tuxedos."

He flushes. "It seems better than getting married in work clothes. Anyhow, we should match."

That's when my heart stops.

I need a wedding dress.

I need a wedding dress.

This is awful. I need a wedding dress.

Okay, so it's not that bad. Since it's a surprise, I don't need the full regalia with a crown of daisies. It just needs to be a dress. Hal says to make his relatives happy, it should be white. And to make my own mother happy, it darn well better be white.

I'm in trouble. On the best day of my life, I have trouble shopping for jeans, let alone buying a wedding gown. I'm doomed. Doomed.

I'm not going to think about it. Instead will go to work, fix cars, and figure out where to stash a wedding ring all day while I stick my hands into engines. Other mechanics say their key rings work fine. Leave the ring on your hand and you stand a pretty good chance of leaving your finger in an engine or just stripping off all the flesh right down to the bone. Although even that sounds good compared to wedding-dress shopping.

That night, I return to my apartment to make phone calls.

Beth is on the computer in the living room, so I call from the kitchen. First it's my mom. She's not home yet. I phone Randy instead.

I get Corinne. I run it by her like this: "Hal and I were wondering if you could come for dinner—all five of you—the Saturday after next."

Sure, she says, but adds that they're quite a crew.

"It's going to be a lot of people, actually." My heart hammers. If I can't handle inviting Corinne, how am I going invite my mother? It's a struggle to keep my voice steady. "You know how Hal loves to cook. Well, he wanted to try out a new recipe for everyone, and—"

Bucky appears, his eyes dark.

"Hold on." I lower down the phone. "What?"

"Remember you said you didn't want to start a marriage with a gamble?" He opens his hands. "Don't start it with a lie either."

"I started the relationship with a lie."

"Oh." Bucky raises his eyes to Heaven. "That makes everything perfectly fine. My mistake. Carry on."

He vanishes. "Jerk," I mutter. I get back on the phone with Corinne. "Okay, the truth is, Hal suggested getting both sides of the family together for a big dinner."

Then I have to yank the phone from my ear to avoid permanent damage from the way Corinne screams.

"Corinne, don't read too much into it."

"This is terrific!" she's babbling. "You can bet we'll all be there. What can we bring?"

Hal decreed that if anyone offered to bring food, we must shut them down. We're not having a pot-luck reception for our own wedding; how tacky would that be? After I've finally convinced her it's a point of honor with Hal to feed everyone only food he's made himself from scratch, that he's even now tilling the wheat to grind into flour to bake into bread, she relents. But they'll be there, she insists.

One down, five to go.

My other two brothers react with less enthusiasm, but they agree because they're guys and guys know better than to turn down free food.

Now for my mother.

"Lee! I'm so glad you called!" My heart cringes. It is entirely possible she has five bridesmaids' dresses laid out on her bed, ready for me to pick women to fit. *"Now dear, don't get stubborn on me. You just have to make two friends who are a size eight, one who's a size six, and two who are size ten. Make sure they look good in coral.*"

My voice wavers. "We...Hal and I wanted to invite you to come to dinner a week from Saturday."

She gasps. "He's going to ask for your hand in marriage!"

"What?" I blink. "Do people do that nowadays?"

"Of course! A proper gentleman approaches a lady's parents for permission to marry."

This is a revolting development. Does it matter that I'm hardly a lady?

"It's not just you, though." I wish my cell had a cord I could wrap around my finger as I pace the dining room. "He wants our families to meet."

I endure a long, deep silence from my mother. She must have figured it out.

She says at last, her voice a cathedral hush, "He's going to propose."

Well, she figured out *something*.

My mother starts planning what she should wear, whether she should hire a videographer (gee, should we do that? Wouldn't normal people think it odd to video a dinner?) and then she says, "You need to shop for a new outfit."

I'd rather chew ground glass.

"It has to be tasteful but alluring, and just a bit romantic. I'll go with you to make sure—"

Bucky!

Praying.

She pauses mid-sentence. "You know what? I'll take you to that place you've had such good luck with before."

My eyes are wide as golf balls. "I really don't think—"

"I want to do this." She's in drill sergeant mode. Actually, drill sergeants take lessons from Mom. "He's going to propose, and we need to make sure he does it right."

Dear God, I pray, *please don't let this happen.*

Honor your mother, Bucky says.

I glare at him. *Don't trot that out at me.*

I'm not trotting it out. I was told to tell you to honor your mother. I'm telling you. Honor your mother.

So I honor my mother, and before I'm off the phone, my mother has ramrodded her way into my Tuesday. We're going shopping, and then we're going to have dinner together. Just a mother and a daughter and an ulcer.

As I sink into a chair, I find Beth, puzzled, in the doorway.

"What's this all about?"

"My mother." I put my head in my hands, then look up. "Hey, can you and Stuart come to dinner the Saturday after next? Hal's cooking."

"Sure, ply me with free food and I'm available." She takes a seat. "Here or there?"

"Church hall. He wants both of our families, and I need you to protect me."

That's the first moment someone sees right through the plan. Beth stares into me, and I shrink inside.

Slowly she says, "I'll make sure Stuart comes too."

"Thanks." I swallow. "You know, free food."

"Cake too?"

Hal spent fifteen minutes planning the cake. Yes, there will be cake.

Beth stares at the tabletop.

"You've been a good roommate," she finally says, and then she leaves for her room.

"Hey, Uncle Mickey!" A pause as he recognizes my voice and we exchange pleasantries. "Have you got a minute?"

As it turns out, he does. "I hope you're not calling to tell me you finally destroyed my car."

"The State of New York says it's *my* car, because of that whole purchase and sales agreement and the way you transferred the title to me." I'm lying on the living room futon with my feet up on the back. "I just tuned it up yesterday. She runs like a dream."

Cripes, was that really yesterday?

"One of those bumpy dreams, like you have sleeping on a bus." Uncle Mickey laughs. "If you're not calling to invite me to the car's funeral, then what is it?"

Ouch! That was a little too close for comfort. "I was wondering if I could have you and Aunt Mary come for dinner a week from Saturday." I've gotten very used to saying it by now. "Hal wants to get both sides of the family together, and it would mean a lot to me if you could come."

Uncle Mickey says, "I have tickets to a Yankee game a week from Saturday."

My heart bottoms out.

"It sounds interesting, but I'm afraid I'll have to pass."

"Oh."

I can't think of what to say. In my plan, everyone was supposed to have one hand on the phone, pining for a social engagement. Not have their own lives.

"Are you sure?"

He says, "It's the Red Sox. A huge game."

More silence.

"I'm sorry. I didn't realize you wanted me there."

"I really kind of did." I don't think we can change the date now. "Could you exchange the tickets?"

Uncle Mickey says, "It's that important to you?"

"I'm sorry. I shouldn't have asked that. That was rude." My voice is way down. "You should go to the game."

"No. We'll be there." He sounds sweet. "There's a guy at the office who would give me a kidney for those tickets, and we'll be there for you."

Chapter Twenty:

The Magic Word: Cash.

Tuesday morning, I give a once over to Hartman's Maxima. (Gosh, there's a pun in there somewhere with those AX sounds in "Maxima" and "axle," but I can't make one stick, and neither can Bucky. I think I've found one of my life's regrets.) We've done everything insurance will pay for (and I've done a couple of things they wouldn't pay for if they knew, but they don't) and we've also had our local body-shop guy come check out the frame. The car's good to go.

So I grab the shop vac and start cleaning out the car. I want Hartman to feel as happy about this car as I do right now, and since the front half of the car is all pretty much new, the inside should shine.

Dashboard: dusted. Windows: washed. Carpet: vacuumed.

And under the seat: screwed.

I don't even move my hand. That's metal. Heavy metal. "Max!" I call. "I want you over here! Now!"

Tim trails Max over to me. I say, "I want you as my witness." And from under the front seat, I slide out a handgun.

It's tiny. On TV they're always these huge heavy things, but this one would fit in your palm, and it's got a pearly white handle. If it weren't so solid, I'd think it was a toy.

I don't know a single thing about handguns except they go 'bang' and you want to avoid the barrel end. Tim, on the other hand, reaches around me and picks up the thing. He slides a bar around, then unloads it of one bullet and sets it back on the front seat. He around the car and puts the remaining bullet in the glove box.

"Thanks," I manage.

Tim grunts at me.

I fold my arms. "Do we call the cops?"

"No," Max snaps. "We leave it here for the customer and we do not ask why he keeps a loaded gun in his vehicle."

"Maybe we should ask why he didn't tell us he had a loaded gun in his vehicle?" I gesture outside. "What if I'd parked the car in the sun and it got hot?"

"Bullets won't explode until at least three hundred degrees." Max shakes his head. "You weren't in any danger unless you shot yourself."

Looking up, Tim says, "Which she could have if she'd grabbed that gun not knowing it was there. That's a Derringer .22. They've got a bad reputation for going off by accident."

My eyes widen. I don't think I've ever heard Tim say so many things at the same time.

Tim adds, "They only hold two bullets, and they fire 'em so slow you can see them in the air, but at close range they can kill you. They were designed for shooting people under the table."

Max says, "Is the customer hiding under the front seat? No. She wasn't in any danger."

"Worker's comp," I say to Max. "I'd have filed in a heartbeat. And even I can add: if there's only one bullet in the thing, that means one was already fired. The kid might have robbed a bank."

Max waves me off. "The car's going away, and the gun's unloaded now. Don't look anywhere else in the car because knowing you, you'll find a rocket launcher and a ski mask. I'm calling it good."

Tim grunts and walks away.

I pull the car into the lot and leave it there for our good friend, Mr. Hartman, who probably hopes he never has to see us again. It's eleven-thirty when he shows up. We take care of the paperwork, and I hand over the keys with, "Have a great day."

Two minutes later he's back. "You left something in the car."

I wait. He says nothing. I play stupid. "What is it?"

He wants me to come with him. Out at the passenger side door, he points to the gun. "You left this in there."

"That's not yours? It was under the front seat."

Dear Mr. Hartman informs me starchly that he has never owned a gun and never will. I say, "Is it your son's gun?"

He folds his arms. "Ms. Lee, I resent the way you continually cast aspersions on my son's behavior. From the time the damage occurred, it's been nonstop accusations, first of speeding and later of reckless driving and now of owing a gun. My son is young, but there's no need to discriminate against him on account of his age. Now please remove this weapon from my vehicle before I drive it from your lot."

I go find Max. "He doesn't want the gun."

Tim retrieves the gun, checks the safety, removes the solitary bullet from the glove box, and heads away. Mr. Hartman glares in my general direction as he gets into the car to put us permanently in his rear-view mirror.

In Max's office, I say, "What are we going to do with that thing?"

Max is putting it in the office safe. "Give it two days. The kid will come back for it."

I say, "Shouldn't we give it to the cops?"

"No, we shouldn't tell anyone it's here because we shouldn't even have the thing." Max smiles at me. "Lee, get out of here before you ask too many questions."

"Then I've got one more question." I fold my arms. "Long lunch? How about the rest of the day?"

Max huffs at me. "Get."

No guy with a Derringer and a maxed-out Maxima ever made as fast a getaway as I do right then. In a flash I'm changed out of my mechanic gear, boots become sneakers, and I become a distant memory. Hello, Manhattan. Hello, plan-in-motion.

Hal and I get the marriage license first. Walking into any of these city licensing bureaus results in the instant loss of one hour of your life. At the end, however, Hal hands over a money order (no, they won't take cash) and we prove we are over age fourteen. That clears the mountain of paperwork and we are equipped with a marriage license, good for sixty days.

And as it turns out, Hal was wrong: even if we'd gotten the license Monday, we couldn't have been married until *Tuesday*. There's a 24-hour waiting period in New York both for a shotgun and a wedding.

"Phone in and take the rest of the day off," I tell Hal, since the city government just consumed the entirety of his lunch hour. "Let's get the rings."

The F train takes us to 47th Street, Manhattan's "diamond center." Between 7th and 8th avenues, it's a flea market for gold and diamond sellers, one shop after the next after the next after the next. Most of these guys are wholesalers who don't like dealing with individuals, but they will to make a quick buck, and the prices are good.

Bucky, any input on which guys are crooks?

Inside, sarcastic laughter.

Terrific. But we're here now, so why not?

While I liked the idea of something eye-catching or just strange,[*] it's best for the two of us to just get plain matching bands. Hal because that's more his style, and me because you really can't trust my ability to keep an ornate ring clean. My college ring had a perpetual layer of toner in the nooks.

At a random store, I turn in. A case the size of Hal's kitchen island is the whole store, but it's crowded with wedding rings. Loud metal fans blow hot dust at us.

I point to a pair of rings, Hal agrees, then points to another. By the time we've settled on a style, the greasy-looking owner puts down his paper. "You want something?"

No, it's just a hobby of mine, to find closet-sized shops and gesture at the merchandise.

Hal asks for the rings. Mr. Greasy gets out one and then the other. "Fifty each."

We still like them after knowing the price. Hal's fits. Mine is too small.

"Can you size this up?"

Mr. Greasy shrugs. "Come back tomorrow."

"That's too bad." I put the ring back on the counter. "Because I have the cash right now."

---

[*] *I wanted The One Ring until Hal pointed out that "in the darkness bind them" isn't the best sentiment for one's marital union.*

That was the magic word: cash. Suddenly Mr. Greasy remembers he has a machine right here that sizes rings, and what size am I? I pull a hundred bucks out of my wallet, and by the time the cash is in my hand, the ring transforms into a size seven. The Greasemeister scrawls random numbers on a receipt pad, and in three minutes, Hal and I are back on the street.

Hal blinks in the sunlight. "Did that really just happen?" He stops. "Wait—he didn't charge sales tax."

"Look around you. I don't think legality is necessarily Job One."

You can tell during the whole walk back to the train that Hal is weighing the immorality of denying New York State eight dollars and twenty-five cents in sales tax, and whether we've just purchased our wedding rings from Satan. (I doubt it myself; the Bible describes Lucifer as beautiful, so he'd know how to use shampoo.)

The result is two more items checked off the list. We now have a minister, guests, a license, and rings. Hal is going to rent a tuxedo tomorrow night while I am—save me, God—shopping with my mother.

"Lee, this would look just darling!"

I've never gotten into heavy drinking, but situations like this may be why rational people make that choice. Bucky has appeared several times to urge me not to take actions I will regret, such as:

- gagging my mother with a clothes hanger
- starting to scream and never stopping
- alerting the police to a hostage situation in a clothing boutique.

My favorite sales gal is on duty. Shari, the only person who ever successfully helped me shop for clothes, turns it into a game. Not so my mother. Unless you consider what Roman gladiators did to be a game.

Shari is of the opinion that clothes are fun. My mother is of the opinion that this is her last and best chance at turning me into a woman, and by golly she isn't going to blow it.

Shari has already informed my mother (bless her) that pastels give me a washed-out look, and that I look better in "autumn" colors. I had no idea colors were seasonal, but there you have it.* Dark hair and pale skin plus pink make for a wraith-like Lee.

This explains my childhood photographs, I tell Bucky.

The photographs faded, silly. He's wearing a smile. *Let Shari battle your mother. Wander around the store and get a breather.*

I banish myself to the shoe nook where I won't be fending off floral prints.

And here's the best part of this little outing: I'm going to have to repeat my performance solo later this week to find a wedding dress. I hate this. I wish God would drop a dress out of the sky. I should get married wearing nothing but a paper bag. I wonder which stores still use white paper?

My cell phone rings. It's Hal.

"Are you still alive?" he says. "You sound tense."

"Mom and I are still shopping."

That's all the explanation he needs.

"I'm very sorry. I was hoping she'd get lost en route to Park Slope. Say, do you know Randy's measurements?"

"Huh?" I sit on the trying-on-shoes bench.

---

* *Speaking of seasons, it's mid-September and all the clothes are already heavy winter fabrics with long sleeves. There are snow boots in the window, and they even set the air conditioner to "arctic."*

"We could have a best man and a maid of honor. At first I thought of Stuart and Beth, but then I thought, I have a perfectly serviceable sister, and you can have your brother be the maid of honor. He'd just have to sign as a witness."

I look up to see Bucky grinning. *I think it's a great idea.*

"But I need measurements for Randy if I'm going to rent him a tux."

He can't see my eye-roll over the phone, so he'll have to infer heavy sarcasm by sound alone. "Of course I know my brother's inseam measurements. Who doesn't?"

"Thirty-two, thirty-four," Bucky says.

"Hold on," I say. Then I look at my guardian angel. "You know Randy's measurements?"

Bucky shrugs. "Who doesn't?"

I toss a display shoe through him, and he laughs. "Neck is fifteen and a half. Sleeve is—"

"Hold on. Hal, write this down," and then I repeat after Bucky in as low a voice as I can manage.

"Thanks." Hal pauses. "Is Bucky sure?"

Bucky sighs.

"Yeah, he's got mad skills with a tape measure. Love you."

"Love you too. I'll call you at the station house when you're under arrest for aggravated assault."

"I'm aggravated," I say, "but I'd never assault her. I'm here because Bucky told me to honor her, and you can't do that with your hands around her throat."

As I shut the phone, I look at Bucky. "You collect measurements on everyone you meet? Doesn't that seem like a waste of brain cells?"

"I don't have brain cells, and anyhow, what color is your brother's hair? How about Hal's? You pick up these things without making an effort to remember." He looks over his shoulder. "You've still got some time. Shari and your mom are debating whether paisley qualifies as a print."

As I wander out of shoes, the clearance rack catches my eye. Why don't they have circular racks anymore so I can sit in the middle like when I was a kid, waiting for my mother to notice I was missing and call mall security?

When I reach the rack, I stop, staring. I part the hangers and pull out a dress.

A white dress.

An ankle-length white dress with short sleeves and a lacy frill around the neck.

Dear God, thank you very much—I have found my wedding attire.

Best of all, it's marked down to nineteen ninety-five.

I'm about to take it to the counter, singing and twirling like Maria in *The Sound Of Music* when Bucky says, "Stop! Think for a minute!"

I do stop. *But—it's perfect! I won't have to shop again! It's nearly the right size, even!*

"And your *mother* is right *there*. Do you want to explain why you're buying a summer-weight white ankle-length dress?"

Oh, crud.

"Let me take over." Bucky folds his arms. "You did pray for your mother to be out of your hair, so I have some authority here, and I'm sure this benefits your soul somehow."

I stand with my hand on the dress, waiting for the Heavens to open and strains of celestial music to emerge.

Instead strains of "Copacabana" emerge as my mother gets a call on her cell. She apologizes to Shari and takes the call.

You're good, I tell Bucky.

"Don't I know it?" Bucky replies.

It's a good thing I learned humility from other sources, isn't it? Or maybe he's being sarcastic. It's hard to tell because he's accurate.

Shari finds me. "How are you holding up?"

"I need help." I thrust the dress at her. "Hide this behind the counter. I'll be back after dinner to pick it up."

"Oh, this one." Her voice lowers to match mine. "It's so pretty, but no one ever wanted it because it looked too much like—"

Her eyes glimmer, and she leans close, her voice as soft as the nature-sound waves over the stereo system. "He's not *proposing*, is he? You wicked girl. Be back before nine. Our alterations person drops off her work just before we close. She'll fit it for you."

I swallow. "We have ten days."

"It'll get done," Shari says as my mother says goodbye to her caller.

As Shari smuggles away my salvation, Mom comes up with the eighth perfect outfit in as many minutes, and I consent to try it on.

The net result:

By seven o'clock, my mother has purchased a forest green set for me to wear to get proposed-to in. She and I have dinner and then my mother drives home, aglow with the knowledge that she has saved my future. I return to Luxuriant to purchase my wedding dress, where I end up with pins stuck all over my outline while a seamstress tucks and bastes and measures everything that doesn't get out of the way quickly enough, including for some reason my head.

Not bad for a night I didn't want to happen at all. I know it says *Honor your father and your mother, so that your days may be long in the land that the Lord your God is giving you,* but maybe those are all Hebrew homonyms for "so that you may find the perfect wedding dress for the wedding you're throwing as a surprise." Maybe.

Chapter Twenty-One

I checked my calendar, and it's not 1378.

Bucky says "a wise man" claims the way to make God laugh is to tell Him your plans. Actually, he only said it once. I rejoined, "Why is it a wise *man* who always says these things rather than, say, a wise woman or a wise girl or a wise boy?" Followed by, "And then why do you get upset when I don't plan things, if God's just going to mess everything up anyhow?"

"Wow," Bucky replied. "That's a profound school of theological wisdom I never heard of before, but which is nevertheless utterly wrongheaded."

I said, "You just said some wise guy declared it. How wrong could it be?"

After that, he never said it again. I don't know why.

At any rate, our plan is awesome: I will marry Hal and then move. Once married, I won't be at the house any longer for Francisco to lie in wait for me. In fact, once I get married it will only be honorable for him to quit trying to go out with me. And at that point I can block his phone number without feeling bad, seeing as married women shouldn't be dating other guys.

This is great! I would have gotten married sooner if I'd realized it would get Francisco out of my hair.

Do you hear that sound? That's God chuckling.

Hal has come up with a shopping list detailed enough to colonize a continent. I'm not sure if he thinks Jesus will rapture Key Food aisle by aisle as we pass through purchasing food products,[*] but he doesn't want to go back for a second pass. We've got five days before the food needs to be prepared—to my mind, that's five more shopping trips. Maybe six.

We're not going to get any produce here, though, because Hal says it's "sad." He'll go to the Korean grocery store two blocks over, where the nice lady gets her product shipped in daily from Eden.

In the "baking needs" aisle (I've only ever *needed* to proceed straight to the actual bakery, thank you) Hal puts flour and sugar into the cart, then powdered sugar, and then he sighs.

You'd have to have dated him for seven months to know how nervous he is, and not about the marriage. It's the food. Specifically the cake.

"I don't know," he says, picking up a bottle of orange extract and then putting it back.

Last Sunday he brought cake squares for the coffee hour. He made three different kinds. He made me try a piece of each, and I will happily go on record to say they were all fluffy, flavorful, and frilly. And then he corrected me: in actuality, they were garbage.

"We're going to have an awful cake for our wedding."

I pat him on the hand. "We'll just have to fire the caterer."

---

[*] *Of course Hal organizes his shopping lists by grocery store aisle. Don't pretend you didn't know that.*

He's mid-recoil when he stops. "Oh, I thought you said *hire* a caterer. No, I guess we'll do okay. I just wanted to give you something fabulous."

I lean closer. "You're not something fabulous?"

He narrows his eyes at me. "A fabulous cake, okay? Everyone remembers the cake."

"You can say that about every part of this shindig." I shrug. "Everyone remembers the flowers. Everyone remembers the dress. Everyone remembers the music. Whatever. I just want to get to next week so we can remember it at all."

We keep traveling the aisles, filling the cart, until a box of Fruity Pebbles waylays us in the cereal aisle. I put it in the cart. Hal puts it back.

"They're rainbow-colored," I say.

"They're of the devil."

I shake my head. "The rainbow is a sign that God won't destroy the Earth by water."

Hal says, "Only because we'll destroy ourselves with sugar and food coloring."

I put it back in the cart. "Jesus would have eaten these for breakfast if He'd been born into 21st century America."

"Hard choice," Hal says, removing the box again, "between the Cross and daily insulin injections."

"He's the Son of God, Hal. I doubt he's going to keel over from type II diabetes."

Hal's putting back my cereal when Francisco comes around the corner.

Too quickly, I pull backward, and Hal instinctively turns to see what's caught my eye.

In the course of a second, Francisco looks surprised, then angry, and then he puts on his smoothest smile. 40-weight motor oil would get jealous at the smoothness.

He comes up to me and puts a hand on my shoulder. "Hi, Lee. It's been a while."

I step away from his touch. "I told you to leave me alone."

"You say one thing and do another." He takes another step nearer, and there's nowhere to go. Where is the "undo" button on my life?

Hal intercepts his hand the next time he reaches for me, and he shakes it. "And you are...?"

"Francisco." His eyes are dark. "Her boyfriend."

Hal nods. "And I'm Hal. Also her boyfriend."

I glance up for the security cameras, sure this is going to end up on Facebook. The only way this can end is Hal and Francisco heading off together, arm in arm, hating me and discovering they both had this previously-unknown affinity for Alaskan cuisine.

Francisco smirks at me. "Is this guy why you've been avoiding me?"

I fold my arms. "Perceptive boy. I avoided your phone calls and told you I didn't want to talk to you ever again. That's commonly known as a *hint,* and it's not my fault you failed to take it. Should I have gotten out a restraining order?"

Francisco gives Hal a sizing-him-up stare. "No, Babe. Take it as a compliment—you're fun and we're good together." Then he looks Hal straight in the eye. "You know, I could take him."

Before I can say anything, Hal says, "I'm sure you can. What you can't take is *her.* I checked my calendar, and it's no longer 1378. The knight who wins the tournament doesn't carry off the princess." He shrugs. "Nice meeting you."

Francisco glares at me. "So you have me for fun and that guy for the money?"

Hal looks absolutely composed. Much more than I am. "If she wants to take off with you, I'll write her a check for five grand on the spot, and I'd consider it cheap compared to a divorce." He folds his arms and narrows his eyes. "By the way, what's her day job?"

Francisco looks startled, and he doesn't answer. Hal snorts and pushes the cart away. "Nice try. You never had a chance with her."

I'm about to follow when Francisco picks up the Fruity Pebbles. "You forgot your cereal."

"Leave it." I don't look back. "I'm giving up junk food."

On the next aisle Hal has busied himself comparing two identical products, different brand name, and I want to stop time so I can go somewhere and do something less painful, like stand under the lift and lower a Chevy onto myself.

He picks one over the other. "I love meeting your boyfriends. You have such eclectic taste."

"We were never really going out." I'm shaking. "Please don't break up with me in the middle of Key Food."

There's a long silence between us, and then Hal says in a low voice, "Wait, was that serious? I thought you'd gone out with half of Brooklyn. Should we move to California?" He runs his finger beneath my chin and coaxes me to look up at him. I avoid his eyes anyhow. "If that fails, there's always the moon."

I look up both ends of the aisle, sure we're being followed. We aren't.

He looks me in the eyes. "You're shaking."

Mouth dry, I nod.

"Come on." He pushes the cart to the front and leaves it there, then ushers me outside.

My cellphone vibrates in my pocket, and I don't even need to look to know who it is. I push the button to send the call directly to voicemail, then turn off my phone.

I slump against the brick wall, but Hal says, "Not here. That guy has you rattled," and walks me across the street to an old stone church. We go around the corner to where

Francisco won't see us, and I huddle on the steps with my face in my hands.

Hal sits beside me. "Talk. Were you dreaming of inviting him to our wedding?"

That's how he found out his first fiancée was cheating. "He's a mistake. I was bored one night. We went for a joyride, and he won't leave me alone."

Hal sounds tentative. "And...?"

"And he brought the Shadow. I don't know how to get rid of him. He keeps turning up. He won't listen."

Hal wraps his hand around mine. "Are you lying to me? Because I'd rather find out now."

"I don't want a check for five grand."

He sounds rueful. "I don't have my checkbook with me."

I laugh. "You told him off pretty good."

"Not bad for an accountant who can't change a tire." Hal kisses me on the cheek. "Tell me the rest of it. How'd he bring the Shadow?"

He puts his arm over my shoulders, and I bury myself in him. "You don't believe any of this."

"Bucky talked to me, remember? Try me."

"The Shadow is infidelity." I close my eyes. "Don't be mad at me. I'm sorry. But the more I didn't want to get married, the harder he'd push. It's like he knew."

Hal said, "You were being unfaithful?"

I cringe.

He goes on. "You always had a couple of guys on the hook, right? You didn't think you were being unfaithful then. So what's different about him?"

I open my hands and shake my head. "It's... I don't know."

"But don't you see? That means you changed your mind. You can't be unfaithful unless you were trying to be faithful." Hal sounds relieved. "So even when you didn't want to be married, are you saying you did?"

My voice wavers. "Usually I understand what you're talking about."

"No, no, listen. This is good." Hal squeezes me. "If you never had any intention of being faithful, you couldn't have done anything you'd feel guilty about, right?"

My brow knits. "Okay..."

He says, "You wanted to marry me. You just didn't know it yet. That's more than I hoped."

I meet his eyes.

"I wasn't sure of you." He looks pained. "I wanted you, but all along I wondered if I was just fun, and when the fun ended, you'd be gone. Sure, maybe you'd agreed to marry me from pity or because your mother was hounding you. I wanted it to come from *you*, but even now, maybe it was coming from Bucky, and I wasn't sure."

I wrap my arms around him. "I'm sorry."

His voice is soft. "I'm not exciting enough for you. That's always going to be a worry."

"I should be more steady."

"It's not all on you." He squeezes me. "I need you to help me be more spontaneous." He pauses. "Did you kiss him?"

I nod. "I did. I'm sorry."

He leans over and kisses me. "How many times?"

I say, "Twice?"

He kisses me again. "Maybe three times?"

I shiver. "You'd better be sure."

He kisses me again. "It's okay. We're going to be okay."

"I didn't ruin everything?"

"You ruined my perfect shopping trip." He makes a downcast face. "I'll have to start over."

"The only danger to that cart is rust." I squeeze his hand. "We can head back for our twentieth wedding anniversary and it'll be in the same place. We'll just have to see what's expired."

Hal raises his eyes to the Heavens. "Well, there goes the Mac and Cheese."

I snicker. "Mac and Cheese lasts forever. It's powder."

Hal shook his head. "Sadly, I picked out the organic kind."

"Organic means nothing if Kraft sells an organic Mac and Cheese."

Hal bites his lip. "That's a sad harbinger of the future." He squeezes me. "Are you okay now?"

"Better." I glance at Key Food. "Do you think he's gone?"

"I'll finish the shopping, and you go home. I'll even buy you the Fruity Pebbles if it makes you feel better."

"No Cheetos?"

"No Cheetos." He smiles. "If I see him in the store, I'll smirk menacingly and tell him my GRE scores or something equally lame while you're making yourself some tea and reading that *Serenity* fanfic Mrs. Smith sent you."

"Actually, I want to finish reading *Taking Charge Of Your Fertility*. Did you know that at eight days post-ovulation, both luteinizing hormone and follicle stimulating hormone levels are exactly the same, and if they're not, you can't get pregnant?"

"No, my Corporate Restructuring professor failed to mention that. A concerning omission on his part." He kisses my forehead. "I'll call when I get home, and you can come help with the food prep."

Hal goes back to the store, and I head down the hill. I'm halfway down the block before I realize our tactical error: my escape plan was predicated on the idea that Francisco stayed in the store. Francisco might be waiting for me on the steps.

I could call him and tell him to leave me alone. Maybe he left a voicemail and I can listen to get the gist of whether he wants to win me over or whether he's griping me out. The latter is what I'd want. If I talk to him again, the object of that conversation will be to make him so mad that he dumps me. Effective, but tough to pull off.

I need help. Beth: maybe she can check the front steps. I turn on the phone to a series of disasters: first off, Francisco is blowing up my phone with texts. Secondly, Beth isn't answering. Thirdly, I've got five voicemails, and they're all from Francisco. Bet me he's on the steps.

"Bucky," I say into the air, "are you up for surveillance duty?"

Bucky appears. "What do you want me to do?"

"Figure out if Francisco's waiting for me." There's no back door to the brownstone, not unless I climb eleven fences and then scale the fire escape to break in the window. Actually, that's not a bad idea.

Bucky says, "Why?"

I pause. "Well, I'd rather use the front door. Maybe I could scale one of the other buildings and cut into the apartment through the roof."

Bucky stares at me. "I mean, are you really going to get married to Hal? Because if you're not, you shouldn't get rid of Francisco."

I pivot and look right at him. "Are you serious? I thought you wanted me to get married!"

"I only told you to think seriously about it. But typical for you, you haven't considered all the ramifications of your actions."

Bucky never talks to me like this. My gut clenches in fear. "Ramifications?"

Bucky sighs. "Look, you have to make a choice. You can't make an eternal promise to Hal when there's someone you love more."

I draw myself up. "I don't love Francisco at all!"

"I mean me."

The bottom drops out of my world. For a moment I'm standing, ears ringing, in the middle of Carroll Street struggling to draw breath.

"You have to make a choice." Bucky's voice is absolutely flat. "You can't have it both ways."

I hunch my shoulders and keep walking "Are you saying if I marry him, I can't ever see you again?"

Bucky doesn't answer, but his eyes drop.

"That's insane! Why would you do that?" I'm shouting, and I don't care if anyone hears me. "Why would God let that happen? Why would you ever let me date anyone in the first place if it meant losing you?"

"I'm your childhood friend." Bucky shoves his hands in his pockets. "I never thought it would go this long. When you started serial-dating, I encouraged it because I didn't want you to stop talking to me. I'd mess things up if they were going too good, so it was always just you and me. But now you're on the edge, and it's going to be goodbye. You need to know that before you commit."

"Go talk to God! Tell him this is insane!" My hands are in fists. "Damn it, Bucky! This isn't a game. I'm not going to do anything that makes you leave! I don't care if Hal's heart breaks—why didn't you tell me this before?"

I stalk forward, unable to see through the tears. I want to get the heck home. I want to hole up in the shower and sob, maybe scream into my pillow, then kick the couch cushions.

Why would Bucky have brought me to Hal in the first place if loving Hal would lose Bucky? Bucky left me once before, but that was my fault. Getting married isn't wrong. It's not evil. I'm making a promise, not violating one.

This isn't right. This isn't right.

Wait a minute. No, it's not right.

I know what to do. But what if I'm wrong? *God, help me.* I don't want to blow this. What happens next is everything.

I steel myself. And then I snort. "Leave."

Behind me, Bucky stops cold. "Lee—?"

I turn. "Get out of here. Leave me alone. In God's name, I'm ordering you to go."

Bucky goes pale. "You're choosing Hal over me?"

"I'm choosing commitment over infidelity. You have nothing left to say to me."

It breaks my heart, but I step forward and try to avoid the pain in Bucky's eyes. "You said you're going to go if I choose Hal—well, I'm not choosing you, that's for sure."

Bucky's wings flare.

"Out of here." I wish I could look ferocious. I'm not even carrying a handbag I can swing. "Now. Go. You're a liar, and you have nothing left to say to me...Shadow!"

Bucky vanishes.

It's quiet. I'm utterly still inside.

I'm shaking. What if I really sent away Bucky? Shouldn't I call him back?

No, no. Brace yourself, Lee. If Bucky was that much of a jerk, then Bucky had to go anyhow. There's no way around that.

But what if I was wrong?

Well, if I was wrong, Bucky wouldn't leave, would he? He'd know the difference between me thinking he was serious and thinking he was being impersonated.

That all sounds nice, but I'm still alone in my head.

Inside, a twinge: *I didn't throw out Bucky fast enough—God is angry that I would have chosen Bucky over Him.*

I frown, then retort, *No, because God sent away the Shadow, and God wouldn't have done that if I'd just pledged myself as a bride of Satan.*

I imagine a demon muttering, "Good point."

I quirk a smile. Then I stall.

Oh, God, this one's going to be rough, isn't it?

Because yes, I've rounded the corner and there's Francisco on the stoop of the brownstone. And I have to handle him without backup.

I remove my keys from my purse before I approach. That's New Yorker Jujitsu.

"Hey." Francisco stands as I approach. "I want to talk to you without your lawyer present."

"There's nothing to talk about. I'm getting married in a week."

Francisco laughs. "That's not a problem with me."

"It's a problem with me." I sidle to the side as he puts out his hand. "I'm beyond serious. I should have been honest from the start that Hell has a better chance to host the Winter Olympics than you have with me, but I'm doing it now. Leave me alone."

I unlock the glass doors. Francisco says, "You can't just leave, Babe."

"I don't owe you anything except an apology." He tries to follow, and I block the entrance. "But the thing I'm sorriest is that I didn't throw your phone number out the window."

He says, "Because I'm irresistible?"

"Because you're pushy."

"Don't you deserve more excitement than some straight-laced white guy with a button-down collar?" He laughs. "Is he an accountant?"

Ouch.

"You know what I deserve, Francisco?" I drop my voice. "I deserve a guy who respects me when I say no."

He says, "Give me a chance."

And I don't answer him—because if I expect him to respect when I say no, then I'd better start respecting it first.

Although my mother would vomit if she saw me do this, I shut the door in Francisco's face, then let myself in through the inner doors and lock them too.

Before I reach the third landing, I've deleted his voicemails unread. He's texting me again, so I pause at my door to block his cell phone and delete every text he's ever sent.

I shut the apartment door behind me. *Bucky, I really could have used you back there.* Still silence inside. I hate being the only one in my own head. *Like if you could have done that trick like you did when you yelled at Hal.*

In my heart, I feel, *You did fine on your own.*

I give a relieved smile. *Yeah, but if I could bottle what you did to Hal, I'd make a million bucks.*

A million bucks is over-rated. I'd do worse than that if it kept you from ruining your life.

I grin. "Thanks."

"No problem." He appears at the table. "I have to admit, I was worried you wouldn't see through the Shadow's game."

"Why'd you let her imitate you?"

"Yeah, I *let* her. She came up to me and said, 'I've got a great idea! Loan me your t-shirt!'" Bucky sits forward. "Didn't I tell you to challenge me if I ever said anything that sounded off? I knew she'd try that, and I knew when she did, I wouldn't be able to stop her. She's kept one attack in reserve for an opportunity like this, and God ordered me to stand down because God wanted you to choose. I'm pretty cool," he adds, "but I'm not your ultimate good."

"And you're modest, too."

"Don't I know it?" Bucky gives a bright smile. "You had a rough minute or two, but that's the kind of rough minute that gets you into eternity. You didn't refuse to sacrifice what you wanted in order to obtain something greater."

Chapter Twenty-Two

So There.

It's two o'clock in the morning, and I'm lying on my side in the dark.

Tomorrow's the day. No, wait. By now, today's the day.

I'm aware of Bucky's presence the way you're aware of the edge of your bed, the way you're aware of the television in the next room or the rhythmic clank of train cars as you rumble through the tunnel toward Manhattan.

I'm listening to traffic, listening to my heartbeat and the distant muffled sound of a clarinet. All these years and I've never figured out which building the sound belongs to. I'm going to move out never having figured it out. It was never important enough to ask Bucky, always intriguing enough that I kept my eyes open for someone carrying a clarinet case.

I grope for the phone and dial Hal's number.

He answers at the third ring, groggy.

"It's me. I'm sorry." My voice is little more than a husky whisper. "I just—"

"I love you," Hal murmurs into the phone. "I love you so much."

With my eyes closed, I nod. "I needed to hear it."

"We'll be okay," he murmurs. "Tomorrow night, if you're worried, you won't have to phone me."

Tomorrow night, I'll be able to reach one arm forward and feel his shoulders, his chest. I can snuggle up behind him and rub my lips against the edges of his hair, still sharp from the trim he got yesterday so he'd look nice for me.

"I love you," I tell him.

"I know," he says.

I know he knew. But I needed to remind myself.

Saturday I awaken like a gunshot.

"Good morning!" Bucky's eyes glow in colors like a sunrise. "I thought you might want to get a jump on things."

Staring at the clock, I realize it's five-thirty. "Do I have to?"

"Well," and Bucky sounds a bit uncomfortable, "it would be awkward if you were late for your own wedding. I thought you might appreciate the extra time."

I would, if he could figure out how to give it to me at eight o'clock in the morning instead of oh-dark-thirty.

I drag myself into the shower, and as the hot water blasts me, I have a horrible thought: today I am getting married. Married, as in "getting married," being a bride— *becoming a wife!* I don't even know how to be someone's girlfriend very well, and I'm going to become a *wife*?

I shut off the water. "I can't do it."

Turn the water back on and rinse off the soap.

"I can't." I wring my washcloth until my hands hurt. "Bucky, I must be nuts. I've been playing this huge game of pretend, like I'm an adult. I'm a little kid."

I have to admit, your sudden inability to take a shower does evoke fond reminiscences of your childhood.

Rubbing my temples, I close my eyes. "Why didn't you stop me before now? I can't do this. I have to call it off."

I've got a better idea. Why don't you rinse off the soap and make some coffee, and we'll talk?

"You're not talking me out of this." As I turn the water back on, it startles me by being a little colder than a moment ago, but then it warms right back up. "I'm going to dry off and call the priest and have him call Hal."

I'm not going to talk you out of it. Just rinse off.

I finish my shower, get dry, throw on a bathrobe, and head to the kitchen. Coffee. I can't handle this without coffee.

As I'm making coffee, I think of Hal's coffee roaster and the coffee maker that grinds the beans, adjusts the water temperature, and recycles the steam—in fact, does everything short of growing the cocoa plants. Hal's so cute that way. It's a tradition, he says, to bake pumpkin muffins for the first snowfall. On rainy Sundays, we baked cookies, and that was always fun. He'd send me home with "half" that was really far more than half the cookies.

What was I possibly thinking? I can't call it off. I'd break his heart. I'd break my heart. Am I insane?

I set my coffee cup on the counter with a bang. "I can't do it."

Put the sugar in the mug and get out the milk.

"I can't," I say. "Bucky, I must be nuts. I can't call it off. I'm an adult. I'm going to go through with it."

Get the milk out of the fridge.

Rubbing my temples, I close my eyes. "Why didn't you stop me before? I nearly made a terrible mistake. I have to go through with it."

I've got a better idea. Why don't you finish making your coffee, and we'll talk.

"You're not talking me out of this." As I get the milk out of the fridge, I'm startled because there's not as much in it as I expected. "I'm going to have coffee and get dressed and get over there."

I'm too nervous to eat. When I'm halfway through the coffee, I nearly drop it. I'm going to get *married* today. Married—just like a real person. I'll be someone's wife, and I'll wear a ring, and I'll file a joint tax return, and when someone asks me out on a date I'll say no, and I'll have dental insurance, and I'll have to figure out whose house we're going to at the holidays. Who could possibly do all that? That's it. I'm calling it off.

"I can't do this," I tell Bucky. "I must be insane."

Bucky replies, *I'm beginning to know the feeling.*

"Are you having jitters?" Hal says.

I look at him, brow furrowed. "Not at all."

It's ten o'clock and I'm at the church with Hal, getting food into ovens.

"That's one of us. I keep forgetting how to boil water." He takes my hand in his and gives a squeeze. "Please tell me this is going to work."

Blinking, I say, "The marriage?"

"The wedding. That this isn't a stupid idea. That people aren't going to yell that we deprived them of the chance of getting dressed up and eating tasteless food."

"That was the point." I kiss him on the cheek. "Only my mother will decry the loss of those things. That's *also* part of the point."

Eleven o'clock: I haul chairs and tables around the church hall.

Twelve o'clock: I pick up the flower arrangements Hal ordered at the last minute.

For all that he got flowers, though, it's not going to scream "Wedding!" It's done up like a nice dinner, the way someone picks out flowers when he has taste and isn't, for example, me. The flowers are autumn colors in glass vases with clear marbles at the bottom. But he couldn't resist a little wedding-frippery. There are corsages.

And one white bouquet with roses.

"I wanted you to have at least one thing traditional," Hal says.

I kiss him. "There are only eleven roses, my overpaid accountant."

He grins mischievously.

One o'clock: we're still cooking. I keep adjusting things on the tables. My iPod is very excited to play music the entire time (although I think Bucky keeps adjusting the playlist to have more Fleetwood Mac). I've got the buffet table set with anything that doesn't need to be kept hot or cold.

One forty-five: We light palm-sized cans of Sterno. Then Randy arrives.

I dash into the meeting room to change into the outfit my mother bought while Hal spends a few moments showing them around. Before Hal is done, his parents have arrived. I finish putting on my necklace and start greeting people as if I know what I'm doing.

You might think getting married is out of my league, but I'm far more prepared to be a bride than to play Miss Manners.

My brother Morgan and his family are the last to arrive, at 2:30. Uncle Mickey is munching on chips while telling everyone how much he must love me to give up his tickets to a Yankees-Red Sox game; Aunt Mary is making pleasant talk with Hal's mother. My own mother is lecturing Hal's father. This could be an utter disaster.

I wanted to have ice-breaker games to get people talking to one another, but Hal said that was silly. It wasn't silly, but right now I'm glad he nixed it. I couldn't lead starving ants to a ham sandwich. Instead Beth and Stuart are facilitating the mingling because they alone know nobody from either family. As they ask questions, they unwittingly draw together people who might otherwise not have gotten to know one another.

Hal kisses me for good luck, and we declare dinner served.

I don't go through the buffet line until the very end. Like that's a problem. My stomach feels like someone put a bunch of rubber bands around it. On the other hand, there's the steaming hot rolls; there's the salad with the homemade dressings. There's lasagna (always a favorite) plus chicken florentine and miniature beef Wellingtons. Those look too good not to try; I hope we have leftovers. Hal said when you're cooking for thirty, you're really cooking for forty anyhow; in actuality, I bet he was cooking for sixty. You know how some people freeze a portion of their wedding cake for the first year? Well we won't need to cook for our first anniversary!

And this spread is after people have been munching on chips and dips and bread bowls filled with yummies. All around, there are compliments on the food. Hal looks pleased. My mother looks twice as pleased.

I'm up browsing the buffet again when Hal's mother joins me. "Did you cook any of this, or did Hal padlock himself in the kitchen?"

"I did the set-up and the shopping—well, some of the shopping." Hal has this thing about picking out his own produce, but he's showing me how to find materials up to his standards. "He did let me stir the sauce once while he was taking something out of the oven."

"He's always had that way about him. As if, if only he can do the entire thing himself, nothing will go wrong." She puts her hand on my arm. "Come with me for a minute."

We sit across from one another at a table without anyone near. Leaning forward, she says, "How long have you been able to see angels?"

I gulp. "What?"

"You sidestepped the question back at the Labor Day barbecue, and I just discovered that at least one of your brothers thinks you work as a mechanic."

When I sit back sharply, Hal's mother chuckles. "I thought it odd how Hal suddenly could name all the parts of an engine, but I didn't want to tell my husband he was insane. I'm glad to find out I wasn't the insane one. But you—" She squints at me. "Does Hal know?"

I nod.

"When did it start?"

"I was three." I look at my hands. "I only see one. He's... He's just awesome. I don't know what else you want to know."

"What he tells you." Her voice is strained. "Whether you've tested him."

"I've tested him repeatedly." When I look up, her face is more relaxed. "He warns me when I'm doing something wrong. He tells me not to lie. He encourages me when I'm ready to give up. And he tells me sometimes that God has something He wants me to do, like to honor my mother when I want to scream at the top of my lungs."

"Your mother is overprotective. Even I can tell that." She chuckles. "What does this angel say about my son?"

"He likes him," I say. "He's a lot like Hal."

"But does he let you cook?"

"He has no choice. Angels can't bring you a pizza."

Actually, that would be seriously cool

Don't even think it.

Before I can pout at Bucky, Hal's mother says, "I have to admit, I'm a little jealous. You'll have to tell me more about him sometime."

"He said—" I pause, focusing on my plate. "Back in January. He woke me up, said God wanted me to go to the early Mass. I only ever got to the later one. When I came, I met Hal." I smile. "So he has to be good, doesn't he? If he did that?"

"He must be good." She rests her hand on my head before she walks away.

One of the best, I tell Bucky.

Thanks.

Not "Don't I know it?"

Not this time. You kind of choked me up there.

I chuckle.

Then I have a moment of panic, because Hal's gone.

"Where were you?"

Of all the places he could have run off to in order to escape marrying me, you know where he picked? The kitchen. And he's startled by how I've uncovered his master scheme. It's got to be that he's upset I've foiled his plan and not that he's upset by the panic in my voice.

"Hey." He holds onto me for a minute. "I wasn't going to bail on you. I wanted to get out more rolls."

I press my face against his shoulder.

"Ah." He kisses the top of my head. "You were having jitters, weren't you? And you figured I was, too?"

I look up. He's blurry.

"Well, as a runaway groom, I fail." He looks aside. "Oh, good. You're here."

It's Father Dan. I grab a napkin and blot my eyes. Hal says, "Take a few minutes," and I listen to him head outside with our black-suited-white-collared conspirator. "I just wanted you to meet the guy who let us use his church," Hal is saying. "Otherwise we'd have been forced into a restaurant to eat substandard food." Polite laughter. Father Dan says hi to everyone, and folks invite him to fill up a plate while I'm still calming my nerves.

Well, if nothing else, I guess this tells me I've made the right decision.

And now we have a plan to put in motion.

I need to get changed. Ironically, because of all the doo-dads on a tuxedo, it's going to take Hal longer than me. Randy is going to need to get dressed as well, although he for some reason probably thinks he's already dressed. The guys will change in the kitchen; I'm going to get ready in the conference room.

Hal passes by me and whispers, "I'll need a five minute head start," and I giggle. Yes, he's practiced with a stopwatch.

While the priest is talking to Hal's sister (who actually belongs to this church), my mother comes to me. "When is he going to propose?"

"Don't worry until after dessert." I give my mother's hand a squeeze. "Right now I need Randy."

Over at Randy's table, I grab his arm and say, "You're required in the kitchen," and I pull him.

Corinne starts to get up. "I can help too."

"No!" That's a snag I hadn't considered. "This is man's work."

Randy says, "And yet you asked for me?"

"No one else."

At the kitchen, Hal shuts the door behind us.

He looks good. Even without the whole tuxedo done up yet, he looks really good. Wearing a silly grin, I just look at him, and he looks sheepishly back.

"Oh my word." Randy shuts the door quietly. "What on Earth are you two up to?"

"Here." Hal lifts another tuxedo off a hook on the door. "You're my best man. Or her maid of honor. But you need to look the part."

Randy grabs my arm. "You?"

"Can you think of a better way to get Mom off my back about a big white wedding?" I giggle. "Please, Randy?"

"You couldn't stop me. I'm just sorry I won't be able to see the look on her face when—" He pauses. "Am I to understand from this that there's a little mechanic on the way?"

"I see Bucky." I kiss his cheek. "I haven't seen Gabriel, and that's what it would take."

Randy nods. "Ah, so you're only going off the deep end. Fine by me." He squints. "Have you got a wedding gown to change into?"

"No, dork—I'm prancing down the aisle wearing nothing but body paint."

Hal kisses me, and I open the door to leave—

—and bump right into Avery.

"Mom said I should help—"

I collar her as she begins to squeal.

"Not a word," I hiss, pushing her out the door and shutting it firmly. "Not a single word."

"But—" Her eyes are wide as eggs. "Hal— My dad—"

I guide her into the conference room. "Can you keep a secret for ten minutes?" When she nods enough to give herself whiplash, I open the closet door to reveal my dress.

Open-mouthed, she stares. Then, after a moment, she's jumping in place. "This is so romantic!"

"It's actually practical." I pause. "Can you help?"

Avery has never heard such a wonderful thing in her entire life. She will help.

She and I unwrap the dress, and the folks at Luxuriant really did go above and beyond. Shari knew I had no headpiece; she's included a tiara-type thing with rosebuds that match the pattern on the dress.

I'm choked up. I can't even speak. I have no idea how to put that on.

Luckily, Avery knows. My dress slips on in one minute flat. I'll wear white sandals to match. My bouquet of roses, all eleven of them, sits in a vase at the center of the conference room table. It takes about twenty seconds, and then Avery has redone my hair around the tiara. "You look great." She sniffs. "You know what? I'll go grab mom's camera. No one will see. Then I'll go back out and help distract everyone."

Just like that, she's gone. I'm standing alone.

I look toward the roses, but Bucky stands between me in the table. He takes a step forward, and then he's right in front of me, looking down into my eyes.

He's wistful. Concerned. Proud.

"What's going on?" I stammer.

He smiles. "I just wanted a minute alone with you."

I find myself smiling back at him. He's projecting a bouquet of his own, emotions I could name if I wanted but which I'd rather see in his eyes, in the softness of his smile, in the slight incline of his head. His hands brush against mine against my chest, and he leans forward ever so slightly as if to breathe on me and impart his blessing.

I swallow. "I'll still be able to see you, right?"

"I'm an angel, not a unicorn." He chuckles. "We're fine."

"This is huge," I tell him.

"It's huge." He smiles. "God is bigger."

Then I drop my eyes. "I wish you could walk me down the aisle. You're the one who earned it."

Just before he vanishes, Bucky says, "What makes you think I won't be there?"

The door opens. "You know what I mean," I murmur.

Avery slips into the conference room. "You look wonderful." She pushes me to a more scenic corner. "Terrified, but wonderful."

She starts taking pictures, and I've probably got a smile like you see in a horror movie. She's chattering. "The priest said he's got a slide show on the history of the church, and no one knows how to say 'no' so we've got the chairs arranged with a little aisle going down the middle. Dad is ready. We're going to sneak Hal through the back, and when we hear the music start, we go."

"Music?" I say.

"Hal pulled out your iPod and jacked in his own. He said it's respectable music."

Seriously. Like ABBA isn't respectable.

She takes my hands. "Do you think he'll cry? I love it when guys cry." A moment passes. "At weddings."

I burst out laughing. "At weddings!" Avery insists. "I don't watch the news looking for guys who've just lost their families in a train wreck to see them crying—honest."

It was perfect, just what I needed to bust up the tension. Then there's a knock at the door, and Randy motions for Avery to leave. She dashes out with the camera.

"You're gorgeous. Are you ready?"

I nod.

"Don't forget the flowers."

I grab my bouquet.

"Don't try to talk. You look petrified." He takes my arm, then kisses me on the forehead. "I remember when you were born, you silly thing. You're far too young to be getting married. But if you insist, I think it's time."

A burst of commotion, and Randy chuckles. "Yep, definitely time. Sounds like they saw your groom."

"Holy cow," I whisper as we walk to the door. "My groom. I'm getting married."

Out in the church hall, everyone turns toward the back to see me. Where's Hal? I can't see him because Morgan and my mother are in the way.

Uncle Mickey approaches, and he moves Randy away from me. "Pardon me, son, but this is where I take over."

Randy bows his head, and Uncle Mickey gives me a hug. "Are you ready, little lady?"

Randy stands at the front. Beth and Stuart give me a thumbs-up; she alone doesn't look surprised.

I grip Uncle Mickey's hand like a lifeline. He wraps his other hand around my forearm, and he escorts me.

Between the last row of chairs and the first it's a hundred miles. Morgan steps back, and in that moment it's me facing my mother, who is whiter than the paper this book is printed on.

A moment passes, and then there's a hand resting on her arm. It's Hal. "Mrs. Singer," he says in a voice smoother than satin, "may I ask for the gift of your daughter's hand in marriage?"

My mother's eyes well up, and she rushes me. Uncle Mickey lets go in time for me to hug her.

She turns to Hal and chokes, "Yes."

Uncle Mickey guides me to the front, but by now I'm no longer shaking. Hal is here, his eyes brilliant, his smile outshining his eyes, and he's holding one solitary white rose – the last of my dozen. Randy takes that and my bouquet, and Hal takes my hand. *Hold his hand,* Father Dan urged when we blocked this out. *Not only is it sweet, but that's the best way to steady each other.*

Holding hands, we face the priest. Hal squeezes my fingertips, and I squeeze back. It's our secret. It's not so secret any longer.

The priest reads from Genesis, a man leaving his parents, a woman taken from her home. He reads from

Isaiah. He reads from Luke. And then he turns to me. It's time for the vows.

I don't wait for the prompt. "I, Juliet Singer, take you, Hal Baxter, to be my lawful wedded husband, to have and to hold, from this day forward, for better, for worse, for richer, for poorer, in sickness and in health, until death do us part." I stick out my tongue at him. "So there."

He smirks. "I, Hal Baxter, take you, Lee, to be my lawful wedded wife, to have and to hold, from this day forward, for better, for worse, for richer, for poorer, in sickness and in health, until death do us part."

The priest asks for the rings, which Hal's sister has in her pocket (thank heaven—I would have had no idea where they were.) He blesses them, then has Hal put my ring on my finger, and I slip Hal's onto his. Other than that moment, we've had our hands in one another's the entire time, and then we're back to holding on for dear life.

Father Dan says, "By the power vested in me, before the witness of God and this congregation, I pronounce you man and wife."

Hal leans forward and brushes his lips against mine. He may kiss the bride. It's gentle and sweet and permanent.

There's applause from our families—our *family*. My mother is sobbing. Hal's mother is beaming, but his father is dabbing his eyes with a tissue. Avery looks to have filled an entire memory card with pictures. Corinne is battling tears, and behind Hal, his sister is biting her lip, holding her sleeping baby against her shoulder.

Uncle Mickey kisses me on the forehead.

"Was it that bad?" I say, and everyone breaks up with laughter, and then we're surrounded by people offering congratulations, mock-scolding us for pulling such a stunt, some saying they "knew it all along." But they didn't, and they know we know it.

Hal still hasn't let go of my hand. I look at him, and when he meets my eyes I know that no matter what happens for the rest of the day, it worked, and we're married.

The fifteenth time was the charm for Hal, who not only baked the perfect wedding cake but also managed to frost it in buttercream roses and little silver dots. I'm so nervous feeding him a bite of cake that I get frosting on his nose. So I kiss it off.

We have Fleetwood Mac's "Sweet Little Lies" for our first dance.

When I toss the bouquet, it's to all the singles, not just the females. Much to his horror, Brennan catches.

I have already answered questions about my fertility five times, but for some reason no one wants to hear about rising progesterone levels and how to read your cervix signs. I always get interrupted with, "Then when are you two going to have kids?"

Father Dan has been sitting with Mom for ten minutes while she cries. I wonder if my mother made a deal with God ala Simeon that she wanted to live long enough to see me married off. Maybe we should have had an ambulance standing by.

Corinne shakes Hal's hand and then kisses me on the cheek. "I love you like a sister," she says, "but I'm going to hate you forever because you managed to escape enduring your mother for a bridal shower, registries, an engagement party, and endless shopping trips."

I snicker. "Jealous?"

"Beyond jealous. They need a new word for jealous."

"Where are you going for a honeymoon?" says Avery.

I'm about to say we're not having one when Hal says, "Where else? We're going to Six Flags: Great Adventure."

"We are?"

Family members have started going home, and we're cleaning up in the church kitchen, kind of rushing things, but without exactly saying why. Hal keeps looking at me.

Morgan and Randy (who has escaped his tuxedo) have been loading the car with our (our!) dishware as we finish. Corinne has boxed up leftovers for everyone to take home; cake has been put in the church refrigerator for tomorrow's coffee hour.

And the next thing I know, we're back in his condo— our condo—and everything is put away, and he's looking at me with a heart-stopping intensity.

I manage to say, "Have I told you how much chicks dig guys in tuxedos?"

His face falls a little. "I hope not as much as chicks dig guys without tuxedos."

I break up laughing, and he embraces me, his black jacket pressed against the white of my dress.

Chapter Twenty-Three

Now you can remember me living somewhere else

And just like that, it's over and it's begun.

Hal drives us out to Great Adventure where I introduce him to the wonder that is "riding the same roller coaster fifteen times in a row because no one else is in line." We do that dozens of times. I also introduce him to the concept of "funnel cakes," which I'm horrified to say he'd never tried before. (He says 'successfully avoided,' but seriously? Why would anyone do that?) We get sunburnt and exhausted and soaked on the water rides and then finally home giggling. Oops, did we leave our cell phones at home? Yes, we did. Why? Because we love our families, but we also didn't want to hear from them. That's our honeymoon.

On Monday, we turn on our cell phones to discover a disturbingly large number of voicemails from folks with their ears to the grapevine. There are five calls alone from my mother, begging for reassurance that it wasn't a joke. That's in addition to the two calls she made Saturday evening before Hal's executive decision to turn off all the phones.

It's Wednesday before Max's wife Allison notices the wedding ring on my key chain and demands, in front of five customers, to know exactly when that happened, and then the customers demand to know exactly when getting to their cars will happen.

Hal's office-mates have been laughing behind their hands at how their mild-mannered accountant snuck off and got hitched. Julie of the Five Faces Of Doom first screamed at him, then burst into tears over how romantic it was, and finally asked him about three checks that needed to be cut on Monday (naturally, she hadn't thought of it until Sunday) and could he please get to them now before she murdered him.

In other words, life is back to business as usual. Or business-as-unusual. I mean, it's my life, after all.

Max comes into his office where I'm changing my income tax withholding forms, and at his back is the younger Hartman. My eyes widen, but Max opens the safe and pulls out the gun.

I say, "Can you prove that's your gun?"

Max says, "No, and he doesn't have to."

"What if it's not his?"

Max snaps, "It certainly isn't ours."

The younger Hartman stares at the floor. I say, "Look, the car's repaired now, so spill. You didn't just drive through a construction zone."

Max says, "Unless it happens to be a construction zone in Afghanistan."

I add, "We won't tell your father. He wouldn't believe us anyhow because you walk on water."

The younger Hartman laughs, and it's rueful. "No, he wouldn't."

"Well? Confession's good for the soul, and we're intensely curious."

When Hartman says nothing for a moment, Max says, "Take a seat. This sounds like a good one."

Hartman surprises me by sitting. "Look, I know I screwed up. I didn't mean for all that to happen."

Oh, that's a surprise. I'll bet everyone thought the Little Prince went out that night intending to do five figures worth of damage to his dad's car.

"My car is a Prius," he says. "Dad told me to take the Maxima because we wouldn't fit as comfortably in a small car, and his is bigger."

"When you say *we*..." I say.

"My cousins." He swallows hard. "We went to see a Disney play on Broadway because they're visiting from Iowa, and my aunt thought I should take them. They're like eight, ten, twelve and fifteen, and they really like Disney stuff."

Great: speeding with four kids in the car. This story gets better and better.

"But my aunt is a bit of a worrier." He weaves his fingers together in his lap. "So she gave me her gun because she said I'd need to protect her kids. Because you know, it's New York and we all do crack and belong to gangs, so of course no one goes anywhere without a gun, and obviously I'd know how to save the day with one."

My eyebrows raise. "How'd she bring an out-of-state gun into New York?"

He shrugs. "Like I know. I just stuck it under the seat because who the hell needs a gun to drive to Manhattan? It's not like we're in the Old West. So we saw the play, and then on the way home, my GPS screwed us up and we ended up in the middle of freaking nowhere, and the kids were wailing at me because half the buildings were abandoned and there were people standing on the street corners even though it's midnight."

His brow furrows. "Anyhow, the car was a lot bigger than I was used to, and they're all making noise, and I'm lost, and then we hit this pothole and someone shot at us! I just floored it. The kids started screaming, so I ran red lights and I have no idea how fast I was going on the street because I was like, crap, someone's really shooting at us! The car kept lurching and I just kept going because I didn't want to pull over and get killed, and finally we got somewhere I recognized, and I called my father to come get us."

Max laughs out loud. "You panicked."

"Well, who wouldn't panic? Someone was shooting at us." The guy is flushed crimson. "And now that I've told you, I need my aunt's gun back."

"But if someone shot you at that range, why wasn't the car damaged?" And then it occurs to me. "Um, did you maybe drive over here in the Maxima today?" When he says yes, I say, "I want to see it one more time."

In the front lot, I get down under the front seat and probe until I've got it. Derringers: according to Tim the guns most likely to go off after a sudden impact. "Max," I say, "I'm not sure the airbag sensors are functional anymore. There's a bullet hole under the seat."

Hal and I, and Beth and Stuart, have gathered in Mrs. Goretti's kitchen while she talks Hal through the process of making veal scaloppini.

Hal may actually be floating a few inches off the linoleum floor. Mrs. Goretti's kitchen smells of meat, of broth, of capers, of white wine. A scent of tomato sauce lingers on the edges, and if you inhale with your eyes shut you can detect decades of garlic, onion, and mushrooms: a lifetime of menus.

"You should have seen the looks on everyone's faces!" Beth laughs out loud. "No one knew what they were planning, so they tried to laugh it off at first, but then it kept looking more and more like a wedding."

Stuart snickers. "I knew something was up."

"You knew you were up to your eyeballs in dinner rolls," Beth snaps.

Mrs. Goretti looks at me over her shoulder, tsking. "I can't believe you just went and got married like that."

I ignore the way she keeps examining my profile, making sure I'm not Heavy With Child. Everyone's been doing that. *No, really, we thought it would be more fun to do it the other way around.* Instead I say, "You told me I shouldn't let him get away. I figured it was part of the lease."

Hal adds, "She didn't want you to worry yourself sick again about her being single."

In between taking notes, Hal catches my eye. We're going to recap this meal three times in the upcoming week as he embeds every detail in his brain for easy recall. Do I mind? Heck no. That's one cool thing about being married: I eat dinner on a regular basis. The first night I suggested having just cereal was not well-received.

Mrs. Goretti says, "I knew being married would be good for you."

Of course she did. "It's not all that different. I mean, I don't come back here at night." And we've gotten some wedding gifts in the mail, too. That's pretty cool. My mother sent me a bridal-shower-in-a-box. Thankfully, none of the shiny, satiny things had days of the week embossed on them. My mom's been trying to get me into lace and satin since I was four years old, and this time Hal encouraged me to put them on too. Then he wanted me to take them off. Make up your minds, people!

Mrs. Goretti says, "Someone did come looking for you, but I told him you'd moved."

My eyes widen. "Wait, was that—"

Beth says, "Loser-boy. Yeah."

"You didn't tell him where I moved to, did you?"

"He was so unrefined." Mrs. Goretti clicks her teeth. "He asked if you'd married 'that white lawyer guy,' and then he told me to give him your address." My aged, sweet landlady shakes her head. "So I told him to go to Hell."

I choke on a laugh. Bucky says, *That's not nice. I don't want anyone in Hell.*

Bucky's been joking around with the other guardians. When I haven't felt him directly, I've still been picking up the overflow of his laughter. Whatever angels do during a dinner, they're having a good time.

The Shadow hasn't returned, has she?

Not at all. She can't even get close.

Good. That means I'm keeping my promise, and I did promise Hal *for keeps.*

And forever is a long time.

Stuart says, "Hal, dude, you're the one that surprised me. I figured you'd plan out everything."

"I compressed the planning into a two-week window." Hal makes more notes as he watches Mrs. Goretti's technique. "It's more surprising that Lee agreed to a life of boredom and predictability."

"No, it's an adventure, trying to figure out *forever* the way you'd figure out how to climb a mountain. Or the way it would look like a long way to the ground if you're skydiving."

Beth says, "There's a place you can get married while skydiving."

"I told you!" I say to Hal, who's rolling his eyes.

Mrs. Goretti says, "Well, I wasn't at your wedding reception, so you get to have another one right now." And thus dinner is served. There's the veal, plus crusty Italian bread, Mrs. Goretti's magic stuffed mushrooms, plus some peas with onions (you can't win 'em all). And in case any of us is in danger of starving, there's a bathtub-sized basin of pasta.

For dessert, I brought pastries from an Italian bakery Mrs. Goretti loves. Bucky assured me the cannoli cream won't damage her heart any. *After this long, her arteries would probably collapse without regular infusions of solid cholesterol.*

She beams. "Oh, these are wonderful! You didn't have to!"

"Of course we did," I say, cutting open the bakery string. Believe me, I know this woman: if you buy dinner from a restaurant, it's because you don't love someone enough to cook for them, but if you cook the dessert yourself instead of bringing in pastry, it's because you don't love them enough to buy for real. Excepting the lemon cakes she used to make for me and Beth "just so we'd have something nice." Those fit into a category all their own because they weren't for dessert—they were "for special."

I add, "Hal wanted to make you something, but I convinced him you would much rather have these."

Hal looks askance at the box. "You never really did convince me."

I ended up having to distract him. We haven't been married very long, so he's pretty easy to distract.

Hal gets up to pour the coffee.

Beth says, "Oh, I found some more of your things, so I boxed them up. Stuart, go get them."

I stand. "Here, I'll go."

The stairs creak all the way up three flights of steps as I make the hundred-yard dash one more time, and I let myself inside with the key I keep forgetting to return to Beth.

The apartment smells familiar in a way that's already becoming unfamiliar. I can't explain it so much, except that Hal's condo...I mean, our condo...is retrofitted into a factory and has no aura of aged wood, a century and a half of family laughter and lives lived in every square inch. Instead of new money, this around me is an old world, one I've left to head to the dream of the new one.

Beth left two boxes and a shopping bag stacked against the pantry door, but I don't take them right away. Instead I walk through the apartment again, my footsteps creaking in the semidark of the shortening nights. There are the eight-foot windows, the nick on the door where the corner piece came off.

I lived here for so long. I didn't intend to. I just kept renewing the lease, one year of my life at a time given away to the top floor of a century-old brownstone.

"Goodbye," I whisper.

When I turn, I see Bucky with a wistfulness around his eyes.

"Don't give me that." I force a smile. "Angels don't get attached to places because you're a sage higher-order being who knows the whole world's going to be consumed by holy fire or somesuch. You saw entire civilizations come and go. An apartment isn't that big of a deal."

He looks surprised. "It's not the building. It's that I remember you living here."

I smirk. "Well, now you can remember me living somewhere else, too."

Bucky says, "Don't sell it short. I was a pirate here too."

I gasp. "Now I can't leave!"

Bucky nods. "I knew you'd see it my way. There's nothing wrong with a little piratical sentiment."

Hal comes in from the hallway. "I figured I'd help you carry down your stuff. One last hurrah?"

I expect his voice to echo, but it doesn't. The apartment is only empty of my stuff, and shortly it's going to be empty of me too.

"Just checking the place over." I take his hand. "Apparently I'm living somewhere else for a while."

"These things happen." He takes me in his arms, and he kisses me.

For a long time we're quiet. A family of pigeons coos foraging advice to the plastic owls on the roof while a sunset flares out the back window, and I've got a new husband and a lifelong best friend and an eternity in front of me.

"We should get back downstairs." I tuck my head against Hal's shoulder. "People will talk."

"Oh, and the things they'll say." Hal chuckles. "Mrs. Goretti wants to teach me to make espresso, and I figured you might want to be down there to learn exactly what goes into coffee so strong the spoon flattens itself in self defense."

"It actually dissolves the spoon," I remark as we divide the boxes. "All those demitasse spoons? They started out as tablespoons."

Hal laughs, and Bucky does too, and I'm the last one out. The door locks behind me with a click, and then we creak down the stairs to a warm kitchen, a rich dessert, and an even warmer and richer future.

The End! (Or is it...? No, probably not.)

Oodles And Bunches

"Rejoice, O Highly Flaky Woman."

Acknowledgments

I'm always amazed by how much help everyone gives as I take a story through the journey of becoming a book. I'd like to thank my early readers and critique partners. In particular I'd like to thank Ivy Reisner, Wendy Dinsmore, Maria Franzetti, Heather Turner (who is an excellent proofreader!) and finally Roseanne Wells who pointed out a flaw that would have destroyed the story.

Many thanks as well to Evan and Madeline, and to James Lebak who supplied helpful critique and lots of hilarious commentary.

If you enjoyed Lee and Bucky, I would love to hear from you. Please consider joining my mailing list at http://eepurl.com/bcnCNX. I don't send out much on the list, but I'll use it to notify readers of any new books, potential discounts, and ask for people who want free books in exchange for honest reviews.

Speaking of honest reviews, good books can always use them. Forget what Mrs. Miller told you in third grade: a book review can be a couple of lines and doesn't have to be anything more than "I laughed so hard I fell off the subway bench" or "Boring. Don't bother." You can post a review on the book's page at Amazon.com or Goodreads, and I hope you will.

Thank you for the gift of your time and the privilege of allowing my angels into your home.

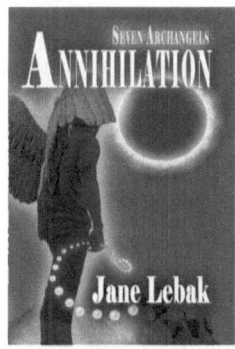